Houston, Texas

"Cade, I'm afraid I have bad news. Your uncle was killed this morning. Hit and run."

Cade Youngblood's heart skipped a beat then thudded against his ribs as he prayed he had not heard the man right.

"I'm sorry to have to tell you on the phone. I'm sure your family can make the funeral arrangements from this end. Everybody will understand if you prefer not to come back."

"My family?" Cade said. "What family?"

"Well, I mean your stepmother. Or Nick. I doubt Trish will be fit to take care of any business for a while. It might be better if you...you know...stay away...let sleeping dogs lie."

The black fog in Cade's brain cleared enough for him to understand the detective's implication: Don't come back—even for your uncle's funeral. That would be the easy way out, and Rickey Chambers was offering it to him like a neatly wrapped gift. Damn it to hell, he had never intended to set foot in Cumberland Cove, Tennessee again in his life.

"You can wake the sleeping dogs, Rickey. I'm coming home," Cade said. "And I'm damned sure going to expect some answers when I get there."

Other Novels by Elaine Grant

ROSES FOR CHLOE

MAKE BELIEVE MOM

AN IDEAL FATHER

NO HERO LIKE HIM

THE
CAVERNS

A TENNESSEE MOUNTAIN HOME NOVEL

ELAINE
GRANT

Mountain Writer Publishing

THE CAVERNS

This is a work of fiction.
Names, characters, places, and incidents portrayed in this novel are either the product of the author's imagination or are used fictitiously, and any resemblance to actual persons, living or dead, business establishments, events, or locales is entirely coincidental.

Book and cover design copyright © 2013 Mountain Writer Publishing
Cover art copyright © 08-03-07 Rob Broek
Edited by Amy Knupp, Blue Otter Editing

Published 2013 by Mountain Writer Publishing
www.mountainwriterpublishing.com

ISBN: 0988333333
ISBN-13: 978-0-9883333-3-8

To all of my family and friends
who will celebrate this book's publication!

Acknowledgments

This book never would have come to fruition without the input of many people. Some shared technical information and advice, others read and reread the manuscript, enhancing it each time. Still others offered faith and support, necessary sustenance for any writer.

Thanks to my writing and critique buddies and dear friends Eleanor Cocreham and Sylvia Rochester for never tiring of rereading and tweaking this manuscript in all its various stages.

Also thanks to the following for their varied input in different areas:

Crime/Police: Major Greg Cooke, Maryville, Tennessee Police Department; Roy Paxton, East Baton Rouge Sheriff's Department; Ronnie Ward, LEO; Wally Lind, LEO retired; Robin Burcell, LEO; Crimescenewriters Group, John Foxjohn

Caves: Wade Berdeaux

Tennessee Legal System: Dr. Judy M. Cornett, University of Tennessee

Computer Hacking: HLWegley and Orblover from Crimescenewriters

Faith and Support: My husband, Tony; my son, Justin; my mother, Julia; my Aunt Grace, and my many friends who patiently listened to my woes and triumphs. Thanks to you all!

Any information or advice I received from these generous sources was in turn interpreted by me in a work of fiction. If, in the process, I got something wrong, it's my mistake, not theirs!

THE
CAVERNS

A TENNESSEE MOUNTAIN HOME NOVEL

All of us, whether guilty or not, whether old or young, must accept the past. It is not a case of coming to terms with the past. That is not possible. It cannot be subsequently modified or undone.

—*Richard von Weizsaecker*

DAY 1

CHAPTER 1

HOUSTON, TEXAS

SOMETIMES the small things drive a man over the edge—and tonight the flashing red light on the phone was doing the trick for Cade Youngblood. Switching off the sound didn't disable the red call indicator. Without missing a keystroke in his typing, Cade looked up in irritation. Would the blasted thing never stop blinking!

The clock on the wall of his office showed 9:15 p.m. He gave a frustrated grunt. It had been one of those days. Rain had delayed his helicopter flight from the Gulf of Mexico to Houston. Then a rough landing during a downpour and a freeway that resembled a parking lot had marked the rest of his morning, forcing him to go straight from the airport to his client's boardroom.

After a month in the wilds and less than six hours' sleep in the past forty-eight, he had looked more like a zombie than a businessman seeking a multi-million-dollar contract. It was a wonder the "suits" of World Com Oil gave him the time of day...but sometimes what a man could do trumped how he looked, and today turned out to be one of those days.

He'd gotten to his Houston office only a couple of hours ago after grueling hours hashing out the details. Showered, shaved, and refreshed, with a half-eaten deli sandwich on a plate nearby, he glanced at the lucrative contract on the desk and grinned. A long, stressful day, but so gratifying in the end when the CEO gave him the go-ahead on the Gulf project.

The phone light went dark, thank goodness. Cade rolled his head a couple of times to work the stiffness out of his neck.

Tonight he had to fine-tune his strategy to tap into the enormous oil pocket trapped deep beneath the Gulf of Mexico without damaging the environment or violating any of the current government restrictions on offshore drilling—no easy task. Tomorrow afternoon, after a follow-up meeting with World Com's CEO, he could board a helicopter headed back to the field.

Cade concentrated on the 3-D seismic survey spread across his laptop screen until the colors ran together like psychedelic art and he had to rub his eyes with the palms of his hands to focus again. The rest of his night would be fueled by strong black coffee and anything else that would keep him alert as he devised a method to get the crude oil to the surface. Oil to guarantee the future of his fledgling exploration company—*and provide energy for the damn phone light to keep blinking.*

From the corner of his eye, Cade saw the flashing light start up again. Losing his train of thought, he cursed under his breath and raked a hand through his hair, shaggy and in need of a decent cut.

Mentally, he flicked through the shortlist of people who might be calling the office this time of night. Basically, that would be nobody. The few casual acquaintances he had made over the years drifted away when they realized that workaholic Cade didn't socialize and spent most of his time out of the country on exploration jaunts or crunching the data he brought back. His engineers would have called his cell.

Ten p.m. That blasted light shattered his thoughts again. Enough! Cade grabbed the receiver.

"Hello."

Silence.

"If you want to talk to me, talk. Otherwise don't call back."

"Wait, don't hang up." A male voice with a strong Southern accent came across the line. "I'm trying to reach Cade Youngblood."

"And you are...?"

"Cade? It's Detective Rickey Chambers. From Tennessee...the Cumberland Cove Police Department."

Swallowing the sour taste in his throat, Cade swiveled around in his chair to stare out the window at the Houston skyline silhouetted in the moonlight. Rickey Chambers? After all these years? From long-honed habit, his fingers traced the thin scar that snaked along his hairline. He tried in vain to stem the onslaught of nightmarish memories that suddenly burst through his mind like flashes of a jerky black-and-white movie. "What do you want?"

"I've been trying to reach you all afternoon," Rickey said. "I left messages at your office when nobody answered, and your cell phone is going automatically to voice mail."

Cade leaned back far enough to dig his cell phone from his pocket. Off. He'd turned it off before his meeting and his secretary was ill today. There would be nobody else in his small office to answer the phone.

"I'm afraid I have bad news. Your uncle was killed this morning."

Cade's heart skipped a beat then thudded against his ribs as he prayed he had not heard the man right. "What kind of perverted joke is this?"

"I'm sorry to have to tell you on the phone...."

Ah. God, no! Cade doubled over like he'd been sucker punched as he tried to assimilate the detective's words. His skin turned clammy with dread and disbelief, his stomach queasy.

"How? When?"

"Hit and run. Apparently he'd gone to get the morning paper. At this point, we don't have any suspects."

A foreboding as dark and impenetrable as the night beyond his window crept into Cade's mind. "And you're the one investigating this?"

After a brief pause, the detective answered, "Yes."

"Wonderful," Cade said. "Do you think you'll have any better chance of solving the case this time?"

"I know you think you didn't get a fair trial, Cade, but—"

"I know damn well I didn't get a fair trial."

"The evidence convicted you."

"Circumstantial evidence. A setup and you didn't do your job."

Rickey fell silent.

Even though he suspected that any news in tiny Cumberland Cove would spread like an oil slick, Cade finally asked, "Does my sister know?"

"I told Trish earlier this afternoon. She's not taking it well. She asked me to call you."

Cade's eyes locked on the chart on his laptop screen as the responsibility of work collided with his anguish. Fury welled inside that some coward had taken his uncle from him needlessly, followed by a moment of selfishness—this was the worst possible time to leave his critical project in somebody else's hands.

"I've got some business I have to take care of first thing in the morning. Supposed to fly out again tomorrow...." Cade thought out loud as he tried to clear his head. To sort out priorities.

"There's no need for you to change your plans. What's done here is done."

"What happens now?" Cade said sharply. "With my uncle...your investigation?"

"Your uncle's body will probably be released to the undertaker tomorrow. Your family can make the funeral arrangements from this end. I'm sure everybody will understand if you prefer not to come back."

"My family?" Cade said. "What family?"

"Well, I mean your stepmother. Or Nick. I doubt Trish will be fit to take care of any business for a while. It might be better if you...you know...stay away...let sleeping dogs lie."

The black fog in Cade's brain cleared enough for him to understand the detective's implication: Don't come back—even for your uncle's

16

funeral. That would be the easy way out, and Rickey was offering it to him like a neatly wrapped gift. Damn it to hell, he had never intended to set foot in Cumberland Cove again in his life. And there was the Gulf project looming....

"You can wake the sleeping dogs, Rickey. I'm coming home," Cade said. "And I'm damned sure going to expect some answers when I get there."

Almost twenty-four hours later, Cade cursed the weather as he pushed the speedometer needle well past the safety zone. White-hot lightning exploded across the inky sky, fragmenting massive thunderheads in the distance. The boom of thunder shook the heavens, and a shroud of darkness fell again as the borrowed Range Rover sped through the night on the glass-slick highway like a wraith bent for hell.

His morning meeting with the CEO of World Com had lasted longer than he had expected, pushing him well past noon getting to the airport. Fortunately, he had been able to save a little time by diverting his leased helicopter as far as Atlanta, where he called in a favor from a business contact with a chain of car dealerships to avoid the hassle of an airport rental car. But the storm that had impeded his progress yesterday had trained east from the Gulf and now hovered over north Georgia, determined to delay him again.

Heavy-duty wipers threw off torrents of rain that whipped in sheets across the windshield. A twisting wrench locked his gut every time he thought about his Uncle Silas. What if his flight hadn't been delayed from the Gulf? What if he'd called his uncle yesterday morning instead of being consumed with business? Would that have changed the dynamics, made his uncle later going for his paper? The automobile that killed him might have passed harmlessly, and his uncle would have gone on with his life like every other day. But that hadn't happened, and somebody was going to pay for leaving him to die like road kill on the highway.

Cade took the last slug of bitter, cold coffee in his mug, his eyes locked on the road, trying to force his past back into the hole where he kept it buried, but ugly memories writhed free, jolting anxiety through him as real and immediate as if he were still trapped in that hot seat in the maw of the Cumberland Cove Police Department seventeen years ago. No answers. No help. No memory, since he had downed enough moonshine the night before to knock out an elephant. Only relentless, pounding accusations of actions so appalling that he couldn't bear the images they conjured. Still couldn't. The terror that usually only plagued him in nightmares now gripped his heart until the pressure in his chest became excruciating.

Suffocating in the close air inside the Range Rover, Cade lowered the window a fraction, let the pelting rain and cold air find their way inside. Drenched within a matter of seconds, with the voices still screaming in his head like banshees, Cade powered the window up and clicked on the CD player. Even with the volume as loud as he could stand it, he couldn't drown out the past. He tipped the coffee mug to his lips, cursed when he realized it was empty.

The beam of his headlights reflected off a marker beside the highway.

Tennessee State Line.

The sign flashed by his window, little more than a green-and-white blur, leaving in its wake an ominous feeling that the gates of hell had just swung open and the devil himself waited around the next bend.

DAY 2

CHAPTER 2

CUMBERLAND COVE, TENNESSEE

O FFICER Scottie Townsend downshifted the Crown Victoria
to save the brakes as she threaded it along the twisting
mountain road leading into Cumberland Cove. Fingers of
early morning mist stretched toward the pale sky above the Smoky
Mountains, making it difficult to discern where the mountaintops
ended and heaven began. Last night's deluge had passed on toward
North Carolina, leaving the mountain air rarefied and clean.

Low-level static crackled over the squad car's radio in raucous
cadence with the dispatcher's voice. The dashboard clock showed
a few minutes before six a.m., her twelve-hour shift almost over.
Working her way back to the station to do paperwork, Scottie listened
for anything that might be of interest to her. Cumberland Cove was a
quiet little town on the edge of the Great Smoky Mountains National
Park, and the general order of business was occasional petty theft or
minor domestic violence.

After five years on the force, Scottie remained the only female
patrol officer in the Cumberland Cove Police Department, the position
hard-won over several young men who thought they deserved it by
right of maleness. She didn't kid herself that having a woman on

the force bolstered the department's minority numbers, but with her former experience on the Atlanta PD, she knew she was as qualified as the others and had no qualms about taking the job.

The crackling sound of the dispatcher's voice broke through. "Raising one-eleven. Raising one-eleven. Over."

Scottie acknowledged the call.

"Morning, Scottie. Report of a suspicious vehicle on Caverns Lane off the Old Knoxville Road. The resident who lives across the highway saw a black SUV turn in sometime after midnight, and it never came out. She claims that road's posted and nobody lives there. Over."

"I'm on it. Over."

Scottie U-turned at the next scenic overlook and headed back up the mountain. Large "NO TRESPASSING" signs were nailed to trees on both sides of a graveled road that ended at the entrance to the long-barricaded Cumberland Caverns. Overhead, the still-barren limbs entwined like fingers playing a favorite children's game.

"Here's the church and here's the steeple, open the doors and see all the people," Scottie murmured softly.

She knew this road well though she had not traveled it recently. A left-hand fork just ahead led to an old mountain cabin, which had not been used in years. She skipped the side road for the moment to circle the cruiser in the overgrown clearing at the entrance to the caverns. The padlock was secure on the door of the lean-to that guarded the opening of the main cave. She backtracked and turned off the graveled road toward the cabin. Wide, deep tire tracks cut into the rain-soaked dirt. Scottie slowed the cruiser, approaching cautiously, even though she was pretty sure who she would find. As the underbrush cleared, she spotted a late-model black Range Rover with a Georgia dealer plate parked in front. The driver was slumped in the seat, profile blurred by the dewy condensation on the window. As a precaution, she called in the license number on the SUV.

A couple of minutes later, the dispatcher returned. "It's registered to Peach State Enterprises, a conglomerate of car dealerships in Atlanta. Do you want backup?"

"Not yet. You might have Jimmy float this way just in case. I'll call if I need him." She clicked off and made a visual assessment of the immediate area. Nothing suspicious. The cabin door appeared locked and secure. Scottie eased from behind the wheel and slowly approached, laying a hand lightly on the Glock service pistol holstered on her belt.

She tapped on the window. Immediately, the man stirred and jerked upright. Scottie stepped back as the driver's door opened. She thumbed the holster release, just in case, and tightened her grip on her weapon.

Shading his eyes from the rising sun, the man eased out of the SUV, standing a good six feet tall, broad shouldered and well built. Black cashmere sweater, soft black leather jacket over jeans, expensive driving boots. Range Rover. Not your usual bum, anyway. Besides, she knew who he was even after all these years.

"What did I do, Officer?" He scrutinized her badge. "Townsend?" His sleep-hoarse voice, tinged with a trace of Southern accent, struck a long-silent chord in Scottie.

"We received a trespassing report," she said.

A stubbly beard shadowed the chiseled face that used to turn the head of every teenage girl, and some of the women, in Cumberland Cove. He lowered his hand from his brow, and she stared into those familiar, brilliant-blue, come-hither eyes that could steal a woman's soul. That had once stolen hers. He glanced at her hand still on her gun.

"Do you shoot people for trespassing around here now?"

"Ordinarily not. But you could call these extraordinary circumstances."

A slight twist of Cade's lips might have passed for a smile.

"Never thought I'd see you in a cop uniform, Scottie," he said, studying her face with an inscrutable stare that put her on edge. No sign of the wide grin that used to split his face whenever he saw her; instead, an impassive look about his eyes and the set of his mouth turned him into a stranger. "I guess some things change over the years."

"And some don't."

Things like destroyed futures, a young girl's life taken too soon that could never be given back. What Scottie wanted to say, she couldn't, so she retreated to neutral ground. "So I guess you'll claim you're not trespassing."

"This is my property from my grandfather. Always has been. You knew that." Cade crossed his arms and leaned against the Range Rover, still staring at her as if he could read her mind.

"I had to check out the report regardless. Most people probably assume it belongs to Silas." Scottie caught herself. "I'm so sorry about your uncle, Cade. I...I would have called you, but it happened while I was off duty. By the time I reached Trish, she said she'd already asked Rickey to get in touch with you."

Cade took a halting breath, the first hint of emotion he'd displayed. "What happened, Scottie? Have you found out who hit him?"

"No, not when I came on duty, anyway. Rickey's on it."

Cade ran his fingers through his dark, tousled hair and gave her a cynical look. "You know that gives me a lot of confidence, don't you?"

"Rickey's a good detective."

"He must have improved a hell of a lot, then."

Scottie saw no point in going there. "You drove all the way from Texas?"

"I hitched a ride on a corporate helicopter and picked up a car in Atlanta. Rickey tried to talk me out of coming."

If any softness remained inside of this man, he kept it well hidden. His eyes held an edge of tempered steel, and his lips looked cold and hard as stone.

Determined not to be intimidated, Scottie said, "We have a motel or two now. You didn't have to sleep in your vehicle."

"I only got here a few hours ago. Besides, I like it out here."

"Always on the fringe," Scottie said before she thought.

Cade's voice lowered to a rumble. "From the look on your face, I guess you agree with Rickey. I shouldn't come home, even to bury my uncle."

An uneasy feeling squirmed in her stomach. "It's going to be hard for everybody, including you."

"Hard?" Cade gave a short grunt. "Darling, I doubt you know the meaning of the word. I'm here to do what has to be done—to take care of business. And to see that the Cumberland Cove Police Department does the same. Whoever doesn't like it can go to hell."

The undisguised vitriol in his voice rankled Scottie, but not as much as his insinuation. He didn't have a clue what she'd been through in the past seventeen years. At least he would be gone in a few days, and hopefully she'd never see him again.

"I finalized the funeral preparations on the phone," he said when she didn't respond. "Uncle Silas had prearranged most of the details with the funeral home years ago. He wanted to be brought home for the wake, and I agreed. I guess I should tell Trish, for whatever it's worth. Does she still live with Johanna?"

"She does...but Cade, go easy on her. She doesn't cope very well. When I talked to her yesterday, she sounded a little out of it again. Silas's death threw her for a major loop."

Cade gave her an inquisitive frown. "Out of it? What does that mean?"

"She takes prescription drugs off and on. Antidepressants and tranquilizers. She'll be okay for a while, then something upsets her, and she'll hit the tranquilizers pretty hard. She never was the same after you were—were gone so soon after your father died."

"Are you trying to dump my sister's emotional problems on me, too?" Cade shoved his fists in his jacket pockets and muttered, "Maybe Johanna had something to do with it?"

"Probably Johanna tried to do what was best for Trish under the circumstances."

Cade's glare ate into her like acid. "I never heard a word from any of them after I went to prison, and they were the only family I had left, other than Uncle Silas. I do blame her."

"Johanna didn't want Trish to know what was happening to you. She was trying to help the child get on with her life."

"Sure she was. Even after I was released, she wouldn't let me talk to Trish on the phone or come to see her. She cut me off from my sister, made it clear there was no reason for me to come back here. If it hadn't been for Uncle Silas—" Cade's lips cut an inflexible line into a tanned and hardened countenance. "Don't worry about it. It's my problem."

Scottie studied his face, ravaged from lack of sleep. Exhaustion clouded his eyes, and deep within, before he shut her out, she glimpsed a restless, haunted look. He was walking into the lion's den alone, and they both knew it.

Regardless of what had happened in their adult lives, she and Cade had shared a pure and innocent love as young children and later as teens...but those days were long past, and nothing would ever be the same.

"Are you planning to stay out here? I'll notify the dispatcher so you won't be reported again."

Cade glanced at the barred and shuttered cabin and shook his head. "No, I have a key to Uncle Silas's house."

Cade reached out to touch her badge. Scottie flinched, but she held her ground. "S. Townsend. Not Thomas anymore. Obviously married."

"I'm widowed. Almost five years now. That's why I moved home."

He nodded slightly but offered no condolences. Why had she expected that he would? The face was familiar, but this was not the same Cade who had left Cumberland Cove as a teenager. Prison changed a man. She'd been in law enforcement long enough to know that.

And after all that had happened, there would be nothing left of what they'd once had together. Best not to rip open old wounds and leave them bleeding long after Cade was gone again.

"I need to get back on patrol. What time is visitation?"

"Four until seven this evening."

"I'll come by."

Cade nodded. "Can you give me Trish's number before you go?"

"You give me yours, and I'll have her call you," she countered.

"Figures," Cade muttered. He handed her a couple of business cards from his wallet. "Give one to her, and keep one in case you need to get in touch with me. My cell number's on there."

Cade eased behind the wheel of the Range Rover and waited until Scottie turned around in the clearing then followed her to the main highway. She went one direction; he went the other.

CHAPTER 3

A FEW minutes later, Cade pulled into the driveway of his uncle's house, turned off the ignition, and stared at the familiar, two-story Victorian, always more of a home to him than his own father's house. The rising sun reflected off the symmetrical second-story windows with eye-watering intensity. The house hadn't changed much since he saw it last as a teenager on the day he was arrested and the life he knew ended forever. What wouldn't he give to go back to that time in his life and do something...anything...everything...differently?

Cade blinked hard trying to block out old memories that swarmed around him like an angry swarm of bees, so unnerving even now that he couldn't make sense of them. Resting his forehead against his arms crossed on the steering wheel, he gave himself the luxury of denial for a few moments longer. He'd always expected Silas's house to be his haven, his uncle there waiting to welcome him home. Cade raised his head to stare at the empty windows. Tingling dread told him he was wrong this time.

The vibration of his cell phone startled him. He took a couple of deep breaths before he answered.

"Scottie told me to call you." His sister's hoarse voice brought Cade's emotions down another notch. "I can't believe you're here after all these years."

"It's been a long time, Trish." Cade opened the door and stepped down from the driver's seat, approaching the house as he talked.

She gave a harsh laugh. "You think I don't know that? I see you made it back for Uncle Silas, even if you never came to see me."

Cade frowned then considered that Trish probably had no idea Johanna had warned him off. "I'm really sorry, Sis."

"Don't call me Sis, and don't bother to be sorry at this late date."

"Well, I am sorry. I never wanted it to be this way between us."

"Right. Anyway, Scottie said Uncle Silas wanted to go home for the wake and for me to call you."

The callousness in her voice hurt Cade, but he let it go.

"Yes, I'm at the house now if you want to come over and help me get things ready."

There was a period of total silence on the other end.

"Why should I?" Trish said finally. "He didn't love me."

"Of course he did."

"No, he didn't. I had to beg for money, and even then, he gave me precious little. Nicky said he sent you a lot of money. And Nicky says if I haven't heard from Uncle Silas's lawyer yet, that means I'm not in the will. So I still don't get anything."

"A little advice, Sis. Don't listen to Nick."

"I told you, don't call me Sis. And I suppose you're going to take care of me after all these years? Forgive me if I'm not convinced."

"Why were you begging money from Uncle Silas anyway? Didn't Johanna take care—"

Trish slammed the phone down in his ear.

Cade exhaled heavily, unsure how to proceed with his sister—especially if Nick was still poisoning her against him. He searched his key ring for the house key Silas had given him years ago upon his release from prison, along with a note saying, "You can come home any time."

Holding the screen door ajar with his hip, Cade slid the key into the lock and opened the front door. The familiar wood-fire scent seeped from the pores of the old house, and a whiff of Old Spice hung on the motionless air. He shivered with a sense that his uncle had walked out of the room only the moment before, a feeling so strong that Cade called out softly, "Uncle Silas?"

The answer he craved didn't come. In the silence, he eased the door closed behind him, rooted to the spot by grief and overwhelming abandonment in a house where he never had thought he would feel alone. The reality of his uncle's death sank into his gut, cold, hard, and eternal.

He gazed around the living room and through the arched opening into the kitchen. Not much had changed over the years. After a quick pass through the downstairs area, he returned to the SUV to retrieve an overnight bag. Instead, drawn to the scene of his uncle's death, Cade walked down the path toward the road, his shoes making soft imprints in the wet soil. His stomach lurched, and the muscles in his neck took a death grip on his throat when he saw the dark blood soaked into the faded asphalt, leaving a rusty stain across the white centerline of the road.

Cade forced himself into the mental isolation he'd perfected in prison in order to survive—a numb, focused state of mind that blocked out pain, fear, and confusion. One that he used even now when he had to concentrate on the task at hand, regardless of emotion or risk, to go forward when his instincts screamed run.

Crossing the road, he stood beside the newspaper box as his uncle had probably done. He stared both ways as far as he could see. In good daylight, vision was limited by the twisting road and low-hanging branches. But in the predawn darkness when his uncle was hit, headlights would be visible long before a vehicle rounded the bend in either direction.

Why hadn't his uncle waited for the car to pass? Had his vision worsened in his old age? No, Cade thought not. His uncle had bragged about winning a turkey shoot in the fall, a testament to his sharp eyesight. Then why? With no sure answer, Cade returned to move the Range Rover to the back of the house out of sight. He took his travel bag inside to get ready.

Showered and dressed for the visitation, Cade stood at the open back door, staring through the screen as he waited for his uncle's body to be delivered. Meticulously maintained and freshly waxed, Silas's beloved red pickup truck, an antique now but bought new, sat forlorn and forsaken under the aluminum carport. What would he do with that truck? Silas would turn over in his grave if Cade sold it, but it didn't need to rot from disuse, either.

A hawk, Silas's favorite bird, circled gracefully on the currents then alighted in a tree not far from the house. Cade stepped outside onto the planked porch. A chill skittered down his back as the regal creature sat perfectly motionless on the topmost branches and cocked its head toward the house. He sensed the sharp eyes boring into him and stared back, allowing the memory of his uncle to fill him like a living presence. As with many mountain children, Cade had been raised on tales of ghosts, haints, and the supernatural, and he could easily believe the hawk might be Silas reincarnated.

Cade watched as the hawk took flight and disappeared into the wilderness. His gaze lingered on the natural beauty he had missed so badly. The Smokies were a part of him, as much as his heart or soul. He always felt displaced on flat land, yet he had chosen to live in Texas for the past several years, on some of the flattest land around. A self-inflicted penance for his sins? Or merely a loathing to return home to face down the devil, as his Uncle Silas warned he'd have to do at some point in life?

A vehicle stopped out of sight on the driveway beside the house. The engine shut off, and two car doors slammed. Cade's gut knotted as he recognized the voices approaching from around the corner.

His stepmother, Johanna, stopped in her tracks when she saw him standing on the porch. Her lips, creased from a lifetime of smoking, pursed in disapproval. Age had etched fine wrinkles into her face and sprouted gray roots along the part in her dark hair, but time had not changed the brazen hazel eyes. Critical, heartless, unforgiving eyes—eyes that still turned Cade cold inside.

Johanna's son, Nick Baskins, rounded the corner of the house and almost rear-ended her.

"What are you doing here?" Nick demanded of him.

"More to the point, what are you two doing here? Visitation doesn't start until four."

Nick approached the porch, putting himself between his mother and Cade. The two men faced off warily—males sizing up the opponent, forming a battle plan. An imposing man a couple of inches taller than Cade, Nick still had the thick neck and powerful body of a football lineman.

Every muscle singing with adrenalin, Cade tensed, fists loosely clenched, watching his stepbrother's slightest move for any hint of physical aggression, recalling fights from the past that always left Cade with a bloody nose, black eye, or aching ribs. For the moment, Nick fidgeted and glared at Cade but kept his distance.

"I talked to Trish a few minutes ago," Cade said. "She was spouting some nonsense you fed her about my uncle's will."

"I'm warning you, don't try to steal Trish's inheritance. I won't put up with any of your crap."

"Warning me?" Cade said with a caustic grunt. "Exactly how's that going to work? And how do you know anything about Silas's will?"

"I got my information from a good source."

"Why don't you crawl back into the hole you came from?" Johanna edged beside Nick. "It's Trish's place to be here with Silas, not yours. You know you're not welcome in Cumberland Cove."

Cade couldn't recall a kind word from this woman from the day his daddy married her.

"So, why are you two here instead of my sister? To loot Uncle Silas's house before anybody's the wiser?"

Johanna's face flushed to her hairline. "How dare you, Cade Youngblood!"

"Because I know you too well. You took my daddy for everything he ever owned. And Silas had a lot more than Dad ever did."

"We're here to pick up some items Trish wants as keepsakes. And don't you think about stealing anything. I'll have the law on you. You might not get off so easy the second time around."

Get off easy! Mentally, Cade grabbed his temper and wrestled it down. Eight years of his life stolen from him, and this witch had not said one word in his defense. Cade cringed even now at the pain and humiliation he'd suffered because Johanna wouldn't protect him and even refused to allow Silas to take custody of a kid she didn't want. And now she was threatening him again? No way in hell!

"Get out of here, Nick," Cade said through clenched teeth. "And take your worthless mother with you."

"You can't talk to us like that!" Johanna screeched, her voice like fingernails across a blackboard. "We're going to get what Trish wants."

Nick started up the steps, followed by Johanna. Cade blocked their path.

"Forget it," he said.

"You can't keep us out," Nick said. "Silas was Trish's uncle too. Mom has every right to protect her interests."

"She doesn't have any interest in this house. Not anymore," Cade bluffed. He had not had a chance to talk to Silas's lawyer, but he wasn't about to let Johanna and Nick loot the place before he knew his uncle's wishes.

"What are you saying? That...that the old man actually did cut her out?" Johanna sputtered. "She should get at least half of—"

"Maybe you should have thought about that before you turned her against Uncle Silas, and against me."

Johanna gave a derisive snort. "Did you expect me to drag her up to Brushy Mountain to see you through plate glass? And she could see her uncle any time she wanted. I never forbade that."

Cade forced himself to take a couple of long breaths so he wouldn't choke her on the spot. When he could speak civilly again, he said, "The only time she went to him was for money."

"Which he rarely gave her, I might point out." Johanna toyed with her handbag, pulling out a tissue to wipe her brow. "That crazy old man never had a lick of sense."

"Get off this property," Cade said, his blood burning through his veins, making his skin sting. "Now."

Nick stared dumbstruck at Cade. "Are you claiming to be sole beneficiary? That son of a bitch."

Ah, the look on Nick's face. The big-shot real estate agent was probably banking on Trish inheriting at least half the property. Just allowing Nick to believe he'd lost out was a taste of sweet revenge.

"Trish's lawyer will be in touch with you," Nick said.

"Bring him on. But you two get off my property." Cade stood them down until they disappeared around the house. He waited for the sound of the car backing out of the drive before he relaxed a little. He'd won his first battle, but their unpleasant visit was probably a harbinger of things to come.

CHAPTER 4

W HEN the hearse pulled into the driveway later that morning, Cade answered the front door to a trim gentleman in a neat black suit who offered his hand.

"Mr. Youngblood? John Davis here. My sincerest condolences."

"Thank you."

After a brief silence, Mr. Davis said, "Which room would you like to use for the visitation?"

"This is probably the only one that will do."

Mr. Davis studied the spacious living room. "Yes, we can arrange everything nicely in here."

Cade stood aside as Davis's assistants rolled in the simple coffin Silas had requested and maneuvered it into place, locking the wheels and attaching a drape around the perimeter to hide the mechanism.

"Would you like me to open the casket so you can view the body? Of course, the decision is up to you whether you want to keep the coffin open for the visitation."

Cade nodded. With due reverence, the dignified funeral director lifted the lid and locked it open. Cade forced himself to step forward and look down at the man he'd loved like a father. Heavy makeup covered any trace of injury on his face and hands. For that, Cade was grateful.

"He looks good." Cade winced at his own words. The old people always said that at funerals when he was young—and he'd been to his share. His mother, dead from cancer before his ninth birthday. His maternal grandfather, a scant three months later. His dad, no doubt from the misery of being married to Johanna, when Cade was sixteen. He shook his head that he'd let the words slide off his tongue so glibly, but Mr. Davis appeared pleased.

"Thank you. Would you prefer to leave it open, then?"

"I guess it's better that way. His friends will want to say good-bye."

"A good decision," Mr. Davis said. "Would you like a few more minutes before we bring in the floral arrangements? I suggest putting the guest register on that small table near the front door."

"Go ahead and finish," Cade said. "I'll wait in the kitchen."

Cade started a pot of coffee and rummaged through the refrigerator for something to ease his rumbling stomach. He found a partial packet of deli turkey and wolfed it down while the coffee brewed then poured a cup and sipped the scalding dark brew. The burn from it served as evidence that he could still feel pain in spite of the sense of numbness inside and out.

A quarter hour later, Mr. Davis appeared in the kitchen doorway. "We're done." He held out a card. "My cell phone number is listed. If you need anything during the night, don't hesitate to call me."

"Thank you," Cade said, taking the card and shaking Davis's hand. "I appreciate all you've done."

"Your uncle was a good man. He'll be missed." He gave a slight frown as he gazed around the kitchen. "Are you alone here, sir? Would you like me or one of my assistants to remain?"

"No need for that, thanks."

"Very well. We'll be back in the morning around ten o'clock to transport your family to the church for services."

"There's only my sister and me," Cade said.

"What about Mrs. Youngblood? Mr. Baskins?"

"They're not related to me or my uncle. They can arrange their own transportation."

"Very well."

Cade ushered the man out, allowing the screen to ease closed on its pneumatic hinge but leaving the front door open.

When the hearse drove away, Cade drifted back to the coffin. He touched the marble-cold skin of Silas's face then leaned over and laid his forehead on the old man's crossed hands, wishing they would reach up and comfort him like so many times in the past. Cade's trembling fingers clutched the soft fabric of Silas's navy blue suit. With clenched teeth and closed eyes, he fought the sorrow that threatened to overwhelm him.

After a few moments, he straightened and roughly brushed his cheeks with the heel of his hand. Reaching around his neck, he unfastened a braided silver chain and slipped off a worry-worn St. Christopher's medal. Uncle Silas had folded the shiny new charm and chain into Cade's hand and invoked the saint's protection on the day Cade's mother was buried. While Cade was in prison, Uncle Silas had worn it for him then gave it back the day he was released. The chain had represented a constant link between the two of them and had rarely been off Cade's neck since. Now he slid the amulet off the chain and worked it under Silas's palm, hiding it well from prying eyes.

"You keep it for awhile, Uncle Silas," he murmured. "I'll get it back from you later." He refastened the chain around his own neck, unwilling to give up that last connection to his uncle.

Apprehension swept through him when he heard another car pull up outside.

Here we go. Just get through this and out of this hellhole.

An older man peered through the screen, his hands cupped around his eyes. When he spied Cade, he brightened, stepped inside, and crossed the room, awkwardly holding out a hand.

"Do you remember me, Cade?"

"Guy Storey, right?" Cade said, shaking his hand.

The old man grinned and nodded vigorously. Well over seventy years old by now, Guy boasted a square, honest face topped by thin gray hair, combed straight back. A reassuring smile revealed strong teeth yellowed with age. Guy had been Silas's right-hand man for thirty-odd years and ran Silas's old-fashioned hardware store by himself whenever Silas was absent.

"I wasn't sure you'd know me."

"It's been a long time."

"Too long." Guy's sloped shoulders shuddered as he looked past Cade at the open coffin. "I can't believe he's gone."

"Neither can I," Cade said. He moved with Guy to the coffin and studied his uncle's serene countenance. Cade could only hope that, by the time he died, he would find a semblance of that kind of peace.

Beside him, Guy breathed in jerky fits and starts. The old fellow looked as if he might collapse. Cade guided him to a seat at the kitchen table and poured them both a fresh cup of coffee.

Guy gathered himself after a while and took a swallow. His gnarled hands shook slightly as he set the cup down and looked across the table at Cade. "How are you making it, son?"

Cade lifted his shoulders slightly and toyed with the spoon on his saucer. "I'm not looking forward to the next day or two."

"It's got to be hard on you, coming back like this. There was some talk this morning whether you would hold a wake or not, considering. I'd like to stay with you, either way, unless you want to be alone."

The old custom of waking the dead at home was rarely practiced anymore with the advent of luxurious funeral homes, but, for Silas, the simplicity seemed perfect.

"I'm sure there's talk all over town, but this is not about me. At least it shouldn't be. It's about my uncle and his life. There'll be a wake, but I can keep out of sight if it makes his friends more at ease."

"No, you won't. Silas was so proud of you. What you accomplished in spite of it all. He'd rather you were there beside him than anybody else. If folks can't handle it, so be it. You stand your ground like Silas would expect."

"I appreciate your staying," Cade said.

There was a knock at the back door. Cade opened it to an elderly woman holding a plastic cake keeper. She shifted nervously from one foot to the other and ducked her head to avoid meeting his eyes as she held out her offering. "I'm sorry about Silas. I wanted you and your sister to have this."

"Thank you," Cade said, forcing himself to play the role expected of him. "Would you like to come in?"

She shook her head. "I cain't. I'll come back for the viewing later." She acknowledged Guy, who had risen to stand beside Cade, then hurried off the porch and around the house before Guy could speak.

"Who was that?" Cade asked.

"Miz Melton. She lives about a half mile from here, that next house over toward town. You'd better find a piece of paper to put down the names. I imagine there'll be plenty of food coming in."

Cade followed Guy's instructions. Over the next couple of hours, a steady stream of neighbors and townspeople dropped by, following a long-standing Southern tradition of feeding the mourners. Guy helped him by greeting the callers and introducing them. While Cade did his best to be gracious, it was pure torture to endure the curious stares and stumbling condolences.

Cade wrote down the umpteenth name and the food item they'd brought, along with a brief description of any containers that might need to be returned. He glanced around at the casseroles, pies, cakes, tempting platters of crispy fried chicken, soft drinks, and pitchers filled with sweet tea that crowded the counters and table. Offerings brought to show respect for his uncle. A reverent tribute to the deceased. And no doubt, there was an underlying morbid curiosity about the pariah of Cumberland Cove suddenly back among them.

At the sound of simultaneous knocking at both doors, Cade gave Guy a weary look. "You get the back, I'll get the front."

The well-dressed, silver-haired man outside introduced himself as he held out his hand.

"I'm Gerald Taylor, Silas Martin's lawyer."

Cade invited him inside. He and Taylor had played phone tag the day before and never spoke. The lawyer moved to the casket, looked at Silas for a long minute.

"This is quite a shock to all of us," he said, turning back to Cade. "And I'm sorry to bother you now, but I thought you'd want to know the provisions of your uncle's will since the gossip mill is already churning. Also, I brought the paperwork for your signature so that you can transact your uncle's business immediately. If you would like, we can take care of that now. Otherwise, let's set up an appointment—"

"Now's good for me. I appreciate your consideration," Cade said. "But shouldn't my sister be here?"

"That's another reason I felt we should discuss this sooner rather than later." He glanced into the kitchen where Guy chatted with the latest food donor. "Is there someplace we could talk in private?"

Cade led the way down the hall to the bedroom his uncle used as a home office and closed the door behind them. The lawyer handed Cade a sheaf of papers he pulled from his briefcase. "As you can see, your uncle set up a Revocable Living Trust years ago. You are the successor trustee."

"Living trust?" Cade asked, scanning the legalese. "Is this different from a will?"

"Very much different. For one thing, a trust doesn't have to be probated and made public, which was very important to your uncle when he enlisted me to set it up. Also, a trust is harder to contest in court, especially since your uncle was of sound mind when he set it up."

"I see. I don't know that he had any other relatives to contest it, though. Trish and I would be his only beneficiaries." Maybe this would be the catalyst that brought brother and sister together again.

"Actually, Mr. Youngblood, your uncle very specifically left his entire estate to you and you alone. Your sister is not included."

CHAPTER 5

'M NOT going over there, and I'm not talking to him again."

"Trish, you've got to go, for your uncle's sake. Now brush your hair and put on something nice," Scottie said.

She handed Trish a hairbrush then turned to the closet, sliding the hangers of dresses and slacks aside one at a time looking for a suitable outfit. On one side of the closet, Trish's taste ran from ultra casual to ultra high fashion with little in between. On the opposite rack, new, freshly starched nurse's uniforms hung in testament to her recent graduation from nursing school. While she was currently employed at a local nursing home, that job wouldn't last long if Trish turned back to the prescription drugs that had been her crutch since she was a teenager.

Scottie finally found a dark blue dress that would suffice and laid it on the bed. Trish made a face at her choice but didn't protest. She sat at the dressing table in her bedroom, swiping her short dark hair off her face with impatient strokes. Slender to the point of frailty, Trish's body and face clearly showed the effects of long-term stress and a degree of substance abuse.

"Nicky called me before you got here. He and Mom went over there this morning and Cade wouldn't let them in. Nicky thinks Uncle Silas cut me off without a penny."

"Nick has no way of knowing," Scottie said.

"Well that's what he said. He and Mom have gone to his lawyer to see what can be done."

"Really? I guess that's why Nick didn't answer his phone earlier. I wish he had waited until after the funeral."

"The sooner the better, in my opinion." Trish caught Scottie's eye in the mirror. "You said you saw Cade this morning. What does he look like now?"

"You two could be twins in the face."

It was true. Both had startling ice blue eyes, midnight black hair, and an expressive mouth with a full lower lip that now gave Trish a pouty look as she fiddled with her hairbrush. Scottie had loved Trish from the time she was born when they were neighbors in the country. Because of the closeness of the families, Trish had always been a part of Scottie's life in Cumberland Cove. Once Scottie returned home and started dating Nick, she and Trish renewed their friendship on an adult level.

"I'm afraid."

"Of what?"

"Everybody says horrible things about him. What he did and all." Tears rolled down Trish's face again. She'd been weeping off and on since Scottie got there.

"All that's in the past, and nothing can be done about it now. And Cade's not going to hurt you. No matter how you feel about your brother, you owe your uncle the respect to show up at his visitation, so stop crying and finish your makeup."

Trish's hand trembled as she laid the brush on the dressing table. Her fingers went to her mouth as if trying to hold in her thoughts. Then she took a halting breath and said, "Scottie, do you think he did it? I mean, he went to jail and all, but I...I never wanted to think...he just didn't seem like he..." She broke into hard sobs. "God, I worshiped him back then."

Scottie stooped beside her and took Trish into her arms. "I know. I know."

"You loved him, too. Did you think he did it?"

"No, I didn't."

"But they convicted him. He must have done it if a jury convicted him."

Scottie hugged her tighter, unable to give the answer they both wanted to be true. "There are a lot of innocent people sent to jail for one reason or another. But, to be honest, I haven't seen anything that contradicted the verdict."

Trish pulled back. "You've looked?"

"As much as I could. I don't have access to all the case files, but I don't think there's anything in there to exonerate him."

"Then he did kill Angela," Trish whispered, her anguish washing over Scottie, reviving old memories and the harsh pain that came with them.

Scottie reached for a tissue and wiped the tears from Trish's cheeks. "We need to go. It's your place to be at the house in time to greet the visitors. Cade shouldn't have to do that alone. Especially under the circumstances."

Trish's fingers dug into Scottie's shoulders. "Scottie..."

"I'll be right there with you the whole time."

"Promise?"

"I promise. Get dressed now."

Scottie tried to call Nick again while she waited for Trish, but he didn't answer. When Trish finished dressing, Scottie drove them to Silas's house in her personal vehicle, a late-model white Jeep Cherokee. She had no idea how the reunion of sister and brother would play out, but she suspected it wouldn't hold a candle to the reception Cade could expect from other townspeople. She wished she could avoid him herself, but she needed to stay close to keep Trish from imploding before Silas was put in the ground.

Cade's Range Rover was nowhere in sight when Scottie pulled into Silas's driveway, but Guy Storey's old Crown Victoria was parked on the gravel drive that ran around the side of the house. Had Cade skipped out already? She wouldn't put it past him, considering the way he had looked and sounded that morning. That would make Trish happy, but the thought ticked Scottie off. Cade needed to do right by his uncle.

Guy opened the screen door as Scottie and Trish climbed the steps to the porch. Both women greeted him as he stood aside for them.

"I'm glad you're here," Guy said solemnly. He nodded toward the casket. "Miss Trish, your Uncle Silas looks real peaceful...like he's sleeping."

Trish's eyes welled with tears again. "I don't want to look at him." She turned away to stare out the window.

Scottie glanced around the room and into the area of the kitchen she could see. "Where's Cade? Has he left already?" she said in a low voice. "I was hoping he would be around to talk to Trish."

Just as she spoke, Cade appeared in the dim hallway leading off the living room. A sense of the surreal shuddered through her. He might have been an apparition in the shadows and their earlier conversation on the misty mountainside no more than her imagination—much like the episodes that had haunted her long after he went to prison.

Back then, she thought she saw him everywhere she looked, but the ghostly vision would vanish when she got close. Or she would imagine she heard his voice ebbing and flowing in the dark of night, when she was alone in her bed, sobbing. It had taken years to be rid of his specter. Even now, she half-expected his form to dissipate rather than step into the light of the day.

As their eyes met, her thoughts swept back through the years to a lovely white dress and lacy veil hanging in her closet. Addressed invitations, stamped and ready to be mailed the next week to special friends and relatives, replaced the normal homework on her desk. Back then, all she wanted in life was a simple wedding and a future with Cade. Baby girls that looked like her and baby boys—Scottie clenched her fists and choked out those thoughts.

Cade's lips twitched into a wistful smile as if he might be thinking the same thing. God, he looked good in a dress shirt the color of his eyes and perfectly creased gray slacks. He was clean-shaven and his hair neatly combed but long enough in back to brush his collar and give him that bad-boy look he'd had as a teenager. An intense flood of heat swept through her, and she caught her breath in surprise. *Leave. Soon. Please.*

She couldn't force herself to look away from the intensity of his gaze, but he broke contact, glanced down her body then back at her face. His expression changed subtly, falling into an unreadable mask. What had she seen there for a brief moment? Anger? Pain? Her breath quickened, but she squelched the rise of panic. She glared at him, hoping to stare him down.

"I'm not going anywhere," he said.

Scottie's body prickled. Was he truly reading her mind? That uncanny knack he once had to figure out what she was thinking and get a step ahead of her? Impossible. She wasn't under his spell like she used to be. No way he could know anything.

Trish jerked around, her eyes red-rimmed and round as an owl's as she saw her brother for the first time since she was a child. Confusion, wariness, and something akin to hatred warred in the frown on her face. She bolted for the door. Scottie caught her arm to stop her.

"Trish, you have to talk to him sooner or later," Scottie said in a low voice.

"Not now," Trish whispered breathlessly, looking away, almost hiding her face against Scottie's shoulder. "I'm not ready."

"This is the best time. You can talk without being interrupted before the visitation."

To Scottie's surprise, Gerald Taylor followed Cade into the room. The two men shook hands briefly, and Cade said, "Thank you for making the trip out here."

"Yes, I'll see you later." Gerald mumbled a brief condolence to Trish then hurried out the front door.

Cade crossed to the women, but Trish shrank back, staring at him as if he might be a snake about to strike. Scottie sensed that he wanted to take his sister into his arms but dared not after her reaction.

"Why was Gerald here?" Trish demanded. "It was about Uncle Silas's will, wasn't it?"

"We need to talk, Trish."

"About what?" she asked, belligerent anger overcoming her reticence. "How I was robbed of my share of Uncle Silas's estate?"

"Let's talk in the back."

"I'm not going anywhere with you."

"For God's sake, I'm not an ogre," he said through clenched teeth, unable to mask the hurt that showed clearly on his face.

"Go, Trish. I'll be right here," Scottie said.

"You come, too," Trish begged, clinging to Scottie's arm.

"It's not my business. It's between you and Cade."

Trish's mouth puckered into a pout, and her watering eyes flashed, but she turned and walked stiffly down the hall and into Silas's bedroom.

Cade followed, positioning himself so that she stood closer to the door and could flee at will into Scottie's waiting arms. Damn it, did everybody in town think he was a murderer come back to snatch another victim?

"Okay, what do you want to talk about?" Trish said in a hateful tone of voice that tempted him to live up to her expectations.

"I guess talking about our relationship is a lost cause, but we need to discuss your future."

Trish cut him a hard look then began to wander slowly around the room, watching him warily from the corner of her eye. A framed photo on the bedside table caught her attention. Their family—mother, father, two-year-old Trish, and seven-year-old Cade—stood close together on the dunes at Nags Head, only weeks before their mother was diagnosed with cancer, when things were happy and none of them could have imagined what the future would bring. Cade knew the photo well. It had sat there for years alongside another shot of Cade at sixteen leaning against the dented fender of his first truck, grinning as broadly as if he had a Porsche.

Trish picked up that photo and stared at it.

"Do you remember taking that?" Cade asked.

"Yes," she said. "The day you bought this old junker."

"It was all I could afford," Cade replied. "Johanna and Dad wouldn't buy me anything to drive because I already had a ticket. I worked my tail off to scrape together enough to buy that truck."

"I remember you and Mom arguing, and you accused them of playing favorites with Nicky."

"Strange they could afford that souped-up Camaro for *Nicky* and not a damn thing for me. Not even a three-hundred-dollar piece of crap."

"She said you scratched up Nicky's new car because you were mad."

"Johanna told you that?" Cade said, grimacing inwardly at the thought of the revenge he'd wrought in the middle of the night. The new paint job on Nick's prized IROC-Z after Cade used a nail to redecorate the sides cost a pretty penny—a lot more than the price tag on his old truck.

"After I got older, she told me all the bad stuff you did."

"I'll bet she did. Look, I'll admit I did a lot of things wrong as a teenager. I felt like I had reason back then. But I didn't kill anybody. I just want you to hear that from me."

Trish glared at him, her brow furrowed like a stubborn child. "You went to jail for it. They don't put people in jail for something they didn't do."

Cade made a wry face. "Trust me, Trish. They do. All the time."

"That's what Scottie said," she whispered.

At least Cade thought that was what he heard. "I beg your pardon?"

She set the photo down on the table. "Is that all you've got to say?"

Disappointed, but wondering why he expected anything more from her—or from anybody in this town—Cade said, "Uncle Silas left a letter asking me to establish a trust for you. I've got an appointment with Gerald Taylor tomorrow to finalize the paperwork so I can set up your bank account. I want you to come, too."

Trish set her hands on her hips. "I don't need you running my life. Just give me my share of the money. I'll put it in my own account."

Cade shook his head. "Sorry. That's not what our uncle wanted, and I intend to follow his instructions. He designated how much money goes into your account and how often. I can't change any of that."

"So you can spend my money and just send me a pittance every now and then? That's not fair. You might spend it all, and then I'd have nothing."

"Uncle Silas set aside the amount designated for your trust fund, and it will continue to draw interest. I'm only administrator."

"What about all his property? And this house? I could live here."

"No."

"I have the right to use this house, same as you."

Trish's disrespect toward their uncle irritated Cade as did the influence Johanna and Nick wielded over her. She was almost thirty years old, yet she acted like a spoiled brat. Maybe the time had come for her to grow up.

"Actually, you don't. Uncle Silas left me everything, the house included."

"What?" she squeaked. "That's *so* not right. It's like Nicky said. The mean cuss cut me out of his will for pure spite."

"I'm beginning to think he had good reason," Cade said, no longer bothering to hide the ire he felt. "But, whether you deserve it or not, he left you an ample trust."

"How much is it?"

"More than you need to live comfortably."

Trish's eyes narrowed. "You won't even tell me how much? And I've got no say-so in any of this? Oh, you love that, don't you?"

"Not really."

"Then give me half the inheritance, and you'll be free of the burden."

"Forget it."

Trish stamped a foot like a petulant child. "That's just not fair."

"You'll have a good income the rest of your life because of our uncle's generosity. And I'm still your brother, and I love you, whether that means anything to you or not."

"I've had enough. Nicky was right; I'm going to have to go to court to get what's mine."

"I can promise you that's a waste of your time and money." Cade reached out to her, but she shrank back. "Look at yourself, Trish. Maybe Silas saw this dependency in you—for alcohol, drugs, whatever you're high on today."

Trish's face flushed. "How can you say such a thing? You don't know me. You've never taken any interest in me," Trish shouted. "Don't come here now trying to run my life. I'll get what's mine. You wait and see."

She whirled away from him and fled out the door, meeting Scottie in the hallway.

Scottie caught the weeping girl in her arms. "What's wrong?" she said, wiping the tears away.

Trish shot a murderous sidelong glance at Cade as he came into the hall. "He got everything."

"Is that true?" Scottie turned questioning eyes on Cade.

Cade gave a curt nod. "Basically. He set up a nice trust fund for her."

Trish snatched out of Scottie's arms and flounced away, dialing furiously on her cell phone.

"Mom? Are you on your way over here? I just talked to Cade, and you won't believe what he said...."

Her voice trailed off as she crossed the living room, giving the casket a wide berth to get to the kitchen.

"That went well, I'd say," Cade said sarcastically.

Scottie watched Trish disappear through the archway. Was Silas punishing those who had treated Cade badly over the years? Had he intentionally pitted brother against sister?

"I might react the same way, knowing what I'd missed out on," she said.

49

Cade exhaled and rubbed his forehead wearily. "I didn't ask for this, trust me. Uncle Silas wanted me to look after Trish, and I'm trying. But if she keeps fighting me..."

"Give her time. This is a shock for her."

"Not only for her. I had no idea what he'd done until I talked to the lawyer."

"Looks like Silas opened a can of worms."

"No joke. I'd hoped to reconcile with Trish, but that doesn't look promising."

"I am sorry, Cade," Scottie said, touching his arm lightly. "Is there anything I can do to help you here?"

"I'm doing all right," he said, but dark circles beneath hollow eyes belied his reassurance. "Guy came early, thank God. Otherwise, I wouldn't have recognized most of the people who dropped off food. There's enough to feed an army or two."

"Everybody respected Silas," Scottie said.

"I didn't notice any gesture from the Drakes or the Baskins. Although I know the gesture they'd like to give."

Scottie smiled. "Good point. I guess there are a few holdouts."

Still standing in the dimness of the hallway, they both turned at the sound of the front door opening. Johanna called out for Trish, who answered from the kitchen. Nick and Johanna talked in hushed voices as they went to join her, Johanna's heels clicking loudly on the wooden floor of the living room then fading away.

"They must have been close by." Cade glanced at his watch. "It's almost time. I guess I'd better put on a coat and tie. Wouldn't want to fail inspection on a dress code violation."

Scottie caught the cynicism mixed with pure dread that laced his voice. Probably anything she said would only make him more querulous, so she let him go without comment. But he had a good point. He would be on exhibit as much as his deceased uncle. He slipped into Silas's bedroom for his coat, and Scottie went in search of Nick.

She dreaded Cade's reaction when he realized she was in a long-term relationship with Nick, of all people. Possibly the man Cade hated worst in the world. But why should he care after all this time? Obviously, he'd moved on just as she had. Good-looking as he was, he wouldn't have any problems with women—except maybe from a bad attitude, which he seemed to have cultivated rather than lost. Other than the man being Nick, there was no reason he should give her love life a second thought.

So why did that needle her pride? His life was none of her business anymore, and hers was none of his. She shrugged off the thought as she joined the disgruntled group in the kitchen. Trish's fountain of tears had dwindled to an occasional sob, her face buried against Johanna's shoulder.

Dressed to the nines, as usual, Johanna wore a royal blue silk sheath topped by a short jacket with black soutache trim, pumps dyed to match, and a black pillbox perched on her head, complete with peacock feather and short veil. She gently rubbed Trish's back with a gloved hand. All the while, she glared over the young woman's shoulder at Nick, mouthing what could only be retaliatory suggestions, judging from the red mottling that always rose to Johanna's face when she was overwrought.

"Did you hear?" Johanna said to Scottie. "The old coot gave everything to Cade—everything."

"I know," Scottie said in a soothing voice. "But Cade's—"

"If he thinks for one minute I'm going to stand by and let him steal Trish's half of the estate, he's crazier than I thought." Nick's temper was already high, and his strong voice grew more strident with each syllable.

Trish began to sob anew, as Johanna tried to protect her silk dress by tucking a fresh wad of paper towels between the expensive fabric and Trish's melting mascara.

Scottie laid her hand on Nick's arm in an attempt to calm him. "Let's go outside, Nick. People are starting to arrive."

"No. I'm going to settle this with Cade here and now." He tried to pull away, but Scottie held on to him with a hard, authoritative grip. He looked at her in surprise, the muscles of his forearms bunching reflexively to overpower her hold. "Let me go."

"Nick, this is not the time or the place for an outburst. You're getting Trish more and more upset, and she needs to be able to greet the visitors."

"I...I'm n-not going out there," Trish declared, lifting her head enough to cut her eyes at Scottie.

"Yes, you are." Scottie cast a reproachful look at Johanna. "Why don't you go with her, Johanna, so she won't be alone."

Johanna pursed her lips and stared into the living room, where Cade had returned to stand with Guy. "I'd rather not."

Scottie's patience was gone. She didn't have to be a part of any of this. She'd give her formal condolences to Cade and leave. She needed to be on patrol in a few hours anyway. "Listen to me, all of you. If you make this into a family brawl with Silas lying there waiting to be buried, then you ought to be ashamed of yourselves. You're adults. Act like it."

She turned on her heel, headed for the living room. Nick caught up to her before she reached the arch, blocking her passage. His body was rigid, his voice laced with suspicion.

"You're defending Cade. Why?"

"Where did you come up with that?" Scottie massaged the tense muscles at the back of her neck. "I want Trish to get her uncle buried without an uproar. You can take up any business with Cade afterward. Will you do that for Trish's sake, please?"

Nick relaxed somewhat. "Okay, okay. I see your point." He rubbed his hands up and down her arms. "I just don't want you to get friendly with him again. Knowing him, he might think he can take up where he left off."

Scottie frowned. "I don't see your point, Nick. Cade and I broke up before he was arrested, so I guess you could say we are where we left off."

"Sorry, it's just that he worries me. In a lot of ways." He leaned forward to brush her lips with his, but she avoided him, angry that he'd brought up the past so callously.

"Maybe you'd better get Trish in shape to go out there," she said, pulling away.

"I guess so."

When he moved out of her line of vision, Scottie found herself in the crosshairs of Cade's perplexed stare.

Before Cade could be certain of what he just saw, Guy blocked his view of the kitchen.

"Where do you want to stand, Cade?" Guy asked.

"Texas."

Guy gave him a sympathetic smile. "Somewhere closer than that for now."

Trish approached with a sullen look. "Scottie says I need to be here with you when the guests come in," she said then muttered, "whether I want to or not."

"I can leave."

Trish glared. "Oh, no you don't. I'm not suffering through this by myself. You'll be a nice diversion for the visitors."

She moved to put him closest to the casket, first in the line of fire. Johanna planted herself opposite Trish like her bodyguard. As if she were family. Before Cade could object, the front screen door opened, and anxiety swept in like a gust of winter wind. He forced slow, deep, steady breaths to fight the panic as a small group came through the door, seeming to move in slow motion toward him.

The man at the forefront of the group lingered for a moment before the casket then moved to Cade to clasp his hand. The man murmured a condolence and moved on quickly to Trish, and the first test was over. The fight-or-flight sensation passed as more visitors arrived. Cade responded politely to those who spoke to him—and mentally took names when he was bypassed for Trish.

A few minutes later, a man came through the door and stepped to the side rather than coming to the casket. Cade kept an eye on him as he wended his way through the visitors, finally settling against a wall. He had not spoken to anybody, nor had anyone taken much notice of him, but his attention had been on Cade the entire time.

Cade knew the man well. Ezra Wright. Angela's brother. They had once been friends, when Angela was alive. Had hunted, fished, and drank together.

Ezra had been in the army when Angela died. According to Silas, there had not been a funeral, as such, since there was no body, and her mother was too poor for a ceremony of any kind, other than a quiet memorial on the mountain with family and a few friends. Ezra had not come home then or after, going career military after their mother committed suicide within a year.

Cade's attention was forced back to the townspeople passing by the coffin. When Cade glanced around the room a short time later, Ezra was gone. Mountain man that he was, Ezra had never been comfortable in town, so maybe he had paid his respects to Silas in his own way and left. Nothing wrong with that. Cade was just as happy to avoid what might have been an awkward encounter.

After an hour, the room was crowded. A trickle of people continued to come in, and others lingered to chat with friends and neighbors. Trish and Johanna were surrounded by a wall of supporters. Guy returned to Cade's side, bringing with him two other men whom Cade remembered from his summers working for his uncle. Big'un Johnson was a massive, loud-mouthed, hardscrabble farmer who always spent more time loitering around the pot-bellied stove in the corner of Silas's store than working his farm, and Old Man Peters, a withered and ageless fellow, who had seemed ancient to Cade over a decade and a half ago. They gabbed about the local weather, their crops, and the latest news, including Cade in their conversation as if he were still that kid working in his uncle's hardware store a lifetime ago.

A heavy hand landed on Cade's shoulder. Startled, he swung around to face Ezra Wright. Guy took a step toward them. Ezra's left hand clasped Cade's shoulder with an iron grip, but he offered his right to Cade in greeting.

Surprised, Cade returned the handshake. "Ezra. It's been a long time."

"I'm sorry about your uncle," Ezra said, releasing Cade's hand but maintaining the hold on his shoulder. Cade resisted the urge to knock his hand away, though he sensed the crushing power in those sinewy fingers digging into his skin. While not afraid of Ezra, Cade felt a sudden wariness as he met his piercing gaze. "I wanted to see you, too, since I heard you were in town. I know how bad it is to lose somebody you love. It was hard on me. But I read my Bible until I understood what I had to do to go on with my life. I hope you atoned and asked the forgiveness of God for your past grievances, same as I wish for your uncle."

"Thank you for coming," Cade said, returning Ezra's hard, unflinching stare. His own atonement was none of Ezra's business.

Ezra dropped his hand from Cade's shoulder. "I'll see you again while you're in town."

Cade gave a noncommittal answer, knowing that was not likely to happen.

CHAPTER 6

A PALPABLE hush fell over the room as the two police chiefs of Cumberland Cove, former and current, walked in. With the Drakes there, Cade had more pressing matters on his mind than Ezra Wright. Although Cade inwardly recoiled from those despicable faces and the memories they regurgitated, old Bull Drake and his son, Ray, were greeted warmly all around. Father and son had run the town with an iron grip for so long that any name other than Drake after "Chief" would sound foreign.

Then a throaty giggle corded his gut tighter.

Gina Lambert flitted into the room on black ankle-strapped stilettos that put her close to six feet tall. Smoky gray eyes showed heavy-handed use of shadow and mascara. Too much makeup and a thick layer of hot-pink lipstick on wide, sensual lips couldn't hide the worn look on Gina's face.

The clinging black jersey dress she wore wouldn't pass as mourning attire by any stretch of the imagination. The tight skirt stopped barely short of indecent, molding to the apex of her thighs as she walked. A high neckline pulled the thin fabric taut over soft breasts that had been a teenage boy's wet dream. Cade eased out a breath, knowing exactly what was barely concealed beneath that shimmering fabric.

Bull Drake waited for her to catch up then latched onto her arm. Cade did a double take.

Gina and Bull? What the hell!

Ahead of his father, Ray shook Cade's hand briefly and expressed his condolences more to Trish than Cade then moved on, shaking hands with Ezra Wright, who stood a few feet away. Cade only heard snatches of the conversation, but it sounded as if Ezra must have worked for Ray at some point and was interested in doing so again.

Cade saw Ray shake his head. "I don't have any openings right now."

"Well, if you change your mind..." Ezra said, as they moved out of earshot.

Shaking hands with everybody he met, Bull Drake grinned like the Chessy cat, exposing cigarette-yellowed teeth. Lanky and broad, slightly bent with time, the old man was dressed in the same uniform-style khaki pants he'd worn on the force, but with an open-collared dress shirt and a casual navy sports coat. He looked fit enough, though his weathered face and wrinkled wattle belied his age. Gina tossed back flaming red hair that cascaded around her shoulders and closed her hand over his, posing like a movie star on the red carpet for the staring crowd.

Her gaze swept the room. When she spotted Cade, her face lit like a beacon. She shot him a flirtatious wink and a little wave with her free hand, as if they were at a class reunion rather than his uncle's last visitation.

The problem was, all eyes were drawn to Gina after her entrance. As if orchestrated, those eyes turned in the direction of her gaze and landed on Cade. Their teenage shenanigans were legend in this tiny town, and nobody seemed to have forgotten, judging by the raised eyebrows and the spark of electricity that crackled through the room hot enough to trigger an explosion.

Bull worked the people like the politician he'd always been, seemingly oblivious to the awkward tension in the room quivering like a tightly drawn bowstring ready to snap. The couple stopped beside the coffin, and Bull looked dispassionately at the man inside.

No doubt Bull was glad to have Silas gone. Silas had been an ever-present thorn in the old chief's side for his part in sending Cade to prison. That he and Ray showed up at the house at all was pure decorum rather than an act of respect.

Bull turned and fixed a stare on Cade. The stupid old coot swaggered toward him with Gina still on his arm. The flash of a large diamond and wedding ring on her left hand confirmed what Cade had already figured out. Gina had sold her soul to the devil.

As they approached, Gina pulled away from Bull.

Come on, Gina. Don't do anything dumb.

"Hey, Sugar," she said, reaching up to hug him tightly around the neck, the rise of her dress no doubt giving the room a thrill for their money.

The overt intimacy in Gina's voice sent shivers of apprehension down his spine. All the old familiar curves of her body fit into the right notches on Cade's. Pressed against him like a scorching iron, her heat seared like the fires of hell licking around him.

Cade caught her by the wrists and pulled her arms away. "Gina," he said through his teeth.

"I'm so glad to see you again." She took one of his hands in both of hers and squeezed. "But I'm real sorry about your uncle. Whoever could have done something like that?"

"Get your hands off my wife." Bull's grating voice scraped Cade's nerves, leaving them exposed, tingling.

The room went silent.

A bitter taste rose in Cade's throat, and long-seated resentment overpowered reason. "I think it's the other way around, Bull."

Gina bit her lip coyly and winked at Cade again. "You're so bad," she whispered.

"Just telling the truth." Cade extricated his hand. "Wouldn't want to upset your...husband?"

Crimson spread up Bull's neck then rapidly saturated his face. Cade wondered if the blood in the old man's veins could literally boil.

"You sorry son of a bitch, slinkin' back into town like a cur with his tail between his legs," Bull said, his voice carrying loud and clear. "I was hoping I wouldn't ever see your face again."

"I guess we're even," Cade said. "I was hoping you'd be dead by now."

A gasp ran through the onlookers. Ray started their way.

"That smart-ass attitude's part of what got you sent to prison."

"You sent me to prison, and you know it," Cade said.

"Shut the hell up," Bull snapped. "That ain't what happened."

"I never thought you did it, Sugar," Gina offered in her simplistic way.

Bull jerked Gina by the arm. "And you—keep away from him."

She teetered on the high heels for a second then caught her balance by grabbing Cade. She yanked her arm free from Bull's grasp, staring at him in anger while stubbornly clinging to Cade. Bull's heavy breathing made a snorting sound through his nose.

"You railroaded me," Cade said.

"Prove it," Bull challenged.

And that was the crux of the problem. After all these years of trying to remember, Cade had no more awareness of what really happened that night—what he did or didn't do— than back then. The remote possibility that he might accidentally have killed his friend was torture enough, but it still was a long way from committing murder.

"DNA talks, even on old crime scene evidence. What do you think, Chief? What would the DNA on Angela's shirt say if we tested it now?" Cade had been contemplating the feasibility of DNA testing for years but had never pursued the process.

A cold sweat broke out on Bull's blotched face. His hands clenched and unclenched at his sides, and his mouth worked convulsively as he stared at Cade.

Heart attack, Bull? Stroke, maybe? Be my guest.

59

If Bull fell out on the spot, somebody else would have to dial 9-1-1, because Cade would never lift a finger to save this old bastard.

Gina released Cade's shoulder and caught Bull by the arm. "Zeb? Zeb, you don't look good."

Ray appeared at Bull's side. "Daddy, you okay?"

At six foot four, Ray towered over his aging father. Short, dark hair grayed slightly at the temples; high cheekbones suggested Indian blood. The copper-colored eyes bored into Cade with pure hatred, just as they had on the night he was arrested, when Bull, then the Chief of Police, decided to interrogate Cade in the windowless backroom of the jailhouse. Cade's blood ran cold remembering the predatory gleam in Ray's eyes as he acted on his daddy's orders, intending to do whatever it took to scare a confession out of a defiant kid.

"What did you say to him, Cade?" Ray demanded.

"That he ought to have the evidence in his case DNA tested, whatever that means," Gina offered, fanning Bull's face with her hand.

"You take Daddy on home," Ray ordered.

"Come on, Zeb, let's go," Gina said quickly.

After tugging on his arm for a moment, Gina got Bull to take a step, but he resisted and turned back to Cade. "Don't you do it, Youngblood. Don't go tearing up this town again."

"What are you afraid of? Maybe it's time for the truth."

The veins in Ray's neck bulged. "You'd better back off, unless you want to land back in prison."

Johanna took Trish under her arm and eased her away.

"On what charges? Aggravating your daddy? I doubt that's a federal offense. And I can sure as hell afford a decent lawyer this time around."

"I'm warning you here and now, drop it."

Scottie stepped between the two men and laid a hand on Cade's arm. "Not now."

Cade bit back his words only because of his uncle lying across the way.

But Ray's parting salvo rang out in the eerily quiet room. "My advice to you, Youngblood, is to get out of Cumberland Cove while you still can."

CHAPTER 7

C ADE shook off Scottie's hand, his eyes fixed on the screen door where the Drakes had disappeared. Lingering animosity hung in the air, and the visitors who remained in the room clustered together, whispering.

"You need to be careful," Scottie warned. "He's got as much power around here as Bull ever did."

"I'm supposed to just ignore a blatant threat like that?"

"Unless you want more trouble than you can handle. You picked a fight with his daddy. What do you expect?"

"I didn't pick any damned fight," Cade said, his voice rising a notch. "And I don't have to—"

Nick slipped a possessive arm around Scottie. "What's going on here?"

A surge of an old, unwelcome umbrage swelled within Cade as he realized his first instinct had been right—Scottie and Nick were involved. Hatred of Nick melded with the misery of what Scottie had done to him, and the two became one spiteful entity.

"As for reopening your case, Cade, forget about it," Scottie added. "Ray would never let that happen—and for all we know, there's not enough DNA left to test."

"So even you don't want to know the truth, Scottie? Is that the kind of cop you are?"

Scottie stiffened and pulled out of Nick's embrace. "If I thought the truth was hidden there somewhere, I'd be the first one to say go for it. But it's not. Nothing would change in the end other than stirring up a lot of torment. Ray won't play nice, I can tell you that."

"Ray's never played nice, and neither has Bull," Cade said. "You didn't lose eight years of your life on a trumped-up charge."

The folks in the room inched nearer, ears open for every word.

Scottie's eyes narrowed. "You don't have a clue what I lost. Do whatever you want to." She spun on her heel and bumped into Nick. When he put his arms around her this time, she didn't pull away. Over her head, Nick shot Cade a triumphant look and guided her across the room to where Johanna and Trish now stood at a distance from the altercation.

Nick ushered the women into the kitchen. Soon, Johanna and Trish went out the back door, leaving Nick and Scottie alone. A frisson of jealousy crackled through Cade as Nick draped his arms around Scottie's waist and cupped his hands possessively on her backside. Cade swallowed hard.

"I know what we both lost, Scottie," he muttered under his breath, the bitter taste of her betrayal palpable. "And I know exactly what you did."

Nick leaned down and kissed her, pulled her closer, prolonging the connection. Were they putting on a show just for him? She was as beautiful as ever, her long, tawny hair pulled back at the nape of her neck with a tortoiseshell barrette. The unruly waves and curls tumbled down her back like a silky cascade, and Cade longed to entwine his fingers in the softness and pull her face to his. He remembered when those clear green eyes gazed lovingly at him, not Nick.

Cade's heartbeat quickened as the memories of her taste and her touch hit him like a hot wind, taking his breath. A stiff drink might help, but he hadn't touched hard liquor since the day he was arrested. He rubbed a hand across his dry mouth and excused himself to Guy.

"I'm going out for some fresh air until they leave."

Guy nodded. "Good idea."

Cade left through the front door and wandered around the house toward Silas's long-unused barn. The sun was melting to molten orange as it dropped behind the mountains, turning the sky fiery and casting an eerie glow across the valley.

The barn boards had weathered gray, and the tall door creaked on its hinges as Cade opened it to go inside. A late-model Cadillac was parked just inside, bought before the first trip Silas made to visit Cade in Texas. Cade had offered plane tickets, but Silas swore he would die before he rode on one of those risky tin cans in the sky. But not wanting to put the miles on his old truck, Silas had broken down and bought the new car for that and future trips to spend time with his nephew.

To Cade's surprise, his old, battered pickup truck from the photo sat in the center of the aisle. Silas had never mentioned keeping the truck. Cade peered inside the open driver-side window, recalling many good nights alone on that ragged seat with Scottie. And some wanton ones with Gina.

Cade supposed the truck had been impounded for evidence then released. He leaned against the fender, arms crossed, staring into the dim recesses of the barn, wondering why Silas had kept the worthless truck all these years. Wondering how Angela's bloody blouse had gotten beneath the seat. Wondering still, after all the years, what the hell happened that night.

Desultory thoughts ricocheted from depressing old memories to the negative effect his absence would have on his company and then how unprepared he was for his uncle's death. The loss ate away at him as he stood in the chilly, dark barn, listening to the soft noises around him: a mouse rustling in the corner, an owl's fading hoot, the old boards of the barn snapping as the air cooled.

The image of Nick and Scottie in one another's arms popped into his mind, souring his mood even more. Of all people, why would she choose Nick? Anybody else, and he could have wished her a world of happiness. But not with Nick. The urge to escape Cumberland Cove ratcheted up another notch.

From a distance, he heard the slamming of several car doors and the revving of engines. After the sound of the cars receded, Cade emerged and barred the door behind him. Walking quietly, he rounded the front of the house. Only a few cars lined the driveway now, and the country road out front was deserted.

The windows were up, and the mellow sound of men's low voices wafted out. The sputtering rumble of a truck pulling up the drive and stopping close to the house kept Cade in the shadows of the large shrubs growing around the front porch. A bowlegged man got out of a mistreated pickup that was dented and scraped from bumper to bumper, roof to fender weld. Holding something against his chest, he bounded up the steps and stuck his head in the door.

"Any cops here?" the man said.

"Yeah, Bobcat, I'm here," Rickey Chambers said.

"You off duty?" Bobcat asked.

"Yeah."

"Anybody else coming? Like the chief or anybody?"

"I don't think the chief will be back," Rickey said, affirmed by a couple of guffaws from the others. "Why? You got some 'shine with you?"

"Sho' have. What you think? Bring it in?"

"I'll look the other way tonight," Rickey said. "Long as none of you leave here until you've sobered up."

"How 'bout it?" Bobcat said.

After a general mumble of assent from the men, Bobcat opened the screen door wide and went inside, the jug of moonshine clutched in his hands. Cade knew Bobcat Jones from school. A dirt-poor mountain kid with less than stellar grades and sporadic attendance, he had not ranked high on the high school social ladder. Everybody thought he was off in the head because he loved to stuff things—squirrels, ducks, anything dead he could put his hands on. His nickname came from the road-kill bobcat he'd stuffed and mounted in the bed of his pickup truck. The snarling animal had scared the daylights out of the girls at school and got Bobcat suspended.

Instead of going inside, Cade sat on the bottom step, enjoying the solitude. Lulled by the laughter and quiet talk in the house, he loosened his tie, unbuttoned his shirt collar, and leaned back on his elbows to stare at the bright stars strewn across the black sky.

Almost dozing in the peaceful night, Cade jerked alert at the sound of a hound dog baying out the window of Bobcat's pickup. Bobcat came to the door and yelled through the screen for the dog to shut up. After a couple of whines, the hound circled and plopped down in the seat.

The voices inside drew Cade's attention.

"You reckon he got ever' thing? Nothing for Trish?" Old Man Peters said.

"She didn't deserve nothin'," Big'un Johnson said, his words beginning to slur from the potent moonshine. "I seen her come in Silas's store and talk to him like he was dirt under her feet. That stepmother of their'n taught her against her natural family. But Silas would give her money when she begged and if she looked sober, even though he knew what she was likely doing with it."

"Reckon he got the land with those caverns, too? That's kinda spooky, ain't it?" Bobcat said. "Wonder what he'll do. Maybe sell out?"

"Why? You got a still up there or something?" Rickey asked.

"Now you know better. I git this from my cousin."

"Sure you do," Rickey said agreeably.

"Nah, really. My cousins took over that line of business after my great uncle got shot. You know my grandpappy and the chief's grandpappy used to run moonshine out of them caverns," Bobcat said proudly, as if that connection to the high-and-mighty Drakes elevated his status. "'Course, that was way before my time. But I hunt around there sometimes. Just want to know whose land I'm trespassing on."

The men laughed.

"I recollect that operation," Old Man Peters said. "Bonner Drake and his in-laws had a couple of jacked-up hotrod trucks to outrun the revenuers. 'Course, that was long before Bull got to be top cop around these parts. Imagine the son and grandson of bootleggers running this town for years."

"They've done a good job, though. Maybe because of their background," Rickey said with a twinge of sarcasm in his voice.

"Any of you ever go in them caverns?" Bobcat said.

"You can't get inside," Rickey said. "That lean-to is always locked."

"I used to go in the other way."

"What other way?" Old Man Peters said.

Bobcat hesitated. "Well, now, there's a hidden tunnel up on the mountain, goes in farther toward the back. I used to sleep in the outer cave sometimes when I was hunting around there."

Cade knew the entrance Bobcat mentioned. It was almost impossible to find, even if you knew where to look. For Bobcat to have stumbled on it meant he spent a lot of time nearby.

As if reading Cade's mind, Rickey said, "You sure you don't have a still in that area? Maybe I better have a look around Monday."

"Ain't no need for that. I don't go in there no more, and I don't recommend you do, either. Them caves are haunted."

"Hainted. Like with ghosts?" Big'un barked. A snicker rounded the room.

Cade eased up to the top step, still in the porch shadows, listening with interest.

"That white lightning's rotted your brain, Bobcat."

"Say what you want to, Rickey, but I know there's cave spirits in there. I've heard 'em carrying on. I think it's the ghost of that dead girl trying to find her way out."

"Sounds like you heard a wildcat or something," Rickey said. "You ever heard a wildcat on the mountain? You know what it sounds like, don't you?"

Cade remembered well the eerie cry of a wildcat. Like a woman wailing.

"I tell you, t'weren't no wildcat, and I don't go in those caves no more," Bobcat said.

"No such thing as ghosts," Rickey said brusquely, as if to end the conversation.

A shudder ran down Cade's spine. Angela's ghost roaming the caverns? And here, he thought her ghost had been following him around the world all these years. For not protecting her. For not even knowing what happened to her.

"You think he really killed her, Rickey?" Bobcat said.

A hush fell. Cade barely breathed as he strained to hear.

"Don't go and ask me something like that."

"Pass that jug, Bobcat," Big'un said. "Silas shore didn't think he was guilty. But you was the one doing the investigation. You ought to know."

"I know we ought not to be talking about this," Rickey said. "I did the best I could, but everything in a case isn't always—"

"Cade, what are you doing out—"

Cade held up his hand to silence Guy, who'd walked up on him in the darkness. Guy's face was barely visible in the muted light spilling from the house, but Cade saw the questioning frown. To his dismay, Cade lost Rickey's last words.

"So you're saying not everything came out in court?"

"There's always a hell of a lot more to an investigation than comes out in court. I'm just saying there were some things, small things mostly, that I couldn't make sense of. But Bull didn't seem to think they were important enough to pursue." Rickey fell silent.

"Here, have a swallow of this shine," one of the men said, a voice Cade didn't recognize.

"Better not," Rickey said. "I go to work early in the morning."

"You was pretty new to the job back then, wasn't you?" Big'Un Johnson pressed, his tongue thick with the liquor.

"I'd just been promoted. I admit I didn't know everything. I wanted one of the Sheriff's Department's crack detectives to double-check me, go over my evidence, but the chief said we didn't have the time or budget for it. Said he looked over my report, and I was doing just fine."

There was long, unbroken silence, then Rickey said in a low voice, "I was careful. Didn't think I overlooked anything. I still don't. I just wanted a fresh eye, that's all."

Guy stared at the open window, his head cocked to one side.

"You don't think he did it, do you?" Bobcat asked again.

"Yeah, I think he did it else I would have said so back then. No evidence to the contrary. Even he couldn't defend himself. But to this day, I'd like to know why—and where the body is." Rickey fell silent for a minute then added, "It's over and done, and he's free now. Looks like he's doing okay, and this should be put behind us."

"What about Silas? Got any leads on that?" Old Man Peters asked.

"Not much to go on. Worse thing is they drove off instead of helping him."

"How long you reckon he laid there alive?"

There was a brief silence before Rickey said slowly, "Hard to tell. Hopefully he passed on pretty quick. Coroner's report will be back in a few days...then we'll know."

"Maybe the driver never realized he hit anybody," Bobcat offered.

Rickey said, "They knew."

"Mighta thought they hit a deer or something."

The images made Cade furious. How could any decent human do that?

"That amounts to murder, doesn't it, Rickey?" one of them said. "Somebody driving off like that on purpose."

"Definitely warrants harsher charges for leaving the scene," Rickey said.

"Might never find out who did it," Bobcat mused.

A chair creaked abruptly. "I gotta go," Rickey said.

Heavy footsteps crossed the floor then hesitated at the door. Through the screen, Cade saw Rickey look slowly around at the men.

"I know what I'm doing, if that's what you're all thinking. It won't be like Cade's situation."

DAY 3

CHAPTER 8

CADE and Guy slipped around the side of the house before Rickey came down the steps and went inside through the back door. Guy stopped Cade in the kitchen.

"Your uncle always said that Rickey botched the investigation and Bull was covering it up. I wish Silas could have heard, so he'd know he was right," Guy said.

"Rickey didn't say he botched it."

"Not in so many words. You need to get that evidence tested like you told Bull."

Cade removed his jacket and tie and hung them on the back of a kitchen chair. "We'll see."

"Guy, is that you?" Old Man Peters called from the living room.

Guy motioned Cade ahead of him. "Come on, let's join the others."

A hush fell when Cade entered the room. Quickly, Guy introduced him to the two men he didn't know, Neal Benson and Eli Pratt, Silas's longtime friends and fellow business owners.

As Cade and Guy sat down among them, the conversation turned to celebrating Silas's life. The nearly empty jug was passed, although Cade declined, and the men shared one anecdote after another. Sometime after midnight, cups of strong, hot coffee were interspersed with the last of the moonshine. As the cool night air permeated the room and gray dawn gradually overpowered the sallow lamplight, the men left one by one until only Guy and Cade remained. Together they cleared the house of clutter and washed the cups and plates waiting in the sink. Cade took the stuffed garbage bags out the back door to the bins beside the house.

Bobcat hailed him from where he leaned against his truck while his dog relieved itself on the shrubbery. When the dog saw Cade, he gave a sharp bark.

"Hush up, Killer," Bobcat ordered. He motioned the dog into the truck where the hound plopped down on the tattered seat, tongue lolling from a mouth that seemed to grin.

"You got car trouble, Bobcat?" Cade asked.

"Nah, just wanted to tell you how bad I feel about your uncle. I could always go to him if I was short on cash."

Cade nodded. "He was like that. Thanks for staying the night."

Bobcat shuffled his feet and looked at Cade from under bushy brows. "Some of them taxidermy places, you have to have a credit card, and I ain't got one. I was kinda hoping you'd let Mr. Guy keep ordering for me like Mr. Silas did. I always paid off my bill."

"I'll have to talk to Guy. He knows more about the business than I do."

"Fair enough," Bobcat said then cocked his head. "You know, you ain't changed much."

Cade gave a short laugh. "I was hoping I had."

Bobcat cleared his throat self-consciously. "Well, maybe, in some ways, but you know, when we was kids, I weren't thought much of in Cumberland Cove." He tipped his head and laid a finger on his temple. "Some folks say I ain't quite right. I don't think so, but that don't matter. I just wanted to mention that you was about the only boy who would give me a break. You treated me decent."

"You were pretty good to keep me supplied in moonshine, if I recall. I guess it was mutual."

"Nah, I got 'shine for plenty of the boys. It was like they thought they was high and almighty and I owed it to them or something. You wasn't that way. Just wanted you to know I'm obliged to you for that. And I was sorry you got sent off."

Surprised, Cade gave a slight inclination of his head. "I appreciate that, Bobcat. I really do."

"Guess I'll hit the road." Bobcat pushed the hound over and climbed in then leaned out the window. "You need any 'shine while you're here, I can get you some."

"I'll remember that."

"And you'll talk to Mr. Guy about my supplies?"

"I said I would."

Bobcat started the truck, but as an afterthought, Cade laid a hand on the open window. "Bobcat, I was on the porch listening when you said the caverns were haunted. You don't believe that, do you?"

Bobcat put the truck in reverse and looked Cade in the eyes. "I talk a lot of trash when I'm drinking."

"So you haven't heard ghosts?"

Bobcat's eyes flitted away. "I ain't saying that."

"You said your folks used to run moonshine out of there. I never saw any signs of that."

Bobcat shrugged. "Weren't on your side. Was on the other side."

Before Cade could question him more, Bobcat eased the truck backwards.

Mid-morning, Cade rode to the church alone in the limo reserved for immediate family. Trish had called and agreed to attend the meeting with Gerald Taylor that afternoon. Cade invited her to ride with him to the funeral. She snubbed him and chose to ride with Nick and Johanna.

He tried to convince himself he'd rather be by himself anyway, but Trish's rejection cut deep, another shard of his broken life that he couldn't piece together again. He was lonelier right now than he had ever been in his life.

The car eased to a stop at the side entrance to the church. Cade was ushered in and seated on the front pew. The other three sat apart from him on the second row. Trish wouldn't cast a glance his way.

Scottie came in just before the service began, and Nick made a place for her between him and Trish.

The organ music changed from a muted medley of old hymns to the plaintive strains of "I Am Thine, O Lord," taking Cade back to his childhood when he spent every Sunday morning in this sanctuary in the midst of his family, and later in his youth, when he was out of grace with his father, sitting beside his forgiving uncle. His thoughts lingered on those rare times when he could persuade Scottie to sit beside him until his teasing or flirting made her giggle and her mother forced her to move away.

Cade focused on the preacher as he spoke of Silas Martin's undying loyalty to friends and to family, of his spirituality, generosity, and kindness. Then Guy moved to the podium. With tears running freely down his face, Guy touched on his long-standing friendship with Silas and Silas's love for his niece and nephew.

Staring at the worn, plank floor, Cade sought the strength to endure and get back to a life he could handle. Where he could expend boundless energy in the field physically searching out the elusive oil that was worth almost any price to the petroleum producers of the world. Or face bottom-line businessmen in the hardball corporate boardrooms where he could level the playing field because he had the goods and knew how to deliver. Where emotion played no part and his past had become irrelevant.

He had to fulfill one last request for his uncle then he could rest easy that he had done his duty. In his prearranged instructions to Mr. Davis at the funeral home, Silas wanted Cade to give the graveside eulogy and sing two songs for him: The first, Silas's favorite, "Amazing Grace," and the other a song of Cade's choosing. He and his uncle had passed many a Sunday afternoon on the front porch, with Silas's gnarled fingers flying on the five-string banjo and Cade playing guitar as they harmonized on favorite gospel and bluegrass songs. There was no way he would deny his uncle's wish, though it meant exposing himself to the hostile community that had cast him to wolves and still didn't want him back.

If he had hoped few people would venture to the graveside, he was disappointed. Dozens of cars crowded the clearing in front of the caverns and lined both sides of the dirt road leading to it. Mourners traipsed the mile up the steep mountainside trail to the small family cemetery where Cade's mother and grandfather and several ancestors were buried. Only his father was missing, having been cremated by Johanna. Cade had no clue where the ashes ended up and didn't care. As far as Cade was concerned, he owed nothing to the father who had betrayed and abandoned him. Same for the rest of this town. He owed them nothing.

Silence hung over the mountainside as the mourners gathered round. Scottie took a spot behind Nick and Trish where she had an unobstructed view as Cade stepped to the head of the casket and began to speak, his voice ringing deep and clear across the quiet valley below.

"My uncle was a good man, as we've already heard. Kind. Generous to a fault. Loving. God-fearing. A friend to the community, a guardian of his family. But to me, he was more."

Scottie studied the man Cade had become. Standing tall and erect, he looked fearless as his gaze swept the crowd with eyes so gem pure that even the brilliant sky behind him couldn't compete. There had been a time when Scottie believed she knew his soul, until that day when she told him she hated him and never wanted to see him again.

The last day she saw him free.

The day her nearly perfect world imploded.

Maturity had honed the male beauty of youth to edgy, dark, good looks that reflected the wildness of the mountain he loved. The expensive, tailored suit that he wore couldn't fully disguise the subtle curve of muscle underneath. He was in his element here on the mountain, and any sign of his earlier uneasiness was well hidden now.

"My Uncle Silas was the rock I clung to when I was caught in a current too strong for me to fight alone. His was the strong arm that reached for me when no one else would cast a line."

Cade's gaze never faltered from the townspeople bunched around the coffin, many here to say farewell to a good citizen, but others,

Scottie suspected, curious to see how Cade would handle himself. Few there could meet those blazing eyes, and most heads were bowed. The reproach was well deserved. Nobody else in town had stood up for Cade when he needed help. Not his stepmother or Nick. Not Scottie's parents, even knowing how much she loved him. Nor would they allow her to see him, not even once, before he went to prison.

Scottie had wept when she saw him on TV being transferred to Brushy Mountain State Prison after his conviction. How she had longed to break the chains that bound his wrists and ankles, constricting his long, free stride, forcing him to shuffle awkwardly between the two deputies. She would have paid any price to wipe away the anger and humiliation on his face as Ray Drake shoved him into the waiting cruiser for a one-way trip to hell. She had always believed his situation was a major impetus that drew her into law enforcement. The belief that she could help somebody else, could ferret out the truth. Sometimes she had succeeded, and other times, the truth was nowhere to be found.

"He was the one who encouraged me long after I lost hope. A warrior who came to my defense, who gave far beyond what was expected of him, who never lost his belief in who I was and who I could be."

Scottie felt the sting of his censure personally. She had failed him miserably. Only Silas had remained steadfast in his defense.

"I owe the man lying here more than I could ever repay. Somebody took my uncle from me too soon, and I can't bring him back." Cade's countenance hardened as he deliberately stared down the crowd, and he continued with effort. "But if I believe anything, it's that he'll be waiting for me...in a better..." Cade's voice choked off, and he bowed his head to regain his composure. He looked up again with shining eyes and said, "And now I'll fulfill his last request of me on this earth."

Cade closed his eyes briefly then lifted his gaze to the sky to sing "Amazing Grace." Scottie's breath quickened as his voice touched familiar chords deep within her memory of them sitting on the tailgate of his pickup truck, her legs swinging in time to his music as the night wind soughed through the trees overhead.

An ethereal spirit floated heavenward on the warm current of Cade's voice as each word of "Go Rest High On That Mountain" trembled on the fragile air in final tribute to his uncle. As the last echoing notes wafted away, he laid his hands on the flag-draped coffin for a moment then walked slowly down the mountain without a backward glance.

Once down the mountain herself, Scottie parted from Nick and the others. She'd driven her own vehicle and didn't plan to join the family at Johanna's house, having heard enough whining from all of them about Silas's bequeathal. Cade said he would provide for Trish, and Scottie believed he would.

She noticed Guy sitting in the driver's seat of his old car with the engine off, staring into space. Leaning in the open window, she touched the elderly man's sleeve, causing him to start in surprise.

"Are you okay, Guy?"

He flicked a hand under his eyes. "Good as can be, I reckon. Waitin' for Cade. He wanted to open the cabin and have a look inside. I offered to drive him down there, but he wanted to walk."

"He's taking this hard. I guess he needs some time alone."

Guy shrugged. "Not sure how much he wants to be alone, but I think he's waiting for everybody to clear out of here so he don't see none of 'em."

"How did the wake go?"

Frown lines deepened between Guy's eyes. "Started out all right. A few old friends and Rickey Chambers. Then Bobcat Jones stopped by with a jug and loosened some tongues."

"Something was said to Cade?"

"Not exactly." Guy glanced in his rearview mirror then caught Scottie's eye and glanced away nervously.

"Go on, Guy. What happened?"

"Maybe I ought not say anything...." Guy appeared to screw up his resolve. "Just that Silas always felt there was something wrong with the investigation, and Rickey pretty much confirmed it—at least it seemed so to me."

Rickey was a good cop, a top-notch investigator. Still...

"You want to tell me before Cade gets back?"

Guy stared out the windshield, his jaw working back and forth a couple of times before he went on. "Rickey said some things didn't add up in his investigation. He said he wanted to call in an experienced detective from outside, but Bull wouldn't."

Guy fell silent as Cade approached the passenger side of the car.

"You heard Rickey say this, Cade?" Scottie asked, catching Cade's eye over the top of the car.

Cade got into the car and slammed the door. "We need to get those locks changed tonight, Guy. Take care, Scottie."

She stood back as they drove off. Could Cade have been telling the truth when he professed innocence? Had Rickey covered up for somebody all these years?

Scottie couldn't believe Rickey might have missed something vital. But the skeptical nature that had garnered accolades during her tenure as a detective with the Atlanta PD kicked in. What if the investigation had been botched? What if Cade truly was innocent?

A chill ran over her, standing alone in the isolated clearing. What if...?

CHAPTER 9

"Damn that old man and his will." Nick loosened his tie as he walked into his office on the outskirts of Cumberland Cove. Glass and polished steel furniture gave the suite a clean, ruthless look, like a killing machine that would leave no trace of blood behind. But today Nick felt like the helpless victim in a dangerous world he had created himself.

Nick's corporate lawyer, William Grazer, waited for him at a glass-topped conference table that could seat twenty. Crystal pitchers and water goblets sat close at hand on silver trays. Leather-bound writing pads and silver writing pens lay ready for business, along with thick folders of paperwork on the table in front of Will.

"More problems?" Will asked.

Nick stared through a wall of glass at a panoramic expanse of the Smoky Mountains shrouded in muted blues and grays in the misty morning, but the peaceful view did nothing to calm his anxiety.

"Do you think I called you in here for my health?" Nick said. "As you know, my stepsister's uncle passed away, and I've been dealing with all that."

"My sympathy." Will fanned the papers before him with his thumb. "So what now? Do you know the terms of Mr. Martin's will yet?"

The question hung in the air like an ominous storm front bearing down. Nick cleared his throat. "Silas left everything to his nephew."

"Cade Youngblood? I noticed his name in the obit. And that's a problem?"

Will had only moved to Cumberland Cove in the past ten years, long since Cade had left town.

"That son of a bitch wouldn't sell me an acre of that land to save his life!" Nick slapped his palms flat on the glass table with a resounding whack that shook the glass like a thunderbolt. "What the hell am I going to do?"

Will never flinched. He was an excellent lawyer and had advised Nick to slow down more than once. Warned him not to pre-sell homes on land he didn't yet own or order special fixtures, exotic wood, prime slabs of granite for the upscale touches he'd promised the buyers because he could get them cheaper that way. Told him in no uncertain terms not to use reinvestment capital to buy a large tract of inferior land to utilize as a staging arena for all of the damned expensive land-moving equipment he purchased at auction—which he had paid for with most of the upfront money from enthusiastic would-be homeowners and investors in his upscale, much-hyped development.

Nick knew better than to count his chichi condos before they hatched. But none of his projects had ever failed. Red ink never touched his ledgers. Each project had been far more successful than the one before. And this new project—his crowning glory—how could it be any different?

He was on the verge of making a quantum leap from mere real estate tycoon to the rarefied world of business magnate. He'd planned to out-trump Trump with his high-end, multi-purpose urban village: million-dollar-plus homes topping the mountain; upscale shopping; opulent office buildings; trendy apartments and condos for lease and sale. In spite of the high-profile publicity over Trump's project in Charlotte, when Nick's mega-development came to fruition, the world would sit up and take notice of the esoteric new star that would be

Cumberland Heights. All his to birth and raise, like a favored golden child.

Now about to dissipate before his very eyes, the air spewing out of his blimpy ego just when he could feel the heft of the profits he was set to reap.

Will leaned back in his chair, gently drumming his fingertips on the armrest. "There was a time when you could have given the money back. Found more land. Relocated the project." Will's way of insinuating the *I told you so* Nick knew he so richly deserved.

"Thanks a lot," Nick grumped, feeling like a child being chastised by his father.

"I guess you'd better be coming up with some land and fast. You won't even be able to get a loan if you can't produce a suitable tract of land."

"I'm trying."

"What do you expect me to do?"

"The old man didn't leave a dime to his niece. I think she should have her fair share. Can we sue the estate for her half?"

"Depends on how the will was made out."

"Trish said something about a trust."

Will pursed his lips and shook his head, fueling the acid that fed Nick's ulcer. "If Silas Martin set up a trust and did it right, we'll never break it."

"Damn it. There's got to be a way."

"I'll look into it, but I'd suggest you find another tract of land."

"There's nothing remotely comparable anywhere near here."

"Then I'd say you're up Cumberland Creek without a paddle."

"I don't pay you for sarcasm."

"How much longer are you going to be paying me?" Will cocked his head to one side, raised an eyebrow, and waited.

Nick couldn't afford to lose him. He wished he could kick Cade Youngblood's ass—and Silas Martin's, too.

"You deliver, I'll pay you."

"I'll do what I can, but you might be looking at bankruptcy."

Cold fear crept into Nick's veins. He had been working on this deal for a couple of years, but he'd built his career and reputation for a lot longer than that. Gritting his teeth to keep the emotion inside, he said, "Get back to me. Meanwhile, I'm going to see if Trish can talk him out of her share."

"That might be your best bet."

After Will left, Nick sat staring out the expansive windows. In the distance, he could see the summit of Cumberland Mountain. This long-overlooked area on the edge of the Smokies was prime for financial explosion with the right man behind the project. The virgin of the South, the quiet, unassuming, underutilized Smoky Mountains epitomized Nick's dream; this project would redefine who he was and what he could do. His crowning glory was slipping away all because of one man. Will Grazer was a creative lawyer and wouldn't have time to blink before some other corporation snapped him up. Nick was the one who stood to lose everything.

All because of Cade Youngblood—a mere man, nothing more. A man could be persuaded, bought out...or nullified.

Nick glanced at his watch, dialed Trish's cell phone, and waited impatiently for her to answer. Her meeting with Cade and the lawyer was in an hour, and he wanted to give her a pep talk beforehand. When she finally answered, her voice was slurred and heavy.

"Are you ready for your meeting?"

"Wha...?" Trish said in a sleep-heavy voice.

"The meeting with Cade and Gerald Taylor. Don't tell me you're in bed!"

"I needed a nap," she said.

"A nap? Christ, don't you have a brain in your head? Did you take something?"

"Why do I have to go, anyway? You said we'd have to sue for my half."

"You need to go and at least find out the terms of the will. Accept whatever it is he's offering you, and if it's not enough then we'll sue." He heard Trish take a sobbing breath and knew he couldn't push her without the possibility of a breakdown. Just what he needed at this point. He tempered his voice. "Don't get upset, Trish. Just understand, the more information we have, the better chance of success. Get dressed and go to the meeting."

Trish hesitated. "You talk to him, Nicky. I'm afraid of him."

Nick rolled his eyes. This is what he got for trashing Cade to Trish all these years. But Nick knew Cade wouldn't give him the time of day, so Trish had to come through. "He's not going to hurt you. Don't worry about that. Gerald will be there the whole time. Get all the information out of him that you can. Tell him that all you want is your half of the land. That you won't contest the rest."

"But I don't care about the land," Trish said in a testy voice. "I want money."

"Look, Trish, sweetie, if you get your share of the land, you can sell it and have a lot more money. Otherwise, you're being cheated out of something you deserve, and you'll be flat broke."

"Okay, okay. I'll go. But I need to get dressed first."

"Get a move on. You're going to be late as it is."

And get that land, damn it!

CHAPTER 10

THIRTY minutes of small talk at a hundred an hour wasn't cutting it. Looked like Trish was a no-show. Across the stately polished oak desk, Gerald was antsy, too, fidgeting with his crystal paperweight.

Finally, Cade said, "I apologize. I wanted to give her a chance, for my uncle's sake. Let's go ahead and set up the trust."

He signed papers to give Gerald power of attorney to act on his behalf, set up Trish's account at the bank, and make the first deposit.

Then Cade said, "Gerald, I need your help on one more thing. I need to make a new will."

When they were done with the legalities, Gerald told Cade, "I'll work with her in any way I can."

The intercom buzzed, and the secretary's voice came through. "Mr. Taylor, Miss Youngblood is here."

"Yes, have her come in." Gerald raised his eyebrows at Cade. "Well, better late than never," he said with a trace of resignation as they waited, standing, for Trish to be ushered in.

Trish hurried through the door as if she could make up the lost time. "I'm so sorry," she said hastily, "I can't seem to get anywhere on time these days. I hope I'm not too late." She flashed a pretty, apologetic smile at the men, and neither of them found heart to chastise her.

Cade held a chair for her then sat down, chalking up the time wasted to the way his life was going lately. He didn't even bother to ask why she was late. From the spacey look in her eyes, it would probably only make him angrier.

"Okay, so tell me what you want me to know," she said as she settled into the chair and laid her purse on the desk.

For the next half hour, Gerald patiently explained the terms of the trust, how it had to be administered, and when she would be able to access the bank account.

She listened, asked a preponderance of questions, and when he'd finished, she shook her head and said, "That's not good enough."

Cade leaned back in his chair and laced his hands behind his head in exasperation, not trusting himself to speak.

"What don't you understand, Miss Youngblood? I'll explain it to you again," Gerald said.

"We're Uncle Silas's only relatives. I should have inherited half. Money and land, both. This way Cade gets everything and even controls the pittance I got."

"This is a generous trust set up according to your uncle's wishes," Gerald said.

"Yes, but I have to wait for my long-lost brother to dole it out."

"Your uncle had the right to leave his estate to whomever he wished. The fact that Mr. Youngblood is willing to share with you is a testament to his generosity."

Cade leaned forward. "It's exactly what Uncle Silas asked me to do, Trish, to the letter."

"When? When did he ask you to do that?"

"He left a letter with Gerald. Even if he hadn't, I would have set it up anyway."

"Like I believe that! I don't want you in charge of my business."

"Very well, we can change that." Gerald's patience was impressive. Cade's was wearing thin to the point of snapping.

Trish smiled triumphantly. "Great. Do it. I want my brother Nicky to take care of my business."

Did she call Nick her brother out of spite, or did she really think of him that way, Cade wondered. Either way, that arrangement was not going to happen. He waited for Gerald to deliver the *coup de grâce* as far as this trust was concerned.

"If you remove your brother as administrator, he will be the one to choose an alternate." Gerald glanced at Cade and almost winked. "And I'm afraid your uncle requested that certain people not be retained as administrator, Miss Youngblood, and Mr. Baskins is among them."

"That's just not right," Trish squeaked.

"Miss Youngblood, the fund has been set up already. No matter who administers it, the terms of the trust won't change in any way. And in truth, your brother might prove more lenient toward your 'emergencies' than anybody else."

"I doubt it," Trish snapped. "I need a house of my own. And a new car. I'm tired of living with Mom. I should at least get Silas's house if I don't get any land. What if I take this to court and demand my share?"

"You could put this money to much better purpose," Gerald advised. "A court battle like this would generate significant legal fees."

"I would win," she insisted.

"Highly unlikely," Gerald said. "I worked with Silas to set up his estate, and there aren't any loopholes. Take my word for it, Miss Youngblood."

Trish sat back in a huff, staring at the landscape painting behind Gerald.

"I'm not going to cheat you, Trish," Cade said. "If you want a house, we'll buy you one."

"Why can't I just have Silas's house?"

"No, I'm keeping that. But any other reasonable place. We'll go look. I can stay another day or two."

She turned her gaze on him, and he could have been looking into his own angry, defiant eyes. "I don't want anything from you."

"It's not from me. It's from Uncle Silas. He set things up this way so you wouldn't get ripped off. Why do you think Nick wants you to have that land instead of money?"

"Because it's rightfully mine."

"Do you honestly believe that? How did he get rich? From helping people keep the land that was rightfully theirs? No. By buying it out from under them and reselling it for top dollar to the property developers already lined up on the side waiting. You've been here the whole time. Isn't that what he's done? Don't you think his sharks are waiting right now for Uncle Silas's land?"

Trish sucked in quick breaths through her nose and fought to keep her chin from trembling. "That's not true. He doesn't want to steal my land. What's to keep you from selling it if somebody offers enough? You just don't want Nicky and me to benefit."

"I sure don't intend for Nick to profit. Uncle Silas left the land in my safekeeping, and there it'll stay." Cade studied her pretty face for a minute, noting the dark circles under her eyes, the pale skin and premature lines that attested to her self-indulgent lifestyle.

"Why don't you look at the positive instead of seeing this as a negative?"

"What positive?"

"You'll have plenty of money to live on. You can get out from under Johanna's thumb and be independent. You won't have to depend on her for anything."

"I don't depend on her. I've got a job," she countered defensively.

"I didn't know that. Where?"

"I finished nursing school last year. I work at Stony River Nursing Home in Sevierville."

Maybe there was hope, Cade thought for the first time since he'd reconnected with his sister. "That's good. Then why don't we look at houses over there?"

"Nick's a real estate agent. I bet he could—" She cut a look at him and made a wry face. "Guess you wouldn't want to use Nick."

Cade smiled. "Guess not. I'll find an agent if you want to go looking tomorrow."

She shrugged thin shoulders. "Okay, we can try."

"Good. Are you hungry? Is Nelda's still operating?" Cade asked, wanting to keep her open to him as long as he could.

"Sure. Best food in town."

"Gerald?" Cade asked.

The lawyer patted his stomach. "Not me. I just lost a couple of pounds, and one meal at Nelda's will put it right back on." He stood and shook Trish's hand politely when she offered it. "I think you're making an intelligent decision, Miss Youngblood. If there's anything I can do to help you out, do come by. That's another perk from your brother—free legal advice."

Cade and Trish drove separate cars from the rapidly expanding business section on the outskirts of Cumberland Cove to the quaint, core village that now served more as a tourist attraction with gift shops, art galleries, and walking tours of the historic buildings, including the centuries-old grist mill. Cade hadn't pressed when Trish insisted on taking her car, and he was glad he wasn't riding with her when she gunned the engine of her old Honda compact to pass him as soon as they pulled out of the parking lot. The smoke that roiled from her tailpipe almost obliterated his vision. She definitely needed a new car and driving lessons.

As he parked beside her, she was smacking lipstick between her lips. She blotted, crushed the tissue into her ashtray, and got out. When brother and sister walked into the café, heads turned.

Cade squared his shoulders and acknowledged the stares with a nod, until the gawkers turned away. The café owner, Nelda Greer, waited a table near the door. She gave them a double take then hurried over, catching their hands in hers. Nelda had sent food to Silas's house, had attended the visitation and the funeral, yet she and Cade had managed only a few words in the tumult of those two days.

Nearing her seventies, with iron gray hair tucked under a hairnet, she had shown nothing but kindness toward Cade and Trish since their mother died. He'd wished on more than one occasion that his daddy had married Nelda instead of Johanna.

"Look at you two! I never expected to see this sight again. Oh, if Silas could be here. Poor, dear man. That black wreath on the hardware store door just tears my heart out." Nelda dropped Trish's hand to grab her apron and swipe at her moist eyes. "Have they got any idea who hit him?"

Trish shrugged.

"Not that I know of," Cade said.

Nelda rallied. "Well, this sight would've made him proud. Oh, for heaven's sake, give me a hug, both of you." She pulled them together against her soft bosom, clutching brother and sister as if they were her own two long-lost children.

When Cade managed to extract himself, he smiled and said, "I hear the food's still tolerable here."

"Oh, shoo," Nelda said, swatting him with her hand. "Tolerable? You know better. Come on. Sit down at this big table right here."

Cade motioned toward the back. "How about that booth?"

"Sure. Go ahead. Wherever you want."

All the while, Trish held her peace, but the look on her face told him she wasn't enjoying the public reunion and would rather be anywhere else. He understood perfectly.

"What's her problem? Old busybody." Trish rolled her eyes as she slid onto one of the benches. "I already know what I want. I always get a steak."

Nelda returned with menus. "Haven't seen you in here lately, Trish. You want your usual grilled chicken Caesar?"

Trish glared at her.

Cade said, "I think she wants a steak today."

Nelda raised her eyebrows. Cade glanced at the menu and noticed the steak was by far the most expensive item on the menu. He almost chuckled. Was his sister trying to bankrupt him with a steak?

"How do you want that cooked, honey?"

"Ummm...well done...I guess."

"What about you, Cade?" Nelda asked, as always, committing the orders to memory instead of writing them down. Cade recalled his dad complaining that she was going to get the orders wrong, but she never did.

Cade pointed to an item. "This pulled pork barbecue sandwich, is that the same one you used to make with the sweet homemade pickles on it?"

"Very same."

"I haven't had barbecue that good since I left here."

"Of course you haven't. I guess you want my seasoned curly fries, too, like you always did."

"You bet. Now you've made me hungry."

"I'll put a rush on it, just for you."

Nelda started for the kitchen. Trish called her back.

"You know, I think I want that chicken Caesar after all."

Nelda smiled. "Sure, honey. No problem."

"You're welcome to the steak," Cade said when Nelda was out of earshot.

Trish made a wry face. "I don't like steaks all that well. Don't know why I thought I wanted one."

Cade looked around the café. Not much had changed. Checkered tablecloths covered the rough-hewn plank tables, and almost every seat was taken. Catsup, salt and pepper, hot sauce, and Nelda's own brand of spicy chow-chow sat in a cluster in the center. Nelda flitted from table to table taking orders, bringing food, refreshing drinks, operating the cash register. Nothing flustered her. In a few minutes, she brought their drinks—water for Cade and a cola for Trish.

"You still run this place single-handed?" Cade asked.

"Pretty much. My nephew cooks, and my niece comes to help out on weekends. That's the way I like it. I'm going to keep going till the good Lord sees fit to take me. Where do you live now? I never could get a word about you out of Silas except how good you was doing."

After all these years, his uncle still tried to protect him. "I have a condo in Houston that I rarely use since I'm usually out of the country."

"That so. What do you do for a living?"

Ordinarily, Cade would have considered the questions intrusive, but he knew Nelda was earnest. "Oil exploration. I find oil deposits for petroleum companies."

"No kiddin'? You travel a lot doing that?"

"Probably no place you'd find interesting. A lot of remote, wild locations that aren't in any travel guide."

His sister cocked her head. "So how do you get there?"

"Helicopter mostly. Sometimes we have to pack in on mules or on foot."

"You always did like to explore. I guess that's a good job for you. Who do you work for?" Trish asked.

"I work for myself."

"You own the company?"

"I do."

Trish looked at him with renewed interest. Across the room, a diner caught Nelda's attention.

"I'd better get busy," she said.

When Nelda left, Trish narrowed her eyes at him. "You don't even need Uncle Silas's money, do you? You're just greedy."

She sounded like a damn broken record.

"Let's not get into that again. Has it ever occurred to you that Uncle Silas was afraid you'd be an easy target because of your dependency on drugs?"

"Are you nuts? What makes you think I do drugs?"

"What about the other night at the visitation? If that wasn't drugs, what was it?"

"I took some tranquilizers, that's all."

"Drugs."

"Medicine."

"Whatever label you want to put on it. Prescription drugs can be abused, too. I've also heard that you drink. Put the two together and they can be lethal. But you're a nurse. I'm sure you realize all that. Silas knew you a lot better than I do. Maybe he was worried that somebody would bamboozle you out of anything he gave you." Cade leaned across the table toward her. "At least this way, you'll have to hand over the money a little at a time, and maybe you'll come to your senses before you're completely broke."

If looks could kill, he would have been bloody, but he didn't really care. Before she could take him to task, Nelda delivered their food. Cade allowed the distraction of eating to ease them into silence. Trish pointedly ignored him, picking at her salad. He indulged himself in the delicious sandwich laced with a sauce Nelda kept a close secret. Sweet but with a slight tang, the sauce was a perfect complement to melt-in-your-mouth pork that had been slow pitted over hot coals in a tiny shed off the kitchen. For the first time since his return, something actually felt like home, and he closed his eyes in pleasure.

"Cade," Trish said, "Are you listening to me?"

Never a moment's peace. He forced his attention away from the glorious sandwich and back to his querulous sister.

"Sorry, what?"

"I want to talk about my house."

He hid his surprise, as well as the tiny flicker of hope that she might come around in time. "Okay. What did you have in mind?"

"Well, before now, I had in mind whatever I could find that I could afford. Now I want a really big house."

"Why?"

"Just because I do. I deserve it."

"Will you get over this 'I deserve it' hang-up? It's still what you can afford."

Trish's lips ran out in a pout again. "Yeah, like you, I guess."

"What do you mean by that?"

"You don't have to budget. That jacket costs a fortune and those shoes about three hundred. And you're driving a Range Rover. You're filthy rich."

"I didn't buy one thing with Silas's money. I'm working my butt off long-distance right now to keep my company above water. And I still have to live within my means. I don't have a Lamborghini, and I own a condo, not houses on both coasts. Fact of life, you and I both have to make good use of our resources. Now about this house, you've got two choices."

"Really? And what are they?"

"I'll allot you a certain amount for a house—and a better car, if you want one. But I'm not buying you the Biltmore Estate. You have to decide if you want to buy a house and car outright, which means staying within the budget, or use the money as a down payment and pay off loans for the balance. The same decisions every one of us has to make every day. Live within our means or make debts."

"You keep saying I've got plenty of money," she said with a negligent shrug.

"Fine. Your decision. But think about it before you commit. House and car paid for, lots of extra money to spend on whatever you want. Clothes, travel, landscaping, gas." He held his hands palm-upward like scales of justice and levered them up and down. "Or high loan payments and maintenance on a big house, and you'll be just as strapped as you are now."

Trish pondered that. If he failed to get through to her, he foresaw an endless stream of phone calls whining about money. *Thanks, Uncle Silas.* At least he could escape out of the country often.

Unbidden, Nelda brought them both fresh coffee and a bowl of ice cream. Strawberry. Cade's favorite. Nice way to end what was turning out to be a more pleasant day than he'd anticipated.

Cade's phone rang. He checked the caller ID then excused himself to Trish and answered, knowing the call would be brief.

"Busy?" Scottie asked.

"Just finishing up."

From the corner of his eye, Cade saw Trish lean over her purse on the bench. She rambled around in the depths then quickly put her hand to her mouth, straightened, and took a sip of her drink.

"So, did you get your business with Trish done?" Scottie's voice drew his attention again.

"Pretty much."

"That's good." She sounded sincerely glad. "Have you decided when you're going back to Texas?"

"Not yet. Why?"

"I want to talk to you before you leave town."

"Okay, when?"

"Tonight, maybe tomorrow?"

"I'll be around. Probably best to call first."

As he slipped the phone back into his pocket, he noticed that the battery was low, almost dead. It had been giving him problems for weeks, losing the charge too quickly, and he'd planned to pick up another one in Houston before flying back to the Gulf but had not had time. He'd have to remember to plug it into the car charger on the way home.

"That sounded like Scottie." Trish quirked an eyebrow. "Nicky won't like that."

The muscle in Cade's jaw twitched. "Maybe it's none of Nick's business who I talk to."

"When he finds out, he'll make it his business."

Cade had no doubt of that. "If you want to tell him and make trouble, go ahead. Scottie and I are old friends; it's nothing more than that."

"Right. You were more than friends back when you killed Angela."

Trish's callousness stunned him for an instant, making him glance around as if every eye had turned his way. The diners chatted happily away at their tables, oblivious to the blood draining from his face. His hands clenched into fists on his thighs.

"You took a pill while I was on the phone. What was it?" he asked.

She cocked her head and gave him a sly look. "None of *your* business."

"You need to get off these drugs." He folded his napkin and laid it on the table. "I'm not going to discuss anything with you right now."

"I don't care." Trish leaned across the table toward him. "And, Cade, I've changed my mind. I want my half of everything, and I'm going to get it. Nicky will buy the land from me, and I'll have a lot more money."

Cade didn't need proof that Nick was behind his sister's recalcitrance, but to hear it so blatantly thrown at him drove his blood pounding into his skull.

"No...way...in...hell!" he said, keeping his voice low but making sure she understood every word. "You'll never get an acre of Uncle Silas's land as long as Nick is involved."

Trish twisted her mouth into an ugly pout. She pushed up from the bench and threw her napkin at him. "You are stealing my inheritance from me, and I'm going to get what's mine!" she shouted. *Now* everyone in the room turned their way. "I wish you were dead; then I would get it all!"

Before Cade could respond, she grabbed her purse and flounced out. So much for pleasantries. Nelda watched her go then brought Cade the check. "Temperamental, isn't she?"

"Seems to be. Not the little sister I remember...but then I guess I'm not the big brother she wants, either."

"She's got her problems. Be sure you come in again before you leave town. Now let me get my customers' attention back on eating."

Nelda moved on to the next booth. He took a last sip of coffee and watched through the window as Trish's car shot out of the parking space and took off. At least he wouldn't have to waste time house hunting.

As he slid to the edge of the bench, his knees bumped a set of shapely legs a mile long in six-inch, hot pink spike heels, and at eye level, boobs to make a man drool all over himself.

Trouble in spades.

"I can't believe I caught you here, Sugar!"

A tight, pink, off-the-shoulder sweater molded perfectly to the full curve of Gina's breasts. She had poured herself into a pair of low-slung white capris with a wide pink belt.

"I'm so glad to see you," she drawled as she laid her designer purse on the table and patted Cade's leg. "I didn't get a chance to talk to you after the funeral. Scoot over, darling. Let me sit down."

"I really have to be going."

"Aw, you've got time for a cup of coffee for old time's sake." She raised a hand that clinked with bangles and called out, "Nelda, bring Cade and me another cup of coffee, sweetie."

Again, several patrons angled for a look. Cade could empathize with those movie stars constantly hounded by paparazzi. Reluctantly, he slid across the bench to the wall, hoping to put a little space between them, but Gina was having none of that. She scooted over until her thigh butted against his.

Nelda brought the coffeepot and a second cup. "How'd you escape?" she asked Gina.

Gina frowned and slid Cade a look. "I don't have to escape. Zeb's not my keeper."

Nelda raised her eyebrows at Cade, poured the coffee, and left, clucking as she went. *Bad news.* Cade knew that well enough without Nelda's hint, but he saw no way to get out of the booth without dumping Gina on the floor or making an undignified scramble under the table to the other side. This little tête-à-tête would be all over town before bedtime, possibly replete with clandestinely snapped cell phone photos.

"Aren't you glad to see me, Sugar?" she said, running a long, lacquered fingernail up Cade's thigh.

He caught her hand and lifted it to the table. His eyes lingered on the fancy wedding ring set. "How did you get yourself married to Bull Drake, of all people?"

Gina pulled loose, moving the big brilliant-cut diamond back and forth, studying it. "Interesting story. You might want to hear it sometime." She batted long eyelashes at him. "Besides, I thought you weren't ever coming back, else I'd have waited."

Cade grunted but made no comment.

"I saw Trish leaving as I came in. Y'all on good terms again?"

Cade laid his arm along the back of the seat and leaned away from Gina. His gaze wandered downward. He checked his lustful thoughts sharply and concentrated on her face. "What do you think?"

"Probably not. She's disowned you for a long time now. I told her not to believe everything she was fed, but she thinks I'm trash and wouldn't listen to me if I told her the earth was round."

"She's been influenced by the wrong people."

"I don't know. She's been grown a while. She ought to be able to make her own judgment. Maybe she's just stuck with all she's ever known. Like most of us.... At least you escaped this Podunk town."

"Bad way to do it. You'd think I could have come up with a better idea."

"Not exactly what you had planned after graduation, was it?"

"Not even close. Listen, I really do need to go."

Gina continued as if he hadn't spoken, her voice sultry and low in the narrow booth. "I hated the way they set you up like that. I wanted to be at the trial. I might could have helped you."

Cade sat up, paying more attention. "What makes you say that?"

She dropped her gaze and backed off. "Just thought maybe I could've, but it didn't work out that way."

"Has Bull ever talked about it?" The conversation at the wake echoed loud and clear through his mind.

Gina lifted her smooth, tanned shoulders. Her smoky eyes flirting, she murmured, "There might be some things I can tell you."

Cade cocked an eyebrow. "Okay, shoot."

Leaning on his shoulder, she pulled herself up until her lips brushed his earlobe. A waft of her heady perfume filled his nostrils. Her breath tickled as she whispered, "Not right here, Sugar. Maybe we can go somewhere more private and..."

"Gina!"

Gina's body jerked back violently as Ray grabbed her arm and dragged her from the booth. Cade slid across to defend Gina. She locked warning eyes on Cade, even though her words came out with remarkable calm. "Don't get up. I've got to go home anyway."

"Good idea," Ray said, giving her a slight shove toward the front door. "Tramp," he added under his breath as she left.

He turned to Cade, standing now.

"What were you two talking about?" Ray demanded. The muscles in his thick neck twisted into cords.

"Nothing in particular."

"Take my advice and stay away from her. Daddy's a jealous man where she's concerned—God knows why."

Nelda appeared at Cade's side. "Having a problem, Chief?"

Ray gave a curt nod, his gaze riveted on Cade's face. "Yeah, I got a problem."

"I'd appreciate it if you take it elsewhere," Nelda said. "I don't like trouble in here."

Cade handed Nelda his ticket and two twenties. "I don't need any change."

"Cade, that's way too much," she protested.

"Trust me, it's not."

CHAPTER 11

Gina entered the opulent, immaculate master bedroom of her home. The only reason she was home now was because the shops at the small mall on the outskirts of town had closed their doors for the night, and she had nowhere else to go. Shopping always soothed her when life went south—as it had since Cade's return. She knew better than to be caught with him in public, but when she saw his car parked next to Trish's at Nelda's, she figured she could get away with a quick Cade fix with his sister as chaperon. Unfortunately, Trish had plowed past her as she went in, but by then it was too late. And besides, she really wanted to see him, to brush against him—to get something going with him again.

She stopped short just inside the doorway. *Oh great!* Bull lay sprawled naked on the bed, his raucous snoring reverberating through the room. Determined not to wake him, she passed with no more than a glance at his aging body and those flaccid shriveled parts, his pride and joy, that needed a medical boost to rise to the occasion these days. Even more reason she wanted Cade. She could almost feel him inside her, filling her in ways that Bull never could.

Damn Bull. Damn everybody right now.

Plush carpet silenced her footfalls, and heavy drapes swept gracefully back from a wall of windows overlooking the isolated valley, where no prying eyes warranted closing them. The massive, carved mahogany bedroom suite was originally built for an antebellum mansion, and Gina had spent a small fortune on it, and more still to have the bedroom enlarged specifically to fit the furniture. The entire house was furnished in white—all white, except for Bull's den, which was filled with black leather and trophy animals with sad, staring eyes.

Pristine and orderly, her home was exactly the opposite of the dingy, dilapidated hovel where she grew up with an abused mother too intimidated to protect her little girl from a drunken, lecherous father. From the time she reached puberty, Gina lived with the dread of her daddy coming home drunk and purposefully mistaking her cot for his own bed. She had always felt dirty and at fault when he told her how beautiful she was, too sexy for any man—even her own father—to resist.

She locked the bathroom door behind her and leaned against it, letting the soothing aura of her favorite haven further calm her nerves. On one side of the room, an oversized slipper tub with gold-plated claw feet sat on a raised dais like a throne, while double vanities with golden, swan-shaped faucets took up the other wall. A huge closet at the far end was arranged meticulously by color and article, with ample cubbies for her accessories. As with the rest of the house, Bull had basically given her a blank check to remodel and decorate, and she had not scrimped. Nor did she ever ask where he got the money. Frankly, she didn't care, as long as he indulged her extravagances. She twisted the knobs on her bathtub fully open and dumped in foaming bath crystals for a hot bubble bath.

Usually, her beautiful haven uplifted her spirits, but tonight, the room just reminded her how she got there and the shortcomings of a life spent with an old man like Bull Drake. Damn Ray to hell, and damn his daddy, too. She never should have married the saggy-balled old bastard.

But she really should thank Bull for plucking her out of the gutter and getting her off a serious criminal rap in Chattanooga years ago, about the time she realized Cade was going to prison and was out of her life for many years, maybe forever, if he was convicted of murder. Seeing Bull as a barrier against the vile cesspool where she'd almost drowned, she'd happily accepted his marriage proposal. But if she'd thought being the wife of a has-been police chief could pull her up the social ladder in Cumberland Cove, she soon found she was wrong. Long ago, she'd given up that dream and pretended she didn't care.

Settling in with soft music playing through expensive headphones and a glass of wine close at hand, she tried to relax. She wished she could invite the churning bubbles into her brain, let them scrub her mind clean, rinse away the memories of a lifetime gone wrong. She despised herself because Bull gave her just about everything she wanted, overlooked a multitude of sins, past and present, and strutted like a rooster with her clinging to his arm, yet she cheated on him because he couldn't satisfy her more basic needs.

And then, without warning, Cade was home and nothing else mattered to her. The only man she'd ever loved; the man she'd never expected to see again. And now he acted as if there never had been anything between them. But there had been. He had cared for her, and she wouldn't give up. Cade was her way out.

She played idly with the washcloth, swirling it around in the mass of bubbles in front of her to make designs. Her heavy, slick breasts seemed to rest on top of the froth, hard nipples in dark contrast to white soap. Breasts that men loved. That Cade had once loved. Sliding her hands down their slope, she recalled his touch from long ago and felt heat flow through her like liquid gold. Texas. She'd love to live in Texas. Anywhere far from Tennessee. She still believed she could convince him, if only she could get him in bed once more... She groaned softly at the thought.

A heavy hand grabbed the back of her neck. Gina screamed and snatched off the headphones. She twisted around, saw her broken door handle and the look on Bull's face, and braced for trouble.

"Zeb, honey," she said in the silky voice that usually soothed him like a cat being stroked, "I was going to let you sleep until morning."

"Didn't I tell you to stay away from Cade Youngblood?"

Gina put on her most innocent face. "What are you talking about?"

"You've been with him tonight. Is that what you're washing off?"

"No, of course not."

"Liar. I could smell him on you when you came through the bedroom. I heard you were all over him in Nelda's. Making plans to leave me, are you?"

Gina frowned. "No, Zeb, you're wrong. I...I went shopping. The bags are in the living room if you want proof. Ray shouldn't have told you that, anyway. I just ran into Cade at the diner, and we had a cup of coffee."

"Ray?" Bull's wrinkled brow furrowed deeply. "I haven't talked to Ray. Three people made a point of calling me to be sure I knew what you were up to."

Gina slid down farther in the tub, scowling. Bunch of small-town gossips. "I didn't go anywhere with him. He left for an appointment, and I went shopping. That's all."

"Sure you did. Stand up, Gina."

"Why?"

"Because I said to," he snarled.

Slowly, she rose, her back to him. The tepid water ran down her body, making her shiver. He loved the sense of power that domination gave him, more so after he was asked to step down as police chief. That blow had wounded his ego, made him more determined to prove his virility.

He ran his hands around her waist and slid them across her wet breasts.

"Not tonight, okay, honey?" she said, reaching for a towel.

He snatched the towel out of her hands and slung it across the bathroom. "Any damn time I say."

Gina tensed but made no sound of protest. She knew better. Suddenly, he squeezed her nipples hard, and she cried out in spite of herself. He emitted a satisfied grunt and pressed his swollen cock against her back, moving rhythmically against her, groaning deep in his throat as his lust took over.

"Zeb, you took another Viagra, didn't you? You know the doctor told you not to take any more."

"Like I give a damn what he said. I'm as healthy as I ever was." He pulled her dripping hips toward him. Running one hand between her legs, he bent her over the tub with the other hand, until his fingers found the crevice he sought.

Gina caught the rim of the tub and held on with both hands, trying to keep her balance on the slippery surface as he forced himself deep inside her. Animal urges overpowered him, and he grabbed her by the waist and thrust her against him, pounding like a madman into her yielding flesh, ignoring her whimpers. *Damn that Viagra.* She wished major heart failure on him as his wrinkled flesh met hers again and again with a damp, sucking sound.

"You like it rough, baby. You know you do."

You don't know what I like, Gina thought, trying to block out the discomfort. Nobody knew what she liked, or even tried to find out—except Cade. She'd made herself content during the first few years of her marriage, then things had gotten a little better, mainly because Bull developed erectile dysfunction, which suited Gina fine. She had found fulfillment elsewhere like always until some idiot invented Viagra and made her life miserable. He could get it up any time and last for hours if he took a double dose. Then his heart started acting up, and the doctor told him to lay off—that lasted about a week.

Harder and harder he drove himself into her, panting like a wild beast, cruelly kneading her breasts, her thighs. And all she could do was hang on, grit her teeth, and wish it over.

Bull threw his head back and groaned with pleasure as he shot off in her. He kept her butt against his stomach a minute longer until everything drained from him. Then he pushed her away as if she were disposable. He took up her washcloth to wipe himself clean then tossed the cloth onto the edge of the tub as Gina slowly lowered herself into her bath. She stared straight ahead, silent.

He leaned over with one hand on the rim of the tub. His vindictive expression frightened her. Her teeth almost chattered as he reached out and brushed a damp tendril of hair back from her face. Suddenly, he caught her by the hair and yanked her down into the bathwater. He shoved her head under, holding it as she fought him with all her might, water and fists flying, legs flailing. When she thought her lungs would burst and she would suck in the deadly water, he pulled her up. Gasping for air, Gina caught his hands, begging him to stop.

"If I ever catch you with Cade Youngblood, I'll kill the both of you. You know that, don't you?" He caught her face hard between his hands as if he might crush the life out of her. "Look at me!" The soapy water stung her eyes, but she dared not close them. "Don't you?"

"Yes," she said, fighting back tears, despising herself for her weakness. But she made up her mind then and there—she was escaping this hell. Cade would come around in time if she went to Texas. She could convince him, and she could learn to love Texas in a heartbeat.

As if a switch had been turned off, the tension left Bull's body, and he released her face. He yawned and stretched, everything about him as limp as her wet washcloth sinking to the bottom of the tub.

"I'm going back to bed now," he said, acting as if the last few minutes had never happened. Just like her father used to do. "Don't be long. I might be up for another go by then."

Bull strode from the room. Gina sank to her chin in the tepid water. She'd shrivel to a prune before she got into bed with him tonight—or ever again.

CHAPTER 12

T HERE were six doors in the old house, and Cade and Guy had installed new double-keyed deadbolts on each one. If Johanna and Nick had ideas of pilfering the place, at least they'd have to make an effort. As the last deadbolt clicked into place, Cade wiped his forehead with his sleeve and dropped the screwdriver into a toolbox at his feet.

"Are you planning to keep the house and hardware store?" Guy asked.

Cade shrugged. "I don't know. I've got a project in the early stages that I need to bring up to speed, then I'll have a little breathing room." Cade leaned on the back porch rail, staring into the dusk. "I have to give it all some thought."

Guy laid a work-worn hand on his shoulder. "You know I'll do whatever you need me to do from this end."

"Thanks. And for helping me change the locks."

"It's gettin' late. Why don't you stay the night at my house? I've got an extra bedroom."

"Thanks, but I think I'll hang around here and sort through some of Uncle Silas's belongings. I found his key ring in the bag of belongings the undertaker left." Cade pulled the keys from his pocket. "Maybe you can tell me what's what on here."

Guy identified all the keys for him and explained the security system for the hardware store.

"The business books are in the big safe. If you want me to go over them with you, let me know. I'm sorry I don't know the combination for the other safe. You might need a locksmith to get it open."

"Thanks. I'll get with you tomorrow."

After Guy's departure, Cade tried to stay busy in the depressingly silent house. In Silas's bedroom, he went through each drawer, setting aside treasured items like his grandfather's pocket watch, Silas's war medals, a pair of dress-up cufflinks that had fascinated him as a child, a large box of old family photographs. He would have gladly shared the moment and Silas's belongings with Trish if she'd given him the chance.

He thumbed through the files in Silas's office, keeping out the ones that seemed of any importance, along with the bills from the tray on his desk. Guy could pick up the mail and pay everything out of the store account for now. Cade opened a large, unlocked strongbox in the bottom drawer of the desk. Inside, he found stacks of legal papers, newspaper clippings, handwritten notes, all from his arrest and trial. He put it with the other items he'd collected. Maybe someday he'd take the time to go through it, see his downfall through the eyes of the outside world. Or maybe he would just shred it all and truly put it behind him.

Moving upstairs, Cade found the guest room closet filled with several of Silas's old suits, miscellaneous pieces of luggage, and a cardboard box overflowing with tarnished and tattered Christmas decorations. Leaving everything as he found it, he moved down the hall to the bedroom he'd often used as a teenager.

His breath caught in his chest when he opened the door. The room looked just as it had the last time he saw it, as if Silas had expected him back at any moment. Exotic car and sports posters clung to the walls with peeling, yellowed tape. A scarred baseball bat leaned in one corner, the memento of a record-breaking homerun season his junior year. His school letter jacket hung on a chair. Cheap, gold-plated baseball and football trophies gleamed from the shelves, showing not a trace of dust.

On the bedside table, a framed picture of young Scottie—his Scottie—smiled at him. Her face was always the last thing he saw before turning off the lamp in this room. Long, tawny hair hung around her shoulders in the ringlets she hated. Bright eyes made his heart lighter. Full, glistening lips invited him to kiss her. For the past two days, he'd had to restrain himself from reverting to the old familiarity of touching her when he wanted, how he wanted. She had moved on, long past her relationship with him. And he had never gotten over what she did to him. Probably never would.

Tearing his eyes from the haunting photo, he opened the closet door to find jeans and tee shirts hanging untouched inside. Hiking boots, running shoes, a baseball stuffed into an outfielder's glove, an under-inflated basketball, and several car magazines littered the floor. Cade reached behind a haphazard pile of baseball caps in the far corner of the top shelf, his fingers groping for what he'd left there. He pulled down a cigar box and opened the lid.

A smile played on his lips in spite of everything. Scottie's love letters were still inside, written on lined notebook paper, folded into that weird triangular puzzle that only teenage girls could master. He sat down on the edge of the bed, unfolded the top letter, and began to read them one after the other. The words he'd memorized long ago spun through his head like they'd done on those bitter nights in a wretched prison cell, when he craved her so badly he ached, and his memories were the only remaining connection to her. Thank God he hadn't known the truth then.

The delicate handwriting blurred before his eyes. In real life, her loyalty hadn't lasted nearly as long as the words on paper. Self-pity smacked into him, like a wall of water bursting over a broken dam, dragging him under with a consuming grief for all that had been stolen from him. His youth, his trust—and his first and only love. His future. Their future. How could she live with herself?

Out of habit, his fingers traced the scar on his forehead, earned his first week in hell. The maximum-security adult penitentiary in Tennessee housed the full gamut of criminals, trapped in a dead-end world. Cade might have been the bad boy of Cumberland Cove, but suddenly he was a naive and terrified kid tossed into a sucking pit of quicksand. Struggling to survive, not knowing the pecking order of the cell block gangs or who he dared befriend, he spent his first night paralyzed by fear.

The second night, cornered by men who wanted more from the new pretty-boy on the block than he was willing to give, he fought back with a primal, battle-to-the-death instinct. He refused to surrender, refused to stay down, until the guards finally heard the fracas and Tased him then dragged him away, bleeding badly and still fighting. A fractured skull sent him to the prison infirmary for a week, then he spent another few weeks in isolation for fighting, but the three bullies who cornered him didn't get the satisfaction of raping him like Bull had predicted.

His body and psyche bore other scars, carved at other times during those eight long years, but that first one he considered his badge of courage—a symbol of the life-and-death struggle he'd faced every day in prison, tangible evidence that he could survive overwhelming odds. For all the ugliness the jagged scar represented, he would not erase it, even if he could.

Cursing the overload of emotion that had gripped him since the news of Silas's death, he scooped up the love letters, crammed them back in their box unfolded, and tucked the box into the corner of the closet. It was too late to fix things now.

In no mood to attempt sleep, he drove into town and parked behind the hardware store. Guy's instructions helped him get inside without setting off the alarm. The telltale odor of age and character filled his senses as he opened the front door, bringing on an onslaught of bittersweet memories.

The establishment had stood on one corner of the crossroads at the center of town for sixty years. Cobwebs adorned the open rafters, pieces of dusty harness hung undisturbed on the back wall, and three pairs of ladies' button-top boots, the brown leather now crackled with age, had been sitting on a high shelf since they were in fashion at the turn of the century. Silas always kept the worthless stuff around to aggravate the antique dealers and collectors. He got a kick out of haggling with them, but he would never sell, much like he probably had teased Nick with the land with no intention of selling it.

Once in his uncle's office, Cade unlocked the desk and went through each drawer before opening the large safe to take inventory of its contents. He removed his uncle's business ledgers and settled behind the desk to look through them. Now and then, his gaze wandered around the room, and he had an eerie sense of connecting with his uncle as he sat in his place, seeing exactly what Silas had seen every day.

He made a quick pass over the accounts receivable, sometimes surprised at who owed his uncle money and how long some of the accounts had been held without any payment at all. Rubbing his chin, Cade pondered whether he would do business with the same leniency as his uncle—or if he even wanted to keep the hardware store. It made little profit, and Cade got the idea his uncle kept it open because he enjoyed the work and because some of the folks in this tiny town needed a sympathetic soul now and then.

Case in point, Bobcat Jones. Cade looked back over years of entries on his account. To his credit, Bobcat paid his bill regularly and usually in full. Cade saw no problem in honoring the mountain man's request for his taxidermy supplies.

Not surprisingly, there were no accounts for either of the Drakes, nor for Nick or Johanna. There were jots in his uncle's handwriting on the cash drawer account, noting each time he'd doled out cash to Trish. Usually a hundred dollars at a time, amounting to four to five hundred a month. Cade shook his head. That wouldn't happen anymore. Cade would instruct Guy not to give Trish money from the store in the future. She could live well on the ample trust, and she had a job now. No need for mooching.

Finished with the store ledgers, Cade stared at the smaller safe, guessing that his uncle's private papers might be in there since he had not found them at the house. He studied the simple combination lock. A few years ago, Silas had sent him a packet of important papers, along with a set of keys similar to the one Cade now carried in his pocket. Possibly the combinations to both safes were in there, but Cade had not thought to bring it with him in the rush to get his business done and get out of Houston.

He was good with locks of any kind, something he'd picked up while working at the hardware store. Within a few minutes, he had the door open. Replacing the store accounts in their place, he locked the big safe before pulling out the envelopes and ledgers in the smaller one. He came across a copy of his uncle's will and reread it before going on to the other envelopes. He lost track of the time as he pored over the accounts—among them a concise, detailed listing of prime real estate tracts and buildings, both in town and for miles around. A second list cross-referenced lease agreements for so many of the major businesses in Cumberland Cove that Cade was certain he had read wrong. He opened a binder that contained hundreds of clear plastic sheet protectors, each containing a legal deed. A second identical binder contained page after page of signed leases. He checked each one against the line items in the ledger, noting the date that each lease expired. His uncle apparently did not believe in long-term agreements, as almost every lease had to be renewed annually. The rare exceptions, Cade noticed, were for the two businessmen who had kept wake last night—Silas's closest friends. Men who had stood with him to the end. Cade would remember those men, too, if ever the occasion arose.

Cade sat back, contemplating his uncle's purpose in leaving everything to him. No doubt Trish's addictive behavior played a part, but Silas could have set up her share of the inheritance without Cade's involvement. Gerald or Silas's banker could have been appointed administrator. Instead, he had given Cade the responsibility for his sister, with only a letter of options, which included giving her nothing at all if he saw fit. Had Silas thought leaving Cade in charge would bring brother and sister together? Cade feared he had been very wrong.

In the quiet store, Cade heard the click of the back door. He straightened in the chair, body tense, senses on alert at the sound of heavy, muffled footsteps crossing the floor. He hadn't turned on the lights in the store, but the door to the office was open, and the light that spilled across the floor would be visible from outside. He should have locked the door behind him, but he'd been more concerned with disarming the alarm than locking himself inside.

Cade eased open the top drawer, where he'd noted his uncle's pistol earlier. As a felon, he couldn't own a handgun, but if he had to defend himself, he would and deal with the consequences later. He didn't trust anybody in this town other than Guy, and that only because his uncle had trusted his friend and employee completely.

He laid his hand on the pistol as a man's large frame filled the doorway.

"What are you doing here?" Ray Drake demanded, his own hand on the heavy pistol in a holster at his side.

Cade eased the drawer closed. No need to give Ray an excuse to arrest him—or shoot him. "Going over my unc...my books. Problem?"

"I heard you got everything. Hard to believe Silas would be that stupid."

"Or that vindictive?"

Ray drew to his full height. "Why don't you get on back to your business in Texas and let this town be."

"My business is here right now. My uncle's dead, and as far as I know, your department is doing nothing about it."

The harsh office light gave Ray's emotionless face a hard edge, but his eyes glittered with a hatred Cade remembered well. He didn't move into the room, but his broad shoulders blocked the doorway, and his hand dropped to that intimidating nightstick on his belt.

"Don't tempt fate, Cade."

Face-to-face with the most powerful man in Cumberland Cove, Cade suddenly understood his uncle's intent. Silas had leveled the playing field for him. He rose slowly, bracing stiff-armed on the desk.

"I haven't forgotten what you and your daddy did to me." Cade ground the words out. "And if you think I can't—or won't—send you and your goddamned baton packing in a heartbeat, think again." Cade tapped the ledgers lying on the desk with immense satisfaction. "Because, you see, according to these papers, I basically own this whole fucking town."

CHAPTER 13

LATER that evening, Nick lounged on the well-worn leather couch in Ray's wood-paneled den, still keyed up from his meeting with his lawyer earlier in the day. Best friends from the first day of kindergarten, when Ray saved Nick from a thrashing at the hands of a second-grade bully, the two were like brothers.

Ray brought Nick a scotch before settling into a nearby armchair with his own drink. He pulled off the tie he wore for work every day and unbuttoned his collar, pivoting his head in circles to ease the tension in his neck, then propped his feet up on the coffee table and sank back into the chair to nurse his drink. "That damned Cade."

"My thoughts exactly. Trish is even more of a basket case with him around." Nick took a sip and leaned into the corner of the couch, his arm slung across the back. "He's buying her off with a house and car so he doesn't have to give her a full share."

Ray grunted. "Sounds like him."

"I checked out that company of his, and it's legit. He pulls down big bucks on a regular basis. I have to wonder how business would fare if his clients knew about his prison record."

"He's too smart to get caught with his pants down on something like that. It's easy enough to find out an ex-con's history, so I doubt he tries to hide it."

Nick arched an eyebrow. "I've got to find some way to get that land. I may have gotten overconfident, but damn it, Silas basically promised it to me."

"But nothing on paper?"

"No, but his generation tends do business by handshake. So I made some bad calls." Nick took another long drink, savored it on his tongue before swallowing. "When the banks and my investors learn the development's a no-go, they'll want their money, and I don't have most of it anymore. And I probably can't get a loan if the banks get a whiff of this mess."

"How much money are we talking?" Ray asked.

Nick slugged another swallow of his drink. "Millions."

Ray whistled softly. "You're pretty much screwed with Cade in control." Ray studied the amber liquid in his glass. "I caught Gina with him at Nelda's this afternoon. When Daddy hears that, he's likely to have a stroke."

"I know that feeling. I didn't like Scottie around him the day of the funeral, either. He need not think I'm going to stand by and let him move in on me." Nick threw back the rest of the scotch and set the glass down on the table hard enough to rattle the ice cube. "It's not going to happen."

Ray took a cigar from the humidor on the coffee table and clipped off the end. Lighting it, he blew a puff of smoke in the air. The gleaming glass eyes of a dozen mounted trophy heads stared blankly from the walls, killed over the years by Ray or Bull. Above the native-stone fireplace, framed by a collection of skinning knives, four high-caliber hunting rifles hung on racks.

"The son of a bitch is using that inheritance to threaten my job, the whole town," Ray said, spitting a jot of tobacco off the tip of his tongue. "I should have shipped him off to reform school back when I had the chance. Then maybe Angela—"

Ray stopped abruptly, but Nick knew that Ray had always felt that his leniency toward Cade as a teenager might have played a part in Angela Wright's death. That burden had changed Ray over time.

Nick contemplated Cade's new status in town. From pariah to proprietor in the time it took an old man to bleed to death on the highway. As much as he abhorred the thought, Nick had to do business with his criminal stepbrother.

"Just imagine how many million-dollar-plus homes could be built on that mountain," Nick mused aloud.

"Over Cade's dead body, apparently."

"Now there's a thought," Nick said with a snort, studying the array of weapons on the wall. "Terminate him. Maybe your old man will take care of him because of Gina." He downed the last swallow of his drink. Nick rolled the idea round in his head like savoring good brandy. Outright murder seemed fitting—an eye for an eye—but not feasible.

"I hope he gets out of town before it comes to that," Ray muttered. "But if he keeps it up..."

"What'd you say?" Nick asked.

"Nothing."

Nick's phone vibrated. He answered to find Trish nearly hysterical.

"What's wrong now?" he asked wearily.

She babbled out an almost incoherent recap of her day with Cade, ending with words that almost made Nick cry along with her. "He's not going to buy me a house because I made him real mad. He said I had to quit taking my medicine before he'd talk to me again."

For once, Nick shared Cade's opinion, although he didn't say so.

"I think he's leaving tomorrow," she whined, "and I won't get my house."

"How did you screw up this time?"

"I said something about him killing Angela."

"Smart move, Trish. Why would you bring that up if you want something out of him?"

"I know, I wasn't thinking right. I told him you wouldn't like Scottie calling him, and he said they were old friends. I said they were more than friends when he killed—"

"Whoa! Back up. Scottie called him? Why?"

Nick could sense Trish's shrug. "I don't know. I couldn't hear most of it, but I think she wanted to talk to him."

This girl was worthless. Like brother, like sister.

"When? Where?"

"He told her he'd be around town tonight and tomorrow. But, Nicky, what about my house and car?"

"What about it? You blew it." Nick was in no mood now to humor her. He wanted to find Scottie and ease his doubts. "I need to go. We'll talk about the house tomorrow."

"What if he leaves?" she wept. "I won't get anything."

As much as Nick wanted Cade gone for good and far away from Scottie, the fact that he couldn't afford to lose thousands of acres of prime real estate weakened his resolve. But maybe the time had come for a new tactic.

"Okay, calm down," he said, thinking. "I talked to some lawyers today, and we're not likely to win a court battle. Silas could legally cut anybody out of his will except his wife, and she's long dead."

"Oh, Nicky!" Trish wailed. Nick held the phone away from his ear and rolled his eyes at Ray.

"Listen to me. I've got an idea that might work. I'll come by Mom's house in the morning and tell you what to do. In the meantime, call Cade and get him to stay another day. Trish, be nice to him, no matter how hard it is."

Nick disconnected, staring into space for a long moment until Ray distracted him. "So what now?"

"Try killing him with kindness, I guess. At least let Trish give it another whirl."

"Good luck."

"We'll need it. Thanks for the drink. I'm going to take off."

"Going looking for Scottie?"

"Yeah."

"Don't do anything stupid. I'd hate to have to arrest you instead of Cade."

***

Answer! Answer! Answer!

Trish thought her head might split from the tension headache. Each faraway ring through the earpiece of her cell phone drilled more anxiety into her already frazzled mind. He was *gone, gone, gone* forever. She was *lost, lost, lost* for eternity.

"Come on, Cade," Trish pleaded, "please answer."

She had been calling over and over since she'd talked to Nick and realized how stupid she'd been to alienate Cade. Why would he have anything more to do with her now? What she said to him about Angela was unconscionable. Why had she said it? To get him to admit his guilt so she could hate him with impunity? Well, he hadn't, and now she'd wrecked everything...again.

Muffled sounds came from the bedroom across the hall. Johanna getting ready for bed. Trish knew the routine. An hour-long soak in a lavender-scented bath, another half hour smearing different creams on her face. A specific one for forehead, nose and chin; another for under-eye bags; yet another for the creping neck. All the while with her dyed-to-a-fare-thee-well hair slathered with conditioner and wrapped in a Turkish towel. Then Johanna would slip into a silky negligee— why? Who knew? The last man who had been in her bed had left on a stretcher, dead of a heart attack. That would be Trish's father. The last of her family that she was allowed to love.

She left another frantic message for Cade, clicked the cell phone off, and noticed the low battery indicator. Plugging it into the wall, she flounced back on the bed, staring at the ceiling. She felt like a thirteen-year-old. Even though she had a decent job, being new meant terrible hours and rotten pay. And afterward, she still had to come back to this house, the only home she could remember, but one that grew more stifling day by day.

Anxiety washed from her brain through her whole system, making her weak and jittery. She hadn't had a Xanax since that afternoon with Cade, and she was feeling the effects. She reached for her purse to find the familiar prescription bottle, but Cade's words rang out as if he were in the room. He just didn't understand. She needed something to keep her nerves calm, else she wouldn't be able to hold down her job or face life stuck in this rut that had no end. That was pulling her steadily toward a life of...of nothing....

She grabbed the cell phone instead of the pills and dialed Cade's number with shaky hands. "Cade, where are you?" she whispered.

When the phone went to voice mail again, Trish left a one-word message: "Please!"

She dropped the phone to the floor. He must have already headed for Texas by now and was ignoring her calls.

She pulled her purse across the bed and rattled around inside until she found the bottle she wanted. Downing more pills than the prescription called for, she closed her eyes and waited for peace.

DAY 4

CHAPTER 14

K EYED up after his confrontation with Ray, Cade couldn't sleep. Like cancer, the old nightmares ate away at his peace of mind, jerking him awake every time he drifted off. In the predawn hours, he gave up and pushed away the heavy quilt. The cold air gave him incentive to get moving. He pulled on jeans and a sweatshirt and padded downstairs barefoot, pushing up the thermostat as he passed. The faint odor of lilies replaced the customary aroma of coffee brewing and bacon frying, reminding him for the thousandth time that his uncle was gone.

Pulling out his laptop equipment from the case he'd brought into the house the night before, he set up the connection through his uncle's wireless Internet access and fixed a cup of coffee while the computer booted. He logged on to his company network, called up his project, and grimaced. The report due to the client by Friday was behind schedule. He had to keep the project on track even if that meant micromanaging his young, inexperienced field engineer. When he was on-site, he could handle problems before they got out of hand. From this distance, all he could do was try to circumvent disaster. He pulled up graph after graph from the network, analyzing the information and making notes for his engineer.

When he was done, he shot a terse email to the engineer with a directive to incorporate the notes into the final report and get it to the client immediately. After copying the email to his secretary, Marge, he called the office phone, where he got the answering machine as expected this early in the morning. He left detailed instructions for Marge to phone the client to assure him that the project would meet deadline, a promise Cade meant to keep. He hung up, disconnected from the network, and closed the laptop, pondering his options, since they didn't include sleep at this point.

As much as he would like to hound the Cumberland Cove police department to find his uncle's killer, he needed to head back to Houston then straight on to the Gulf. That would put him only a few days behind. With that in mind, he gathered all of his uncle's belongings and paperwork that he wanted to take with him and left everything inside the back door.

The nightmares had his mind on Angela again, something he had worked for years to leave behind. The one thing he had promised himself, and Angela, was that if he ever returned to Cumberland Cove, he would go to the site where she was allegedly murdered— the mammoth waterfall secreted in the deepest bowels of Cumberland Caverns. A place beyond the comforting lights and safe footing of the front end of the caves, where his grandfather and great-grandfather had honed the beginning of a vast show cavern that was never finished. The less-developed area leading to the waterfall had rudimentary lighting, and the going was more treacherous. Cade had ventured there as a child with his grandfather only a couple of times.

He wasn't even sure he remembered the way, but he was going to keep his vow. He had to confront the demons that had tortured him all these years. He found a heavy jacket and boots in his closet then went to Silas's workshop in the old barn. He rummaged around until he found a bolt cutter and a new lock with its key attached so he could re-lock the door of the lean-to guarding the entrance to the caves. Arming himself with a couple of flashlights, an electric lantern, and extra batteries, as well as a coil of rope, he picked up a heavy canvas bag near the door loaded with various tools that might come in handy. Putting it all in the back of the Range Rover beside a couple of bottles of water, he headed for the caverns.

Years ago, his grandfather and Silas had a dream to open the wondrous underground world to the public. They had built a lean-to around the opening to the large, main cave to serve as the public entrance. Backbreaking hours had resulted in electric wiring and spotlights strategically placed among the rock formations along smooth pathways. Narrow crevices had been chiseled or blasted wider to make the caverns visitor-friendly. After his grandfather died, Cade had helped Silas out whenever he could until arthritis claimed his uncle's dexterity. Maybe if Cade had never been sent away, Silas could have realized his dreams before he died, but it hadn't worked out that way, and nobody other than Cade cared.

At the lean-to, he tried all the keys on his key ring, but none fit the padlock to the door. The sharp bolt cutter bit through with little effort. The door creaked open, and the cool dankness of the caves seeped out. He moved his gear inside the shack and flicked on the lantern. He crossed to the edge of a steep slope. Before him, the precipice dropped ten or more feet to the floor of the cave. The lantern's beam, though strong, barely penetrated the thick darkness. The timeless formations were as familiar as if he had been here yesterday.

Cade moved the light around to the walls nearest him on the upper level, seeking the door that led to the tool room. Inside the tool room, Cade examined the metal fuse box, finding the fuses dry and tight. He flipped the breaker switch. A bare lightbulb hanging from the ceiling glowed to life. A well-used miner's hat sat on a shelf near the door. Cade changed the batteries and was rewarded with a working spotlight. He plopped the hat on his head.

Stepping outside the small room, Cade found the expansive cavern bathed with golden light as he had hoped. A flicker of an old, good feeling ran down his back like the play of fingertips on his skin—the ghost of long-ago trips into the caverns with his grandfather and uncle.

Tucking a spare flashlight in his belt from his stash by the front door, he closed the lean-to door, slung the coil of rope over his shoulders, and headed down the cut-stone steps to the lower level. He crossed the length of the huge chamber and entered a tunnel, picking his way carefully along a path that he had not traveled for many years. This particular tunnel led to some of his favorite spots.

The low tunnel gave way to a vaulted room, much larger than the one at the entrance. This one was at least a hundred fifty feet high and twice as wide. Huge groupings of rock formations were scattered about the room as if placed there carefully by a talented artist. Cade's eyes drank in the long-missed grandeur of the lofty red-and-gold formations towering overhead and spreading out like a miniature Grand Canyon to the opposite wall. Where the tunnel had been completely silent, this room was filled with a low burbling sound made by a shallow stream that ran along the perimeter of the room. A beach of coarse, reddish sand skirted the stream, and the bed was strewn with water-polished pebbles.

He glanced up at the long, gleaming sheets of stone that resembled the folds of draperies hung at a window. The formation was washed in a shimmering palette of colors ranging from moss green to rosy pink to blood red and dark umber. Ahead, a massive formation of uneven stalagmites gave the appearance of a big-city skyline against the soft, indirect lighting fixed behind it.

Another mile into the depths, he reached the big forest formation, where hardening stalagmites had risen from the floor of the cavern to meld with the source of their existence, the stalactites dripping from above. Once connected, they formed huge pillars extending from floor to roof. Cade had thought it was an underground forest when he was a child, so his grandfather named the formation Cade's Forest.

At the end of the last well-lighted section of tunnel, Cade came upon a stash of his Uncle Silas's long-unused tools and materials—rolls of dry-rotted electrical wire, several floodlights still in damp corrugated boxes, a chisel and mallet, a cracked leather tool belt, and a few coils of rope.

Cade flicked on his lantern to augment the headlamp and started down the tunnel leading to the nether regions of this world he'd thought he would never see again. He could still recall his elders' deep voices telling him the secrets of the underground wonders around him, teaching him to appreciate and protect such works of nature. They had spent countless hours exploring, finding new formations, new paths to follow. Cade often sought sanctuary in the caverns from his miserable home life, comforted by the quiet, cool solitude.

In places, the walls crept in to enclose him like a needle's eye. The absolute silence of the caves became a presence unto itself, a beast that seemed benign in the light but grew oppressive in the semi-darkness.

Loose sand and pebbles rattled away from Cade's boots as he half-slid down a steep incline. It crossed Cade's mind how close to impossible it would be for a strong man to drag a body into these depths, much less a drunk teenager, and he wondered if the same thing ever occurred to Rickey in his investigation.

After what seemed to be miles of maneuvering the twists and turns, the precipitous drop-offs and dead-end paths, the surreal silence slowly gave way to a distant drone. A dull roar filled Cade's ears as he entered a vaulted cave. The cascading water of the waterfall glimmered in the light of the lantern. He swung it slowly around, noticing the steep, downward pitch of the incline leading to the chasm surrounding the falls. His taut muscles seemed to vibrate with the thunder of the falls. So far as he knew, nobody had discovered the origin of the water plummeting over the brink high above nor where it went after disappearing into the black abyss below.

He glanced at the damp floor beneath his feet, contemplating the slickness of the surface. Anybody lugging a body to the edge would be in serious jeopardy of going over himself. Of course, a body could be rolled or, as light as Angela was, tossed toward the brink with enough force to carry it over. But how would anybody ever find this place?

How would a killer manage to dispose of the body and come up with the perfect setup to hide the crime?

It would have to be somebody who knew Cade's habits, Angela's daily walk home, who could intercept her without being seen coming or going. Somebody totally familiar with the area and with these caves. Cade couldn't think of anybody who fit that bill, other than himself. Which was exactly why he had been convicted, even though Angela's body never was found.

As he swung the light around, something caught Cade's eye. Going closer, he set his lantern down by a rusty iron cross that had been hammered into the stone. The letter "A" cut from metal was affixed to the cross. Cade stooped to examine the monument, wondering when it had been put there. A small scroll was attached to the crossbar. He glanced around, struck by a sudden harrowing feeling that he was not alone here in the bowels of the earth where nobody else was supposed to be.

He removed the scroll and unrolled it. The words were scrawled in red ink:

I'VE BEEN WAITING FOR YOU.

CHAPTER 15

A T THE end of her shift, Scottie headed down the back
stairs of the Cumberland Cove Courthouse to the Police
Department located in the basement. The area was spartan
and unimpressive, with bare, two-toned beige walls. Several straight-
backed wooden chairs waited for occupants, most of them kept warm
on weekends by local teens brought in for fighting or drunk driving,
favorite pastimes in this rural area.

In the background, soft country music played, interrupted now
and then by a commercial or the grating static of the police radio.
Marvin McCoy, the rookie duty officer, looked up from behind the
desk as Scottie approached.

"Hey," he said. Brown, ruler-straight hair hung awry around a thin
face, making him look more like a teenager than a twenty-five-year-
old. "How's it going?"

"Same old," Scottie said. "I'll be at my desk."

On her way down the corridor, Scottie checked her inbox and
pulled out several message slips and memos. She glanced into Rickey
Chamber's empty office. He probably wouldn't be in for another
hour or so, which suited her. She'd love to go meddling in his files
but didn't dare—at least not yet. First, she needed to refresh herself
on the evidence in Cade's trial. She hadn't looked at his file since

she first joined the force five years ago. When she had found nothing redeeming, she had put the file away and never expected to open it again.

Farther on, Ray's door was locked. The large, frosted window bore the Cumberland Cove PD emblem and Ray's name and position. Scottie trailed a fingertip along the gold lettering, thinking she wouldn't mind having her name there one day. A bit ambitious for a woman in an old-fashioned village like Cumberland Cove, but why let a little thing like decades of tradition stand in the way? It could happen. Ray wouldn't be there forever.

She piled her armload of paperwork onto her desk, turned on the computer, and went for a mug of coffee. Back in her cubicle, she logged into the system and started an intensive search of Cade's case with an empty writing pad at hand for notes. Forty-five minutes later, her coffee was cold, her notepad barely touched, and she hadn't found a damned thing out of order.

Rickey had done an excellent job of documentation, and all the evidence was duly logged and noted as stored in the department evidence room, even evidence that was introduced in court. She'd seen that happen before, where the court sent the evidence back to the originating law enforcement agency for proper storage, especially a case like this that had seemed so cut-and-dried. Nothing remarkable that might prompt the judge to keep it within court jurisdiction. Rickey was the evidence custodian in their small department, so she would have to involve him if she got that far.

From the computer files, Cade just flat looked guilty as hell from all angles. Angela's bloody blouse under the seat of his truck, the trace blood trail leading deep in the caverns, where apparently he'd disposed of the body. Cade's defense attorney had pled down to voluntary manslaughter, so there was no life term, no death penalty involved to tweak the jurors' consciences. No wonder the jury convicted within six hours, in spite of his age. Disappointed, she closed her notepad and wrote up her shift report.

Hearing someone come down the corridor, she peeked out to see Rickey disappear into his office. Now, how to broach the subject? She knocked lightly as she stopped in his doorway.

Pushing fifty years old, Rickey was married to his college sweetheart, had two grown kids and a son still in high school. The gray in his strawberry blond, thinning hair was well concealed, and he looked much like the ten-year-old photo on his desk except for the ten pounds that made his face fuller and his suit tighter across his chest. He wore a suit to work, went home to his family pretty much on time every day, and was expected to be the next police chief, if Ray ever retired. He seemed content with his life and didn't like anything out of the ordinary that rocked his boat.

"Morning," he said as he flipped on his desk lamp and computer. "Surprised to see you here this late."

"I had to catch up on paperwork I put off yesterday. That was some funeral, wasn't it? I never expected to see so many people at the graveside."

"Most everybody respected Silas, old cuss that he was. Things won't be quite the same downtown now, especially if the hardware closes."

"You think Cade's going to do that?"

Rickey shrugged. "Why not? Why would he want to relocate back here? Folks have long memories for something like he did." Rickey busied himself sorting through his inbox.

"He still claims he didn't do it. You headed the investigation. Do you think he was guilty?"

Rickey straightened in his seat and looked at her. "What kind of question is that?"

"Have you ever thought about the possibility of testing some of that old evidence?"

Rickey stood, pulled her inside the tiny office with barely enough room for them to move, and shut the door. He lowered his voice to the point she had to listen intently to hear, even that close.

"I did a good investigation. The evidence incriminated Cade. You don't know what you'll be stirring up if you encourage him."

"That sounds almost like a threat," Scottie said, boring into Rickey's eyes until he looked away.

"Not from me," he said quietly. "Maybe a warning, though. First of all, you have to get Ray to release the evidence, and he won't. Then you have to get him to agree to DNA testing, and that costs a lot."

"I'd think he'd want to be sure justice was done."

"As far as he and this town are concerned, justice was done. A neat little package that solved the crime and got rid of a pestilence at the same time."

"What do you think modern DNA testing on those bloody clothes would show?"

"What have you been doing? Snooping in the evidence room?"

"I know better than to tamper with the chain of evidence," Scottie countered. "What do you think they'd find?"

Rickey grunted. "Nothing of any consequence. Nothing likely to see the light of day around here, anyway."

"Excuse me?"

"Scottie, you and Cade need to back off on this."

Rickey opened the door, ushered her out without another word, and stalked off in the direction of the coffeepot.

CHAPTER 16

ETRACING his steps out of the caverns faster than he'd gone in, Cade breathed a sigh of relief when he reached the main entrance. He switched off the lights and locked the lean-to with the new lock he'd brought along. He had brought the scroll with him to examine in better light. How long had it been there? And who had erected the monument to Angela?

Outside the caverns, his phone dinged, and his voice mail light flashed on. Ten missed calls? Eight messages? What the...? All the calls were from Trish. To hell with that. He would deal with Trish later.

Cade cursed long and hard when he realized both front tires of his vehicle had been slashed to ribbons. Thoroughly pissed off and not a little spooked, Cade searched the surrounding woods for any sign of an intruder but found nothing.

His first call was to AAA to get the vehicle towed; his second was going to be to Scottie. He hesitated before hitting the call button. Maybe he didn't want to get anybody else involved just yet. He was admittedly paranoid that everybody in town was out to get him, but that was probably an overreaction. That cross and scroll could have been in the caverns from the time during or after his trial when the caverns were not secured.

Instead, he sat in the driver's seat with the door open to wait for the tow truck. He pulled the scroll from his jacket pocket and examined it back and front, holding it gingerly by the edges. It appeared to be simply a sheet of writing paper about five by eight inches. The writing, which had been done with a red ballpoint pen, was simple block print, bold and sure.

He rolled it up again and thrust it back into his pocket, wondering if this was an old threat or a new one.

He jumped when his phone rang. Trish again.

Cade felt like putting his fist through the windshield. He really needed this hassle with his sister, on top of dealing with Gina and Scottie and maybe some wacko going psycho on him. Why were there never any *normal* people in his life? The urge to escape this hellhole ramped up to near panic level.

Just go, fool! Don't worry about what you found in the caverns. Don't worry about what the hell Trish wants. Just get the tires fixed and go!

And let some bastard think he's run me off? Not find out what's behind the note? No way.

Here are the facts, bud. Scottie hates you. Gina's poison. Trish is a pain in the ass. You are in deeper every minute you stay.

Before good judgment got the upper hand, his phone rang again. Cade stared at the caller ID as it continued to ring. Become his sister's patsy one more time or hit the road?

Cade finally gave in and answered.

"Yeah," he said shortly.

"Cade." Trish whined in such pitiful baby talk that Cade wanted to jerk her into adulthood. "I'm sorry about what I said to you."

A decent start, anyway.

"Apology accepted." Cade waited then said impatiently, "Is that all you wanted?"

"No, not exactly. I mean...Cade...I do want to get a house and car like we talked about."

"You said you wanted to go to court. Remember?"

"I didn't mean it. I was...it was...just... I've thought it over and changed my mind."

"Fine, I'll set you up with a good real estate agent—and don't even mention Nick's name to me."

"No, no, I don't want that. I want to *build* a house."

Warily, he said, "Build?"

"I decided I don't want to move away from Cumberland Cove. My friends and all are here, and I want to live on our family land. That's not too much to ask, is it? Since we already have the property. You'll give me enough to build, won't you? Seems like it would make more sense."

Trish make sense? When hell froze over.

When he didn't answer, Trish tried again. "Please? I want you to help me pick a spot. I really want your help."

Torn, Cade leaned wearily against the door frame. "Trish, I have a business to run. I need to get back to Houston."

"Just another day, Cade. Please. I...I want to spend more time with you. We got off to a bad start, and I'm sorry."

Skeptic that he was, Cade wasn't buying Trish's saccharin gloss-over. But he had to get new tires, and that would put him late leaving, anyway, so what the hell?

"Another chance, Cade? Please?"

One more chance? At least then he could honestly say he had made every effort to reconcile with her.

"All right," he said reluctantly. "Meet me at Uncle Silas's house this afternoon around one. If I'm not there, just wait for me. I've got something that has to be done this morning. And don't be late like you were with the lawyer. I'm telling you now, this is the last time I'm going out of my way to help you."

CHAPTER 17

"OKAY, Sis, tell me what you want," Cade said as he ushered Trish into the kitchen of their uncle's house, twenty minutes late.

"I want to stay here. I think Uncle Silas would like for one of us to live on our family's land."

One of us and how many strangers?

"I've already told you I won't let you live in this house."

"That's not a problem. It's old and stinky. I want to build a new house on the mountain. And I want some land around it."

"How much land do you think you'd need?"

"Oh, I don't know. Around ten thousand acres, maybe more," she said immediately.

Far more than enough to build an upscale urban development. *Nick again!*

"What would you do with all that land? Do you even know how much that is?"

Trish shrugged a thin shoulder. "I want enough to hike and stuff like that. Why shouldn't I live on this land?"

"No reason at all," Cade said, with an agreeable smile. "You're perfectly welcome to live here."

"You're kidding?" Trish blurted out.

"Let's take a walk."

She shrank back, visibly concerned. "Why?"

"Look, acting like I'm the big bad wolf about to gobble you up doesn't particularly make me want to help you. If you want to look at the property and find a building site, we can do that. Otherwise, I have other things to do."

"Okay, okay," she said quickly. "But are we going to walk, like, thousands of acres? I have on my good shoes."

Cade glanced down at the spotless white nursing shoes she wore with her light blue uniform. "I noticed several pairs of shoes in the utility room off the back porch. You can probably find a pair that will fit well enough. Go look."

Trish headed in the direction of the porch. Cade put his laptop in the case, set it in a corner near the counter, and went to see if his sister needed any help tying her shoes. He was about to that point with her childishness. She had found a soiled pair of sneakers, and her nose wrinkled in disgust as she tied the second lace. "Ugh," she sniffed.

"Good enough for where we're going."

Trish followed him away from the house toward the fields behind Silas's barn. He kept a vigilant eye around them, unable to shake the uneasiness he felt after this morning. Half a mile later, they turned to follow a broad, fast stream that boasted some of the best trout fishing in the area. Another half mile had Trish complaining, but Cade took her a bit farther, to a deep glade that swept to the base of Cumberland Mountain. A panorama of blue-gray peaks rose around them and enclosed the narrow valley.

Trish sucked in a breath. "I haven't been here in years," she whispered. "We used to come with Momma and Daddy."

Cade soaked up the pristine, quiet beauty. This had been their favorite picnic spot. Almost every Sunday after church, their mother would pack lunch, and they would rattle alongside the stream in their old car. Father and son would fish while mother and daughter read or gathered wildflowers. An idyllic scene. Too good to be true. Too good to last. Right now, Cade could see a trace of his little sister in this bitter woman beside him, but how could he reach her?

"So do you think this would do?" he asked. "You could build a nice house on the rise above flood stage. Bring an access road in from the highway. No neighbors to bother you. Free to hike, or whatever."

"Are there ten thousand acres here?" she asked persistently.

"Trish, as far as you can see in any direction—that's how much land you'd have use of. A lot more than you're talking about."

Trish fell silent, turning slowly to take in the vista.

"I think I remember falling into that pool," she said, indicating a widening of the stream a few yards away, where the water quieted in a protected cove. The pool was deep and cold, with the undercurrent of the stream hidden by a deceptive stillness on the mirror surface.

"You're right. When you were around three."

"I nearly froze afterward, and Momma wrapped the picnic quilt around me and sang to me until I stopped crying," she said then added quietly, "You were the one who jumped in first and kept me from drowning, weren't you?"

Cade nodded, remembering the panic in his baby sister's eyes as her head went under. His father yelled for him not to jump in after her, but Cade knew Trish would drown before his father made it to the bank. "The water was definitely cold that day."

"Bet you wouldn't do that now."

"Jump in and we'll see," Cade said with a teasing grin.

Trish actually giggled in return. "Maybe another time." She strolled around the clearing, picking flowers like she'd done as a child, then sat on a wide rock overhanging the stream.

After giving her a few moments alone, Cade joined her, leaning back to prop on his elbows. "So is this what you were looking for?"

Trish looked around at him with tears in her eyes. "I'd love to live here. It's special to me."

"I was hoping it would be."

"I might never have thought of it again, I was so young the last time we came here, before Momma..."

"Died," Cade finished when she hesitated.

The very hour that his mother succumbed to cancer was branded into his mind. Nobody had explained to him how very sick she was. All he knew was that her hair fell out, and she didn't have the energy to play games with him and Trish liked she used to do. Then one night he went into her room where she stayed in bed most of the time, kissed her goodnight, and woke up the next morning to find her gone. Lila, the maid who served as nanny and housekeeper, told Cade his mother had grown worse and had to go to the hospital.

That afternoon, his father came to take him and Trish to say good-bye. Still not understanding that she was never coming home, Cade hugged his mother as she whispered her love for him and his sister. She laid her head back, closed her eyes, and Cade thought she'd gone to sleep. His father ushered him and Trish from the room and told them that she'd never wake again.

In the interminable days that followed, Cade came to understand the meaning of never. The feeling that she would be in her bed each morning when he peeped in slowly diminished over the days. Their grief-stricken father offered no consolation for two dazed, confused children, and Cade and Trish learned to cope in their individual ways. Trish gradually withdrew into an imaginary world; Cade lashed out in anger and frustration. For him, her death signaled the end of his childhood and the beginning of a long, hard road ahead. His grandfather's death three months later only compounded his troubles. With only a brief respite before his father married Johanna, Cade could honestly say that the only joy he had known since was the time spent with Scottie.

After his stint in prison, he marked the passage of time by material successes, careful not to form emotional ties that might trigger more loss and more grief. If he grew lonely or melancholy, he worked all the harder.

His sister shifted beside him, drawing him from his bitter thoughts.

"But I could never sell this piece of land," she muttered. "It's too special."

"No, you couldn't. Or any of it."

She looked at him with a frown. "But you said you'd give it to me."

"I said you could *use* it. You're free to enjoy all of it. I'll deed you a few acres to build a house. You can live here as long as you want, but you'll only have usufruct of the property."

"What does that mean?" she asked, her brows puckering.

"It means there will be a legal arrangement where you can use and enjoy the property as long as you don't damage it or alter it without my permission. You won't own it, and you can't sell it to Nick."

The anger and belligerence returned. "I can't believe you! Just a few minutes ago, you said you'd give it to me."

"You read too much into my words. I said you could live here. You heard what you wanted to hear. Do you think you and Nick are fooling me?" Cade rose and looked down at her. "I wasn't that blind the day I was born, Trish."

Trish stood and dusted off her butt. "No, I don't imagine you were."

"Why are you letting him use you?"

"He's not using me. He's helping me get what I deserve from Uncle Silas."

"Deserve is a tricky word, Sis. And it seems to be one of your favorites. Explain why you deserve a single acre to sell off to Nick so he can destroy it? That's the last thing Uncle Silas would want."

"Because I'm as much kin as you are. I should get half, even if he hated me."

"He loved you. But Johanna and Nick turned you against your own family, and it hurt him."

"How do you know all that? You never came back here."

"Uncle Silas and I kept in touch."

"Sounds like you talked to him a lot."

140

"As often as I could."

"Did you ever come to see him?"

"We met other places. I wasn't welcome here. Any more than I am now."

Fresh resentment clouded Trish's face. "You never called *me*. Or wanted to see *me*."

Cade fought to quell the battle of emotions warring inside him.

"I made a mistake. I should have kept trying."

Trish bit her trembling lower lip as she glared at him. Finally, she said, "So you're trying to blame Mom? What did she do? Forbid you to call me?"

"Yes," Cade said. "Or to come back to Cumberland Cove to see you."

"Oh, come on. She couldn't stop you from coming back. You're here now. And you could have called anyway."

"I tried for a while, but she blocked my phone number every time I changed it. Were there times when she wouldn't let you answer the phone?"

Trish puffed up and wouldn't answer, but the tightness of her face, the struggle not to cry gave her away.

"I tried for a couple of years, Trish. Then my work took me out of the country for months at a time, and finally, I gave up. I kept up with you through Uncle Silas. And I sent you birthday and Christmas cards every year and gifts, but I doubt you ever saw any of them."

"You are telling me *lies*, Cade Youngblood. Just stop!"

"Believe what you need to. I'm sorry I didn't keep fighting Johanna."

"Why didn't Uncle Silas tell me you tried to call?"

Cade shrugged. "I have no idea."

"Because Mom would have cut him off from me if he had?" she said softly.

"Maybe. He never mentioned Johanna's name to me."

"Since you hated her so much, why would he?"

"You might love her and consider her your mother, but I never have and never will. Nor Nick my brother. You should know that Nick thought Uncle Silas was going to sell him over ten thousand acres for a big development. Ten thousand, does that ring a bell?"

Trish pouted and wouldn't answer.

"Did he mention that he wants to raze the old downtown area and put in office buildings? And top off Cumberland Mountain for high-end mansions?"

"I don't believe you."

"You should. I've been researching this project of his."

"Nicky wouldn't double-cross me. I'm going to tell him what you said, and we'll go to court."

Cade intercepted her as she tried to run away. "Sis, if you would get your mind straight, you might see what's going on around you."

Trish refused to look at him.

"I told you this is my last offer. I'm going to give you a few hours to cool off and make a rational decision, if that's possible. As of tomorrow morning, this deal will be off, and there won't be another."

She sidestepped him and stomped down the path toward Silas's house. Cade let her go, following after a few minutes. By the time he reached the driveway, her car was gone.

After Trish left, Cade crossed the road to the mailbox, reached inside, and withdrew a handful of envelopes. Flipping through them, he found the normal array of bills and advertisement fliers, along with a couple of condolence cards. In the paper tube were the past few days' papers.

He stuck the mail back into the box and walked the path the deadly automobile had taken to run down his uncle. He stopped at the first bend in the road, checked both ways of the highway for traffic, then moved to the centerline. From here, he had a clear shot of his uncle's house and the delivery boxes on the opposite side of the road. Again, he tried to visualize the scene in the early hours of dawn. A driver flying around this curve might not have noticed an old man on the roadway. Even so, the driver would have seen Silas at the last minute in the headlights, would surely have tried to swerve to miss him. He would have felt the impact—could have had the humanity to stop and help or, at the very least, call for an ambulance.

Seeing nothing of note other than the black residue of a multitude of tires that had traversed this road, none of which stood out from the rest, he retraced his steps to the mailbox and continued along the roadside, slowing to a snail's pace to focus on the grassy shoulder, casting back and forth for any sign of disturbance. He stopped at the intersection of the narrow road that led into the mountains then continued down the main road to the next residence, where Mrs. Melton lived.

Cade stopped directly across from her house, looking at her front window then at his uncle's house sitting at a distance in the deep shade of hundred-year-old oaks and sycamores. Scottie had said Mrs. Melton heard something but never saw a car pass. Cade shifted to stare at the side road a quarter of a mile back. Bobcat had turned onto that road the day of the funeral.

Rickey would certainly have checked it out. Then again, it *was* Rickey, and it *was* Cumberland Cove. With little traffic, the narrow side road had seen few repairs over the years. Potholes pocked the asphalt surface, and gravel encroached along uneven edges. Cade stayed close to the shoulder, climbing the grade slowly, listening for approaching vehicles on the winding mountain lane. He scrutinized the tall weeds and wildflowers on the right side; he would check the left side on his way down.

After a mile, Cade was ready to give up. What was the use? Rickey had probably scouted farther along than this. Still, he went forward, step by step, around another tight curve in the road. Before him and behind, nothing but a deserted black ribbon twisting through the lush green of the mountainside. Cade pivoted to start the descent. Frowning, he turned back to stare at the roadside just ahead.

At first, he could not discern what caught his attention, then he noticed a spot where the tall grass thinned under the low-hanging branches of the bordering forest. Cade made his way off the pavement, careful where he stepped, not only because of the snakes that would be out on a warm day like today but also because he didn't want to destroy anything that might be evidence.

He squatted to study a thin, twisted piece of black composite metal then surveyed the surrounding area, but nothing else stood out. Turning his attention back to his find, he identified it as a piece of auto trim, possibly from a headlight, judging from the length and what was left of the original shape. The grass was bent underneath the metal, and no grime had accumulated. The part might have no significance, but Cade did not dismiss it outright.

He hesitated to call Rickey to investigate, imagining the skepticism and snide remarks that would ensue, but he feared the part might disappear if he left it. He glanced at his watch. Scottie should be awake by now.

CHAPTER 18

Trish's heart pounded, and she blinked back stinging tears as she stalked into her mother's house, clammy fists clenched, mind reeling, ready to do battle but terrified of the end result. She wished Cade had never raised these frightening doubts in her mind.

"Mom?" she called shrilly. "Mom, where are you?"

She reached into her purse for her Valium. As her hand closed on the small cylinder and she anticipated the peacefulness the bottle promised, Cade's warning ran afresh through her mind: *If you would get your mind straight, you might see what's going on around you.*

Trish let the bottle of pills drop to the bottom of her purse.

"Mom!"

"In here," Johanna called from the kitchen.

Trish crossed the living room to the spacious, light-filled kitchen where she'd learned to cook on a kitchen chair at Johanna's elbow. Her mom. The woman who had raised her and protected her. And shut her brother out of her life?

Johanna turned from the counter where she was chopping vegetables. She wiped her hands on a nearby cloth and came to Trish immediately, her face full of concern. "What's wrong, darling? You're white as a sheep."

"Mom...." She faltered.

Johanna caught her by the shoulders, steadying her as she had done all the years Trish could recall. Today, Trish pulled away.

"Mom, no." She drew a deep breath, squared her shoulders, and forced the words from her constricted throat. "Did you tell Cade never to call me or try to see me?"

"Whatever gave you that idea?" Johanna said with an air of innocence, but her face had gone pale.

"Just tell me the truth! Did you?"

Johanna untied the apron around her waist, taking her time to fold it neatly before laying it on the counter. "Well," she said, choosing words carefully, "I suppose I suggested that to him when he first got out of prison. I didn't know how he was going to turn out, and I couldn't take a chance on him harming you."

Johanna's eyes pleaded with her for understanding, but the truth only added to Trish's confusion. Of all people to betray her—her mother? Pressing her hand to her mouth to stifle the sob rising in her throat, she waved Johanna off when the woman attempted to reach out to her.

"Don't," Trish choked out. "Just don't. You never even told me he called!"

"Trish, it was for your own good."

"He's my brother!" The words tumbled out on the flood of long pent-up emotion. "You knew how much I loved him. You knew! And he didn't turn out badly. He's...he's..." Trish frowned and balled her fists tighter at her side. "Did you know Nick has a big real estate deal going that depends on Uncle Silas's land?"

Johanna's expression left no need for an answer. Trish recognized the signs of the familiar meltdown she suffered whenever circumstances seemed overwhelming. The mental anguish she normally treated with drugs. But the echo of Cade's words in the face of her mother and stepbrother's duplicity steeled her. What else had slipped her notice while she'd played ostrich? Her uncle had tried to help her more than once, but she had rebuffed him. Loving him and Cade had felt disloyal because her mom and Nick hated them so much. She looked at Johanna with new insight.

"You couldn't stand for me to love anybody but you! Nick has been playing me for a fool, saying that he was just trying to get me what I deserved. And I was too stupid to realize it."

"Cade never should have told you all that," Johanna said, her voice edged with desperation. "What we did was for your own—"

"I know, my own good!" Trish cried. "How many times have I heard that in my lifetime? My own good! Well, I'll take care of myself from now on."

Trish turned and hurried from the room. Johanna caught up to her in the upstairs hallway. "What are you doing?"

"I'm going to pack. I'm going to live somewhere else until I can sort things out."

"What are you talking about? This is your home. We're your family."

Trish glanced around. The hallway where her childhood pictures hung seemed suddenly unfamiliar; the door to her bedroom no longer held the promise of safe haven.

"It doesn't feel like home anymore. And I'm not sure who my family is." Trish flung the bitter words at her stepmother. "I can't believe you did this to me. You and Nick, both. I'm glad Cade told me!"

"Oh, for gosh sake, Trish, listen to me. Trish!"

Trish rushed into her room and locked the door before Johanna could stop her. Flinging herself on her bed, she buried her face in the silky comforter to cry.

"Trish, darling, open the door. Please, dear?"

Johanna tapped persistently on the door, but Trish ignored her. When her tears were spent, she pushed up from the bed and went to her bathroom to blow her nose. Still snuffling, she pulled an overnight bag from her closet and filled it with essentials—underwear, minimal makeup and toiletries, jeans, a couple of tops, a windbreaker for the still-chilly, late-spring nights, and a set of lounging pajamas. She still wasn't sure where she'd go, so the baby-dolls she usually slept in would not do.

The rapping had stopped. Trish eased the door open. The hall outside was empty, but from downstairs, she heard Johanna's voice.

"Nicky? Nicky, call me back. Where are you? You've got to come right away. It's an emergency!"

There was a period of silence, then Johanna dialed again and repeated the message. Nothing like doing the same thing, expecting different results, Trish thought ruefully. Somebody or other had said that defined insanity. How long had she been caught in that hopeless cycle? She crept down the stairs and eased out the door.

Trish threw her bag into the passenger seat and got into her car, praying that the old junker would crank instead of jerking her around like it usually did. Johanna appeared on the front porch as Trish ground the starter.

"Please, please, please," she chanted as Johanna flew down the steps toward the curb.

With a whine of protest, the engine turned over and caught. She slammed the gearshift into drive and floored the accelerator. A glance in her rearview mirror as she rounded the corner at the end of the block gave her a glimpse of Johanna in the middle of the street, beckoning wildly.

As much as Trish wanted to turn around and be enfolded by her mother's comforting arms, she sped in the opposite direction. She still wasn't sure about Cade, and now she was afraid to trust the people she had accepted as family for most of her life. But at least she was deciding her own fate.

CHAPTER 19

WHEN Scottie pulled to the side of the road half an hour after Cade's call, he was pacing like a caged tiger, the set of his shoulders, the angry stride familiar to her. She couldn't deny that she cared for him, even now, in a very primal way that transcended the sexual attraction of youth—a love possibly cemented the day his mother died, when a scared eight-year-old boy told Scottie he was giving her his soul for safekeeping because he was afraid he'd lose it like he lost his mother.

She'd often wondered how different things might have been if he had not screwed up royally—and literally—with Gina. If they hadn't broken up when they did, she and Cade would have been together on the afternoon Angela died, and none of this would have happened. They could be living in that picket-fence cottage she'd dreamed of. She bit the inside of her cheek to stifle the urge to cry. She wasn't here to second-guess the past.

Cade came to meet her when she got out of the car.

"You okay?" she asked.

He stared at her for a long time, silent, angry, then raked his hand across his face, and she could hear the scratch of five-o'clock shadow. "Other than somebody having the balls to slash my tires at the cabin this morning, yeah."

"Somebody slashed your tires? Why didn't you call me then?" Scottie said, pulling a spiral notepad from her pocket.

"You can put that away. I'm not filing a report."

She glanced at her notebook. "What time was it?"

"Sometime around dawn, I guess."

"You don't know?"

"I went in the caverns before dawn. I came out after dawn. The tires were fine when I went in, shredded when I came out."

Scottie knew from Cade's manner that he was holding back, but she knew better than to push him.

"You have no idea who did it, I suppose."

Cade leveled a lethal stare on her. "I'd think you could make that list yourself."

"Help me out," she said, unflustered. "I'm just doing my job."

"Let's see, so far, Bull threatened me about his wife in your presence. Ray has warned me at least twice to get out of town while I could, once in your presence. Nick—well, we know Nick would like me out of the way. I'm sure there are more."

"The list seems to be growing," she said, jotting down his words.

She took as many details from him as he would give then flipped the notepad closed and stuck it in her pocket.

"I told you, I'm not filing a report."

"I know. I'm just taking notes for future reference. You seem to be attracting trouble."

"I'm not going to be run out of town," he said, knowing that now his most pressing reason for staying lay in the caverns. "Not by the Drakes—not by anybody."

"You're treading on thin ice. It's all over town you were with Gina at Nelda's yesterday."

She saw Cade's hackles rise. "I was with Trish."

"I heard Gina. You'd better think twice about messing around with her."

"I'm not interested in Gina."

"Some around here might think Bull would be justified in protecting his wife if he thinks you are."

Cade stared at her, his gaze hard and scrutinizing. Scottie shifted uncomfortably. He could have been carved from the very stone that formed the core of Cumberland Mountain.

"I stand forewarned," he said sarcastically.

"When are you leaving town, Cade?"

"Are you my new parole officer? Did Ray assign you the job?"

"That's not fair," Scottie said. "Can't I be concerned without you getting defensive?"

"I'm good at defensive. Self-protection."

"It's not becoming," she said. "You used to not be with me."

"I could trust you back then."

"And now you can't?"

He gave her a piercing look. "I don't think so."

"I see." She couldn't deny she was hurt by his answer, but she didn't care to delve into his feelings. "I'm sorry you feel that way. Why did you call me out here if not to report the tires?"

"I found something that might be of interest to your department."

He showed her the car part half-hidden in the weeds. Scottie pulled out her pad again and noted the approximate location on the country road.

"When did you find this?" she asked.

"Right before I called you."

She squatted beside the twisted piece of chrome for a better look. The metal was crumpled but not rusted or corroded. And there were niches that might hold evidence—skin, hair, threads from clothing. Scottie took several photos with her cell phone before going to her car, where she retrieved a can of spray paint and an evidence bag. She marked the outline of the part then secured it in the bag. She went a step further and staked the surrounding area with yellow barrier tape to make it easier for Rickey to find.

"Why didn't you call Rickey?"

"You know what I think of Rickey as a detective, and not finding this is just another data point, as far as I'm concerned. Somebody should have found it the first time around."

"I'll take it to Rickey. We'll see what he finds on it." Scottie secured the evidence in the back of her car and climbed behind the wheel. "You want a ride home?"

***

Trish tried to shut off her cell phone so she wasn't tempted to answer the unrelenting calls and text messages from Johanna, but her hands trembled so badly she couldn't push the right button. She tossed it on the seat, needing to concentrate on the curving road ahead. She didn't want anybody to find her—ever!

Sweat trickled down her face, and her heart raced with a fierceness she'd never known. Panic welled as she drove mindlessly on, her once automatic habit of popping the pills now triggering a guilt trip.

Cade and his stupid ideas! She *needed* to take something to calm down. She dug into her purse on the seat beside her for the plastic comfort of a pill bottle. She popped off the white cap and shook a few of the distinctive Valium pills into her palm, steering the car with one finger looped around the wheel. This bottle was about half empty, but she had packed her stash from home, along with her Xanax and Ativan, even a few partial bottles of Vicodin and Oxycodone she'd gleaned from different sources over time, sometimes from Johanna's medicine cabinet. She'd bought from fellow students while she was in college, and now she'd discovered a new source—her patients at the nursing home. But she had to be careful there, because if anybody got wise, she'd be out on her butt and maybe facing charges. Speaking of her job, she needed to be sleeping right now so she could wake on time.

A blaring horn caused her to jerk her head up just in time to swerve and miss an oncoming car. The pills in her hand and the open bottle went flying, scattering tablets across the floorboard.

She'd veered into the opposite lane. She might have killed somebody!

Shaking violently, she pulled to the side of the road. She had to get help. Now! She retrieved her cell phone to call Scottie. Then didn't. Scottie was too wrapped up in Nick and would get him involved, and he'd never cared in the past whether she was high or not. Besides, she'd be hiding in plain sight if she stayed with Scottie.

This time she needed more. She needed a place where she could escape from it all, where nobody would find her and she could uncover who she really was without drugs and dependency on Johanna and Nick for everything in her life. She needed to learn to live again.

But where? Trish didn't have a clue. Nor did she have the money or know anybody who had the money for a nice place like she'd like to go. Well, nobody except maybe Cade.

Carefully she checked for traffic and pulled back onto the road. Caverns Lane, where the old family cabin stood, was only a short distance away. She parked safely in front of the shack, scooped up a couple of the pills from the seat where they'd fallen, and swallowed them down.

She needed help, and she wanted it, but for now she had to have something. As her nerves calmed, she relaxed and laid her head back against the headrest. Just a little sleep. She was so tired. Then she would call her brother and ask him for help—real help this time.

CHAPTER 20

NICK popped more extra-strength aspirin tablets for his monster headache and chased them with expensive bourbon. He relished the wave of cool mountain air that washed over him as he stared at the twinkling lights of Cumberland Cove slashing a ribbon of brightness through the valley beneath his deck. Wired by the likelihood that he faced financial ruin and serious legal action, he hadn't slept in two nights. And some intuition told him that his long-trusted lawyer, Will Grazer, might be having second thoughts about his own future. Nick wondered if he might sneak around and approach Cade independently. Will would call it shrewd business; Nick considered it traitorous.

He was spending every hour of every day calling every contact he had or riding the roads seeking alternative tracts of suitable land for his development. Nothing. Nada. Not a scrap of property that would remotely fill his needs.

His deadline to break ground on the development was bearing down on him like a run-amok bulldozer, and he still had nothing to offer, in spite of his bluster. Nor had he informed his clients or his financial backers of the problem. There was nothing on the market to compare with the expansive, untouched wilderness Cade held in his fist like so much gold. And much of the property bordered Cumberland Cove, prime for development with accessible public utilities and zoning easily approved by the city council. Nick's ulcer was working overtime, and his head pounded harder with every thought of impending bankruptcy and his destroyed future.

He wanted nothing more than to go to bed and sleep several days, but he didn't dare. God knows what would happen if he closed his eyes. He pressed the cold glass to his temple. How the hell did Cade manage to march into town and turn the world upside down? And why should Nick allow his felon stepbrother to destroy the business he'd built up over the years?

Nick poured himself another three fingers of whiskey and threw the drink back, grimacing at the burn down his gullet. He was on the verge of giving up or throwing up—too much booze and aspirin on a two-day empty stomach.

Like a man in a trance, he realized that his cell phone was ringing in the next room.

Grumbling, Nick located the phone on his dresser, checked caller ID, and answered.

"Hello, Mom."

Johanna's hysterical shrieks were indecipherable.

"Calm down. I can't understand you."

Nick paced the length of the bedroom while Johanna babbled out what had transpired between her and Trish earlier.

"I'm sure Trish is fine," he told her. "I'm the one who told her to go see Cade. She's just yanking your chain. She'll be back as soon as—"

"No, no, it's different this time. She was serious," Johanna shrieked between hiccups. "We've got to go find her, Nicky. I'm afraid she'll run to Cade, and he might do something to her. Like he's done before."

"Okay, okay, okay! I'll be right there. See you in a few minutes."

Nick flung the phone onto the bed and put on his shoes and socks then stuffed his personal items into his pockets.

What the hell could go wrong next?

***

At the station, Scottie checked in, intending to get ahead on her paperwork before the shift meeting. Nick's voice coming from behind the half-closed door of Ray's office stopped her in the hall.

"Come on, Ray. You can't wait that long. There's no telling what might happen to her in twenty-four hours."

She continued down the hall, but Ray caught her eye as she passed his door.

"Scottie," he called sharply. "Come in."

Reluctantly, she pivoted and stepped into his well-lighted office. The paneled walls were adorned with a dozen plaques, awards, photos with high-ranking government officials, and a couple of trophy heads from his annual hunting trips.

"I guess you know Trish ran off again," Ray said.

"No, I didn't. When?"

"This afternoon after Cade filled her head with nonsense." Nick's face was strained, his eyes puffy and bloodshot. "He got her all worked up about whether Mom kept him from calling her all these years. She stormed out of the house and left. Now Mom's in a stew about it and thinks Trish's never coming back."

"Trish always comes back," Scottie said.

"I know," Nick said. "But Mom's afraid she's turning to Cade this time."

"I don't suppose you know where Cade might be at the moment?" Ray asked her.

"Not a clue."

Nick looked relieved at that.

Scottie shrugged. "Maybe Cade can straighten her out."

"Christ, Scottie! How can that loser help her?" Nick gave her an exasperated look.

"Did she really not let Cade contact Trish?"

"Sure, she did." Nick said it so matter-of-factly.

"Trish adored Cade. How could Johanna be that heartless?"

"Trish was fragile enough without an unstable, ex-con brother making it worse. You know that."

An unbidden thought crept into Scottie's mind. Had her own mother tried to protect her from Cade like Johanna did Trish, for the same misguided reason? Had she herself harbored an unfair resentment against Cade all these years, thinking he had not tried to contact her after he was free? She would probably never know the truth.

Ray huffed a frustrated sigh and ran a hand over his hair. "I hate to waste manpower on a wild goose chase. Don't you figure she'll come home when she gets through licking her mad spot, Nick?"

"Ordinarily, yes," Nick said. He gave Scottie a quick, wary glance then continued, "But with Cade involved, I'm afraid to take a chance."

"Cade wouldn't hurt Trish," Scottie said.

"You don't know that," Nick growled. "Mom's afraid Cade might have taken Trish into those caverns. Like he did Angela."

Ray stiffened in his chair.

"That's absurd!" Scottie snapped at Nick. "She's probably just run off somewhere to pout."

Nick's eyes grew dark as he stared at her face. "You don't want to believe he's ever done anything wrong, do you?"

"She's done this too often in the past. Just wait for her to come home."

"It's not that cut-and-dried this time, and you know it. Cade's involved, and who knows what he might do to hang on to his precious land. Like get rid of the next in line to inherit."

Ray slid his chair back and stood. "Enough of that. Let's try to locate them before I issue a BOLO for Trish." The muscle in his jaw ticked, and Scottie noticed a tremor in his hand until he clenched it into a fist. "I can't go after Cade just on your say-so, Nick, much as I might like to."

At least Ray wasn't jumping the gun.

"If that's all, Chief, I need to get going," Scottie said.

Ray nodded a dismissal. Nick followed her from the room.

"What's with you?" he demanded. "You keep defending Cade no matter what."

"Why you are so worried about Trish all of a sudden is beyond me."

She turned away, but Nick moved in front of her, blocking her path.

"I'm not finished. You're still hung up on him," Nick persisted.

"This is not the time or place. Don't concern yourself about me any longer. You don't trust me, and I'm not going to be in that kind of relationship."

"Scottie, come on." Nick started to follow her, but Ray appeared in the doorway of his office, a questioning look on his face.

Scottie tucked her paperwork under her arm and headed toward roll call.

"Scottie," Ray called out behind her. "Make a pass by the caverns first thing and see if you spot anything unusual."

"Will do," she called back without breaking stride.

CHAPTER 21

AN HOUR later, Scottie pulled up to the chain with the "NO TRESPASSING" sign across the gravel road leading to the caverns. She unhooked it and laid it on the ground as she drove through. Relieved to find the entrance locked and undisturbed, she circled the car and took the side road leading to the cabin.

The ground, hard packed from lack of rain, showed no distinguishable tire tracks, and nothing had disrupted the leaf debris that had drifted against the porch rails and the front door. Obviously, nobody had been there recently.

She pulled out her cell phone and dialed Trish's number. The call went directly to a voice mailbox. Scottie listened to the familiar voice, and a lump formed in her throat at the thought that something might have happened to her. Scottie left her a message to call right away. Before leaving the area, she checked thoroughly around the caverns' entrance once more, but the door to the lean-to was securely locked.

Wondering if Cade might have some idea where his sister was, she headed to his house. She turned into the driveway, parking behind the Range Rover.

As she walked past the SUV, Scottie peered through the windows. There was nothing obviously amiss inside. Stepping onto the dark porch, she rang the doorbell and knocked. After a long few seconds, she heard him coming.

He opened the door but not the screen. A long-sleeved white shirt hung unbuttoned over jeans, and he was barefoot. He braced with both arms on the door frame as he stared down at her. Sporting a day's growth of beard, he looked tired and unkempt.

"I have to say, I didn't expect to see you again so soon. Can't stay away from me?"

Scottie had to admit there was a time. "Actually, I'm here on business."

"You found something on the car part already?"

"Would you step outside, please?"

Cade glared at her. "Sounds like you've got cop voice mastered."

He flipped on the outside light against the gathering darkness then opened the screen and came onto the porch. He shoved his hands in his jeans pockets, drawing her gaze inadvertently downward. She quickly jerked her eyes back to his face. She wanted to wipe away the smug smile, but she maintained her composure.

"What's this all about, Scottie?" he said.

"Do you know where Trish is?"

"Why are you asking me that?"

"Have you seen her?"

"She came by to discuss a house."

"When was that?"

"Why are you questioning me? Has she accused me of something?" Cade pressed, his eyes riveted on her. "Should I lawyer up?"

"Do you think you need to?"

"You tell me. You're out here in the night with that cop attitude that really pisses me off. So be straight with me, or I will call my lawyer."

Scottie bit back her opinion of *his* attitude.

"Trish had an argument with Johanna and ran off. Nobody's seen her since. Johanna felt, from what Trish said, that she might turn to you."

"Why would she? My sister has barely spoken a civil word to me since I've been here."

"Johanna said Trish was very upset about things you told her."

"I only told her the truth that she needed to know."

"Such as?"

"That I tried to contact her after I got out of prison, but Johanna blocked me. That Nick was using her to get the land he wanted. That she needed to get off the drugs so she'd know what was going on around her."

"It might have been too much to unload on her at once."

"I thought she needed to grow up a little, but I didn't mean to scare her off. Come inside and let me check my phone to be sure she didn't call." He picked up his phone from the kitchen table where it lay beside his computer and a stack of paperwork. He pressed several buttons then shook his head. "Nothing from her."

"Thanks for checking. She's been known to take off before. I'm just afraid if she doesn't turn up soon, the suspicion is going to fall on you since Johanna's already pointing the finger."

"I haven't hurt Trish, and nobody can prove I have."

"They didn't really prove you killed Angela, either, did they?" Scottie said ruefully.

After a missed beat and a hard stare, he said, "Point taken. So what do you want me to do?"

"Call me if you hear from her. Tell her to come home."

"Okay. You do the same for me."

"I will. I'm sure she's okay. Just off with one of her friends like usual."

DAY 5

CHAPTER 22

A FTER a few hours' sleep, Cade woke early. Three cups of strong coffee chased away the fog in his brain, but he wondered if the unrelenting churning in his stomach would lead to ulcers. At nine a.m., he called his insurance agent to file a claim then dialed his secretary.

Once she had caught him up on company business, Cade said, "Marge, I need you to do some legwork for me. I need to find the best criminal defense lawyer on the east coast who can practice in Tennessee. When you find him, put him on retainer for me."

Marge fell silent for a long moment. "Are you in trouble, Mr. Youngblood?"

"Not yet. Better safe than sorry. I'll be in touch in the next day or so."

When he said good-bye to Marge, Cade pulled up his bank accounts on the laptop and transferred half a million dollars from a savings account into his checking account, prepared to post bail if he needed to. He feared that if he ever landed in a Cumberland Cove jail cell, he'd never get out alive.

Worried about Trish, he gave Scottie time to get home after her shift ended before he headed to her house. The more he was around

Scottie, the more he resented losing her and the life they could have shared.

And before he left Cumberland Cove, there was a single question that had tormented him for years—one that only Scottie could answer.

From a distance, the rambling farmhouse appeared to be nestled into the wooded mountainside like a bird's nest in a bush. Scottie grew up in this house, surrounded by whitewashed fencing and neat meadows, after her parents moved in to help Scottie's aging grandfather with the farm work. Cade's family lived across the road until his mother died when he was eight. Then he and his father and sister moved into town, but the children all attended the same school and remained playmates.

A wide porch ran around three sides of the house, with hanging ferns along the perimeter. Two rocking chairs sat at one end of the porch with a table between them; at the other end hung a broad swing surrounded by a tangle of vines climbing a lattice trellis. Sweet memories crept into Cade's mind of playing summer games with Scottie on that shady porch under a canopy of yellow roses. Cade could almost smell the sweet fragrance and hear Scottie's giggles above the low drone of bees in the blossoms.

He followed the driveway to the back of the house and parked beside her Jeep. She answered his knock on the back door dressed in yoga pants and a loose, long-sleeve knit top. Her long hair hung down past her shoulders, the shining curls free to wave and dance for the first time since he'd been back. He closed his fists to keep from reaching out to feather the tresses through his fingers like he'd loved to do.

She looked surprised. For the first time, it occurred to him that Nick might be inside, that Nick might spend every morning with her.

"I'm sorry, I should have called, I guess. I...I wanted to check on Trish."

"No problem," she said, "there's nothing new. No word from her."

"Okay." He knew that it was a mistake to come, that he should turn and walk away. Leave the emotional abyss between them unbridged. Yet, he hesitated. She had been a part of him for so much of his life, and the past seventeen years had been meaningless without her, like the years to come would be.

"You okay? Why don't you come in?"

He shook his head slightly, fighting the subtle, suppressed longing to spend just another hour near her. "I'd better not."

She fell back on an old ploy that had never failed. "I'm making eggs and biscuits."

He laughed softly. "Don't tell me that's still all you can cook."

"You used to like my eggs and biscuits."

"I liked being with *you*. I didn't care what you cooked, or if you cooked at all."

"Come on in," she said. "I cook better than I used to."

"I'm going to hold you to that."

The interior of the house was much the same as he remembered. Scottie had changed very little other than replacing the kitchen counter tops and adding high-end stainless steel appliances. A few pieces of comfortable, modern furniture were intermixed with her grandparents' antiques.

A pang of nostalgia tickled the pit of his stomach. He could walk this house as if he lived here. Scottie's grandmother had been a saving grace for a child who had lost his own mother. He had known he could take refuge here any time and expect a homemade cookie and a hug and, best of all, the chance to play with his young soul mate Scottie.

Scottie had coffee brewing and had been filling a pan with biscuit dough when she was interrupted.

She stuck the biscuits into the hot oven and found a package of bulk sausage in the refrigerator, patted mounds flat, and placed them in a sizzling frying pan.

A carton of eggs sat on the counter. Cade broke several into a bowl, mixed in a dab of cream, salt, and pepper, and poured them into another skillet.

"When did you get so domestic?" she asked, laying silverware beside the extra plate she had set on the table.

Cade shrugged. "Comes with the whole bachelor territory."

The old, comfortable routine of working side by side with Scottie had a calming effect. Never in his most far-fetched imagination had he expected to be in this kitchen again with her. Not after prison, anyway—not after he learned the truth. A heaviness in his heart reminded him that this Scottie was not "his" Scottie. Not the one he'd left behind, the one he'd thought he could trust with his very soul. He couldn't even trust her with his—

"I'll butter these," she said, jerking Cade from his thoughts, leaving a lingering sense of betrayal that warred with the numbing trickle of dread that was finally diminishing a little in Scottie's safe, warm kitchen.

With padded oven gloves, she pulled the piping hot biscuits straight from the oven onto a pad on the counter and set to her task in silence. Cade tried to shake the melancholy that had become a part of him since his return to Cumberland Cove, but the warm aromas swirling around the kitchen filled him with an aching homesickness so strong he had to close his eyes for a moment to ward it off. He thought he had long ago choked those emotions to death. Now to have them inundate him so quickly and so powerfully hammered home the extent of his failure.

"Looks like everything's ready," he said, transferring the scrambled eggs to a serving bowl.

They filled their plates and sat down at the table. After eating awhile in silence, Cade said, "Do you really think Trish just ran away?"

"She has a long history of it from the time she was a young teenager. She usually showed up at a friend's house. When she was older, she would go off with her buddies to Gatlinburg for a few days. The only reason anybody's concerned this time is because you're here, sad to say."

"I need to go back to Houston. I've got a project underway that needs my attention, but I hate to leave with her missing."

"There's nothing to keep you from leaving, really," Scottie said. "Ray wouldn't even issue a BOLO on her because of her reputation."

"Did nobody try to help her over the years? I mean, Johanna was supposed to be a mother to her."

"I don't know, Cade. I wasn't here, either. I've tried to help her since I've been back, but there are a lot of deep, emotional issues with her."

Cade sat back and laid his napkin aside. "I wish I'd known all this earlier. I would have been more tolerant. I do care about her. A lot. Maybe when she realizes what Uncle Silas did for her, she'll be able to put her life together."

"I hope so. If Nick will lay off."

"So when did you get involved with Nick? Looks pretty serious to me."

Scottie made a wry face. "Not anymore. I called it off yesterday."

Cade certainly hadn't expected that answer. "Can I ask why?"

"I'd rather not go into it."

"Sorry, didn't mean to pry."

"I'd better clean up here. I have to get some sleep."

"I'll help. Goes faster with two."

As he brought the dishes to her, she placed them in the dishwasher. The pots and pans were submerged in hot, soapy water to soak.

"What happened with you after high school?" Cade said, hoping she might hint at what he wanted to know in the conversation. "I know you told me you were widowed."

"My dad took a job in Atlanta after...after all that."

Silas had said that Scottie's family moved away almost immediately. *All that*, as Scottie put it, must have been hell for her, too, and probably the reason they took her away. So that she could start anew, so that she could do what she did, and nobody around this town would be the wiser. So that nobody would know to tell Cade.

"You finished school here or there?"

"Here, technically, although I didn't walk for graduation. Dad snatched me out of school right after you were indicted. I had all the credits to graduate, so they mailed my diploma."

"And you went on to college?"

Cade knew all the answers to his questions already, but he only knew *what* she had done. *Why* mattered to him now.

"Yes, I worked my way through college then went to the police academy."

"Your parents didn't pay for college?"

"I didn't want them to," she said, tight-lipped. "My major in college was criminal justice, but I decided to go to the police academy instead of graduate school. I met my husband, Robert, after I joined the Atlanta PD. He was a trooper in the Georgia State Patrol. We dated a few times, found out we got along well together, had common interests in our field, and when he asked me to marry him, I accepted. It was a very comfortable marriage. We both loved our jobs, enjoyed traveling when we could." Scottie's eyes clouded suddenly, and she blinked and swiped brusquely at the tears that threatened to fall. "Then he was killed on duty. Shot by a doped-up punk kid. Senseless, but a part of life, I suppose." She tried to smile, couldn't.

"How long were you married?"

"Six years."

"You must have loved him."

"We had a peaceful relationship. Very easy, no upheavals, no arguments. Mutual respect. I knew he cherished our marriage, and I made a good partner. I think we were both content."

Cade studied her face. She spoke of comfort and contentment, but she never mentioned love. He shifted his gaze to her solemn face. Once, she'd been able to love passionately. He knew from experience. Had he destroyed that in her, too?

"Why did you come back here?"

"I couldn't get over his death in Atlanta. There was always something to remind me of the violence that a big city fosters. I wanted the peace and quiet I remembered here. And Mom never sold the farm, so I bought it. I had good experience from Atlanta, had made detective, so Ray hired me when I applied as an officer. And I guess the rest is history, short though it is." She smiled, but the sadness in her green eyes was not lost on Cade. "End of story."

Not the end of story! Cade wanted to shout. *Not the end of anything!*

"Pat answer," he said.

"What do you mean by that?" she asked, laying her dishcloth aside from wiping the tabletop. "You wanted a rundown, well, that's pretty much been my life since Cumberland Cove."

Why did she continue to lie to him? All of the hurt and confusion and anguish roiled just under the surface, and a pinprick would burst it like a festering boil. He wanted to shake her until she told him everything. What she had done and why. And how she had been so hard-hearted.

He tried another tack. "Look, I've always wanted to apologize to you."

"For what?"

"For hurting you over Gina."

Scottie gave a snort of disbelief. "How can you say that, when you were just with her again?"

"At the café? Come on, you can't be serious. She came in. I didn't go looking for her. Nothing happened, nothing's going to happen. I made a bad mistake when you and I were together that I've regretted ever since, on many levels. But if nothing else, I do learn from my transgressions. So, again, I'm sorry for what I did back then. And I haven't done anything since then to apologize for."

"You know, it really shouldn't matter to me after all these years," she said, "but it does. It's the meanness of what you two did that I can't forgive. So, yes, I guess it still hurts that you would be so open about it. Almost like you want me to catch you two at it again."

"What are you talking about? Catch us at it again?"

"Quit playing innocent. You had the audacity to lure me up to the cabin to find you and Gina...doing it...in the act! Did you expect a threesome or something? Because you ought to have known me better."

"Lure you to the cabin? That's crazy. I didn't know Gina was going to be there. She just showed up and, well, she was hot and all over me, and I was stupid. That's my only excuse. Liquor and ego led to one life-altering mistake."

"The note, Cade! On my typewriter. Like you left me every day in typing class, remember? On that rickety old typewriter you had fourth period and I had fifth?"

"Yeah, sure I know. But I cut typing class that day."

"You did what?" Something inside Scottie seemed to deflate. "That's a lie. The note was there—on my typewriter."

"I didn't put it there, I swear. I cut all my afternoon classes. Smoked a few joints behind the gym with Bobcat and some other guys, then we got up a hunting trip. Afterward, when I went by the cabin with a jug of Bobcat's moonshine, Gina was there. But I never left you any—"

"That bitch! She must have...she..."

"Tricked us both?" Cade offered, realizing now why Gina had been so provocative that afternoon, wouldn't let him alone, wouldn't stop until she seduced a drunken, stupid teenage boy with raging hormones and screwed up his life for good.

Scottie didn't look totally convinced.

"I'm telling you the truth."

An uneasy silence fell between them as things they'd taken for granted for years shifted to expose shaky ungrounded suppositions and an even uglier truth.

"I tried to tell you that day you caught us," Cade said. "You weren't in a mood to listen, and after I was arrested, it was too late. I never heard from you again. *Ever*."

Tears brimmed Scottie's eyes. "They wouldn't let me, and after they found out—"

She cut herself short and twisted away to the counter where she busied herself putting the salt and pepper shakers in place by the stove, wiping the counter until it sparkled. She picked up the sugar dish to put it in a cupboard.

"Found out what, Scottie?" Cade said, moving behind her. Had she almost come clean?

She shrugged him away as if his very nearness annoyed her. "Nothing. Just that they realized we...we...were closer than they knew."

"Closer than I knew, too," he said.

Scottie stiffened, motionless, like a trapped animal testing the wind for the enemy. She didn't turn around, but she whispered. "What do you mean?"

Cade reached for his wallet. Opening it to the photo sleeve, he took out a snapshot of a young boy of about ten years old with dark, curly hair. He reached around without touching her to lay it on the counter.

Scottie stared at the photo then said, "Who is that?"

Surprised at her response, Cade said, "My son."

"Of course. He looks just like you. I didn't know you were married."

"I'm not. Never have been."

"Okay, he's illegitimate. So?" She looked totally bewildered.

So? Was that all she had to say? Perplexed by her nonchalant reaction, he said, "That's an old photo. He's sixteen now." He laid down a recent picture of the boy.

She stood rooted to the spot, but she gripped the dish in her hand hard enough to turn her fingers white. "I don't understand. How can he be sixteen? That would mean he was born..."

"While I was in prison. Exactly. You should know."

Scottie slumped against the counter. "I don't understand, Cade. Gina?"

Cade couldn't stop the explosion of emotion. The rancor overflowed, spilling into the air around them like a deadly venom.

"*Gina!*" He snapped. "This has nothing to do with Gina. That's *our* son, Scottie. *Yours and mine,* and you damn well know it! Admit it, damn it! You're the one who gave him up for adoption. I didn't get a chance—"

The sugar dish slid from her hands and shattered as it hit the floor, sugar flying everywhere. She covered her mouth, and a hard shudder wracked her body as she moaned, "Oh, my God. Oh, my God! It can't be."

"You want to talk about meanness and deceit now?" Cade said with a cruelness born of a long-repressed anger against this woman for what she did. "You gave him away without so much as telling me I had a son. How could you do that, Scottie? How could you—" Cade choked and couldn't get the words out.

The shot was a grainy close-up taken with a telephoto lens, but there was no denying the teenager in the photo. His hair was black like Cade's but curly like Scottie's; his face was the image of Cade's at the same age, with the same brilliant blue eyes.

Scottie turned on him like a wildcat.

"You're lying!" she shrieked, her voice high-pitched with hysteria. "It can't be!"

"Why didn't you tell me? Or let Uncle Silas know so he could tell me?" he shouted back, taking her by the shoulders. "I had a right to know I had a son. I had a right to have a say in what was done with him. I was stuck in that goddamned prison while you just threw him away!" Cade fought back the tears he'd never shed over his loss. "My name's not even on the birth certificate."

"Where did you get those? How do you even know about him? They're fakes. They can't be real."

"You gave away our son!" His grip tightened.

She jerked out of his grasp, her face pale and drawn. "I didn't want to. I didn't want to, I swear," she whispered. "And then later, they told me..."

"Told you what?" Blood pounded through his head, behind his eyes. "Who told you what? You were eighteen years old when he was born. You had a choice."

Scottie just shook her head, picking up the photos to stare at them with her fingers pressed against her trembling lips. Finally, she said, "I didn't. Not when it would have mattered."

Cade forced himself to breathe deeply, to wrestle down that living, squirming demon inside him one more time, to hear what she was saying—to try to understand. "You're going to have to explain that."

"If you're lying to me, if those are Photoshopped, I swear I'll never forgive you."

"You've never forgiven me anyway. What's the difference?"

"My parents forced me to give him up. I *didn't* have a choice, Cade. I was so hurt. You'll never know. I only got to hold my sweet little baby once, for just a few minutes. Then they took him away from me." Her eyes grew huge and dark, her voice shaky. "I can't believe they did that to me."

Scottie's knees buckled, and Cade caught her in his arms.

"This can't be him." She clutched the photos to her heart, her body shuddering. "He's dead. Why are you trying to hurt me again?"

"Why do you think he's dead? That is him."

In a breathless whisper, she said, "They told me he died right after he was adopted."

He eased to the floor with her in his embrace, rocking her on his lap like the baby they'd lost.

Cade held her tightly, kissing the top of her head, trying to hold back the hot tears stinging his eyes at Scottie's heartbreak. "I don't know why your parents lied to you. But I promise you, I'm telling you the truth. He is very much alive. Why don't you call your mother and ask her?"

"It wouldn't do any good. She's got Alzheimer's, and Dad won't even pick up the phone to speak to me. Oh, Cade." Scottie buried her head in his chest, and they sat curled into one another, mourning the child they had lost.

"Why would they tell you that?"

Scottie pressed her face harder against him. "Because they knew I would look for him forever until I found him."

"Just like I did," Cade said. "For a long time, I thought I never would locate him."

The room grew quiet, and Cade could mark the ticking of the grandfather clock in the hallway. He stroked her damp hair and kissed her head again.

"I'm so sorry, Scottie," he said, his throat burning and constricted. "I wish I had known the truth. But he's not dead, I swear."

She looked up at him. "Where did you get these pictures? Where is he? Can I see him? I want to hold him and know he's real."

"I've never spoken to him. I know where he lives, but he's never seen me. He's got a good, loving family, thank God. I've never interfered in his life in any way, and we can't now. We're both bound by the decision you were forced to make. You understand that, don't you?"

She was quiet for a long time, staring at the two photos. Then she nodded without looking up. "I want to look at him," she said then added, "alone. Please?"

"You can keep them." Cade helped her to her feet as he rose. "I'm going to make fresh coffee," he said, "because I've got the feeling we're going to be here a while."

CHAPTER 23

SCOTTIE disappeared into her bedroom and closed the door. Cade could hear her sobbing, and something inside him broke open, releasing the hatred that had poisoned him for so long. He just wanted to hold her again, to tell her everything was okay. But it wasn't—not yet. There was still a lot of hurt between them that had to be forgiven.

Cade stuck his wallet in his pocket and started a new pot of coffee. While it brewed, he visited the guest bathroom to regain a semblance of composure. When he returned, Scottie was sitting at the table, motionless, like a woman in a trance, staring at the boy's pictures in front of her. Cade fixed two mugs of coffee and brought them to the table.

"Are you sure it's him?" she asked quietly as he set her mug close by. "Absolutely sure?"

Cade nodded.

She shook her head sadly. "I don't know anything about him at all. All these years, lost."

Cade eased into the chair opposite her. "His name is Ryan. He lives in Alabama."

"Ryan. I like that," she said softly. "How did you find all this out?"

Cade gave a hard sigh, still reeling from the shock of the answer he had so long sought and so little expected. He started slowly. "When

I got out of prison, I found out where your mother lived, and I called her. She blew me off, just like Johanna did when I tried to contact Trish. She told me you were happily married and to stay out of your life. She wouldn't give me an address or phone number. I was struggling with life right out of prison. I needed some connection to you. If nothing else, just to talk to you, tell you I was sorry for all that happened."

"She had no idea where I was," Scottie muttered.

"She sure sounded like she did."

"After I left home, I never talked to my mother or father again. I bought this house through a lawyer without having to see them. If she knew I was married, she learned it from somebody else."

Cade digested that for a moment. "Okay. Well, I didn't have any way of knowing that, and I figured you'd gone on with your life, so I tried to get on with mine. I had taken as many college courses as I could in prison, so I pushed hard to graduate when I got out, then had to establish a career so I could support myself."

"You said you never married?"

He held up his left hand. "No ring, no tan lines," he quipped. "I've had a couple of relationships over the years, but nothing that warranted marriage. At first, I was busy putting my life back together and making up for lost time. Now I work a lot. There's not much room for anything else."

"So, go on. How did you find out about Ryan?"

Cade sipped the coffee, remembering those sad, overwhelming days when the loneliness and guilt almost killed him even after he'd survived eight years in prison.

"Once I started making money, I didn't have much to spend it on, so I hired a private detective to find you. I honestly thought if I apologized for ruining your life, it would afford some kind of closure." Cade's jaw muscles tightened, and he wrapped his hands around the mug to keep them from trembling. "Instead, I found out you had gone on as if I never existed. At least, it looked that way. And then I learned that I had a son some damn where. Quite a revelation. I questioned

Uncle Silas in a roundabout way until I was sure he had no idea. Your parents apparently spirited you away so fast, he didn't know where you were for some time."

Scottie nodded. "They wouldn't allow me to visit you after you were arrested. I don't know if I could have anyway, legally, but they were adamant. So I told them I was pregnant, thinking that would make them understand why I loved you so much. Instead, my dad went ballistic, and my mom caved like a ragdoll. They clamped down on me, and I couldn't even get out of the house. Then they shipped me off like a dirty secret to my aunt's house in Atlanta after school on the day you were indicted. They didn't tell me ahead of time that I was going; my dad had my things packed when I got home, and he drove me down right then. I didn't have a chance to tell my friends good-bye or anything. So go on, tell me the rest, how you got these pictures without meeting him."

"It took me another year to find out where Ryan was and that he was doing okay. I wasn't about to abandon him like I thought you did."

"Please don't say that again." The hurt in her voice stung.

"I'm sorry. I know now, but I've lived all these years thinking you did, and not able to understand why."

"At least you knew he was alive. I've never had that comfort."

Cade nodded. "I keep check on him. If he needs anything, I plan to provide it, one way or another."

"How can you do that without them knowing?"

Cade grinned. "I have ways. The father owns a fertilizer company, and I bought some landscape operations through a holding company that are some of his best customers."

Scottie gave a half smile. "You're kidding, right?"

"Not a bit," Cade said. "I set it up a few years ago, just for that purpose." Cade faltered then said, "That's the main reason now that I want my name cleared. Just in case he does come looking for us. I don't want him to think his father's a killer."

"Do you think he knows he's adopted?"

Cade shrugged. "I have no idea. My PI said it was a private, closed adoption, and he had a devil of a time getting any information. I've gone to a couple of baseball games when his team plays tournaments in Houston. He's good. A catcher. I keep to crowded public places, where no one would notice. Needless to say, I wouldn't stand side-by-side with him, because somebody might get suspicious."

"I should think so," Scottie agreed, picking up the picture of the teenager to study it closer. "He looks just like you."

"I took that photo at a game with a zoom lens. The PI took the other one once he was sure he'd found the right kid. He's got your hair that I always loved."

"That I always hated, poor kid." Scottie took a deep breath and pressed her hand against her lips again.

Cade reached across the table and took her hand in his. "We lost a lot."

She nodded and squeezed her eyes shut, but the tears escaped anyway. "I can't believe I'm doing this. I never cry anymore."

"Hey, me either," Cade said with a smile, but he knew his eyes were as red as hers, because he was fighting his emotions for all he was worth.

She smiled back, and his heart warmed, encouraging him to take an even greater risk. "I...Scottie, I never meant to hurt you, and I want to say, again, I'm sorry. For everything. What happened with Gina. Deserting you when you needed me most, even though I couldn't avoid that. And especially, this business about Ryan...I mean..." he stammered then went on, "losing faith in you when you didn't deserve it."

Scottie averted her gaze, picking at the tablecloth. "Thank you," she said softly. "It means a lot to hear you say so. I owe you the same apology."

"You thought I killed Angela like the rest of them?"

She shook her head slightly. "No, I couldn't believe you would do such a thing. But after a while, it got so hard to fight the good fight. To keep trying to take up for you when everybody around me believed the worst. My parents either yelled at me or clammed up if I even mentioned your name." She rose to take her cup to the sink.

Cade followed, standing close to her. "I finally just gave up. Can you understand that, Cade? I had to find some way to go on. I couldn't keep living in the past without going crazy. Especially after I lost the baby. I just couldn't." She pressed her cheek against his chest.

Cade rested his chin lightly on the top of her head. "I do understand. The pain can eat you alive. I guess we both chose survival."

"That's a good way to put it."

A loose curl fell across her forehead. Cade brushed it back then cupped his hand along her cheek, lifting her face so that their eyes met.

"What happened, happened," Cade said. "It's in the past."

Cade kissed away the fresh tears that trickled down her face, following their trail until he found her mouth, salty and trembling. She stiffened under his touch for a moment, then pressed against him and returned his kiss. Her fingers brushed through his hair, lingering on the jagged scar below his hairline. She drew back slightly and pushed his hair back, sucking in a tiny breath, but she said nothing.

He lifted her hand from the scar and brought her fingertips to his lips. She pulled back and disentangled herself from his arms.

"I can't do this again," she said, her voice still hoarse.

He held his silence and let her walk away from him, although it was one of the toughest things he'd ever done. Even as she disappeared down the hall into her bedroom, Cade debated the wisdom of rekindling their relationship. The shattering of their familiar world of long-held misconceptions suddenly left them on an entirely new emotional plane. Both of them would need time to regroup.

Cade picked up the shards of the fragile sugar dish and swept up the scattered white crystals. As damaged as it was, could it ever be put right again?

Maybe, with the right glue. He left the dish on the counter, wondering if Scottie would bother to fix it.

Scottie was gone so long that Cade assumed she was sending him a message to get lost. Saddened after hoping they had reconnected on some level, he took his jacket from the coat rack near the back door, was reaching for the doorknob when he heard her behind him.

"Tell me more about Ryan," Scottie said softly. "I want to know everything about him."

Cade gazed straight ahead in silence for a long time, not sure he was ready to share everything about his...their son.

"I love him as much as you do, Cade. I have a right to know about him."

Finally, he turned and said, "I need your word that you won't try to interfere in his life in any way."

Reluctantly, she nodded. "I won't try to contact him. But I have to know more about him."

"First, I want you to see where I'm coming from. I'm suddenly having to do an about-face. On everything." He met her stare. "Especially sharing this secret I've kept for so long."

She came to him and touched his arm. "I need this connection to our son as much as you did. It's nice outside. Let's sit on the porch."

Once he started, Cade talked freely, his pride for their son and his accomplishments overflowing. Scottie listened with rapt attention as Cade described Ryan's family, his home, his pets, his academic and sports accomplishments. She laughed and shed a few tears and occasionally broke in with questions.

The emotion between them spilled over into small confidences. Glimpses into the lives they'd led since they were parted.

"Just think," she mused, her knees pulled up beneath her chin. "If things had been different, you could have been his little league coach. I could have been room mom. We might have had more—"

"Stop it, Scottie!" Cade rose abruptly, pulled her from her chair and wrapped his arms around her. His hand trembled as he smothered her face into his chest. "Don't make me more guilty than I already feel. The past is written in stone, and I can't change anything."

"I'm sorry. I didn't mean it that way. I just wanted to imagine for a moment," she whispered.

"I try not to imagine what might have been," he said, his hands entwining in her hair, drawing her face close to his as he whispered. "I can handle reality better."

Surely he was dreaming. But Cade only dreamed nightmares, and Scottie's sweet breath on his face, her soft, short protest when he kissed her again had no place in a nightmare.

"We should go inside," she whispered.

CHAPTER 24

KISSING her repeatedly, he gently maneuvered her through the house and into her bedroom. He had not truly made love to a woman in years. Sex, yes. He had no problem getting women in bed for short-term gratification, but there was a difference.

Scottie put her hands on either side of his face and drew him into a deep kiss. When her lips parted and invited him in, an irrational, soul-deep lightning bolt almost buckled his knees. She didn't protest when he eased her down on the bed. She pushed his shirt up and nuzzled his chest, her lips working downward. Wanting to be inside her so badly he hurt, Cade shifted over her, but Scottie pushed him onto his back and rose on one elbow. She unfastened his pants and slid her hand underneath the waistband. Her touch sent a hot jolt of lust through him. His body's strong response was immediate and obvious.

Their faces almost touching, her long hair fell in a shimmering cascade that enclosed them in their own shadowy world. He drank in the flush of passion on her face caused by the friction of his five-o'clock shadow and her slightly parted lips, rosy from being kissed.

How many times, trapped in that stinking hellhole of a prison cell and even afterward in self-imposed exile, certain he'd never be with her again, had he willed his body not to remember her touch, her sighs, or the warmth of her breath as she whispered his name? And now, after he had given up hope, she was in his arms again so suddenly, so unexpectedly, that he didn't dare question fate or his own sanity. And no, he had not forgotten her touch or her body.

She withdrew her hand, generating a powerful hunger for it to return. She stripped her tee shirt over her head and tugged off the yoga pants. She had grown even sexier with age. She stretched across his body like a lithe cat as she worked his shirt up and off. He closed his eyes, reveling in the explosion of pleasure her nearness created. Running her fingers gently along the curve of his shoulders, she braced to hover above him then grew still.

"Cade," she said. "Do we...you...need to use protection?"

Cade grudgingly opened his eyes just a fraction, anxious for her to move again. "You mean for babies or disease?"

"I'm on the pill. I mean you."

"I'm clean, I swear it. But I don't have any 'just-in-case' condoms. I wasn't expecting this by a long shot." As much as he wanted to continue, he would not entice her into something she would regret. "Look, I don't want you to do anything you—"

"There are some in the bedside drawer," she murmured, which made him a little sick to know why they were there, though he had no right to rebuke her. He had not been a choirboy, either. He allowed her to slide one on without protest. Anything to make love to her.

Shifting her onto her back, Cade moved on top of her. He recalled pleasures she used to enjoy, curious to see if he could still make her moan. He could. She arched to meet him, his name escaped in a low purr from deep in her throat.

Scottie's hot skin slid against his like satin. Her long, slender legs wrapped around him, and she pulled his body down against hers, forcing him deep inside. Sultry, half-closed eyes the color of a stormy sea delved into his as if she could devour him. The heat that enveloped him was suffocating, snatched his breath, threw his heart against his ribcage in explosive thuds.

Breathing hard, Cade closed his eyes, spent, as he lay between her legs, feeling her damp skin against his—wondering already where they would go from here. The thought that he might never hold her again like this triggered panic. He drew her closer, crushing her to his chest as he buried his face against her neck to breathe in her sweet, clean scent, unable to get enough of the feel and taste of her. He wanted to drown in her essence and never come up for air.

In her arms, for the first time in years, he felt truly safe, as if she stood watch between him and the devil itself. No nightmare could touch him while Scottie held him close. Gently, she caressed his hair, lulling him into a sweet limbo between sleep and waking.

"God, Scottie," he murmured into her ear. "I never dreamed we'd have another chance."

"I didn't, either," she said softly.

"I'm never losing you again," he whispered. "Ever."

***

Scottie couldn't relax. Her mind raced with the sudden and unbelievable turn of events. Making love to Cade had awakened a maelstrom of feelings that she was not ready to try to define, but the likes of which she had not felt since she gave up on him so long ago.

She lay quietly in the crook of his arm as he slept naked beside her, his face as peaceful as she'd ever seen it. Thick, dark lashes brushed his cheekbones, and his lips parted slightly with soft snoring. The afternoon sun sent rays through the partially closed blinds to lay pencil-thin strips of light across his body, defining honed muscle under tanned skin. She allowed her gaze to slide down his bare body from head to toe, memorizing every detail of him. She knew all too well how quickly something you loved could be snatched away, maybe forever.

She told herself she had not meant things to come to this, but somewhere deep inside, she had known what would happen if she let down her guard. He shifted toward her with a contented sigh, and she barely breathed for fear of waking him and ending this sweet, magical moment.

She could envision their son in his face, could imagine Ryan as a baby sleeping in the next room. This could have been their life. Her childhood dreams had included a pristine house, the proverbial white fence, with children and dogs playing noisily in the yard while she prepared dinner. She always assumed that Cade would work for his uncle in the hardware store and take it over someday, since he never talked about big careers or ambitions. And that would have been fine—that was the simple life she wanted, too. Back then. In her naiveté.

Reality check, Martha Stewart! No marriage license was tucked in the desk drawer, no picket fence around the farmhouse she had worked so hard to revitalize. There had never been a baby in the next room and might never be.

"Oh, Cade," Scottie whispered. Her breath mingled with hot tears against his neck. "What have we done?"

Cade jerked upright, the serene expression gone. Confusion and apprehension filled his eyes as he glanced around the room.

"Cade?" she called in concern, reaching out for him. "Are you okay?"

He closed his eyes for a moment and took a deep breath then eased down again on his side, their faces level on the pillow. "Sorry. I don't wake well in an unfamiliar bed," he said with a contrite grin. "Have to figure out where I am and how I got there."

"Oh?" she said, tracing a finger along his lips. "And does that happen often, Mr. Youngblood?"

He kissed the tip of her finger. "Most of the time, in fact."

"Well, that gives me a warm and fuzzy feeling. I'm in bed with a playboy."

The gentle pressure of Cade's warm hand on her back kept her from pulling away. "I hardly ever wake up in a woman's bed. Mostly I wake in a tent or some ratty hotel room in a foreign country. I move around so much it takes me a minute to get oriented sometimes. I have to say, this is the best wake-up I've ever had."

She was willing to accept that. She rubbed away the frown lines between his eyes then touched the chain around his neck. "Where's your St. Christopher's medal?"

He wouldn't meet her gaze. "I gave it away."

She frowned, knowing the significance of that medal, but seeing the distress in his expression, she didn't press, especially since his hands and mouth began to touch her in those ways only he knew, which left her almost powerless to resist. She wriggled away from his exploring fingers and pulled the rumpled sheet between them to discourage him.

"Don't," he mumbled.

"We can't do this all day."

"Why not?"

"For one thing, I have to get some rest before work. For another, we need to slow down and give some thought to what we're doing."

"I've thought about it for years. This is all I've ever wanted."

"Well, it's caught me by surprise. There's a lot more to it than just making love all day long. I have a home here and a career. Your life is all over the place."

"I can run my business from anywhere."

Scottie had not foreseen that answer. "You mean you would come back to Cumberland Cove to live?"

"If that's what it takes."

"You're committing for the wrong reason. Just because we had sex again doesn't mean we can sustain a relationship. And what if it didn't work in the end and you'd uprooted your life and business? I don't want to be responsible for that. It's too big a chance."

"I'm a big boy, Scottie. I understand the consequences. I've gone through most of my life half-living. It's not enough for me anymore. Are you willing to risk losing each other again for fear of what if?" Cade rose onto one elbow, following her eyes with his gaze. "Because I'm not."

She couldn't give him the answer he sought. He wanted more from her than she knew how to give right now. And was offering more than he could afford to lose.

His expression grew somber. "Nothing's ever easy, is it?"

"No." She was quiet for a moment then said, "I have to get some sleep, and I don't think I can do that with you in bed next to me."

"Okay. I've got more than enough work to do to keep my company treading water another day or two."

"We'll get together later, then."

He took her in his arms and kissed her lightly on the lips. "Scottie, don't give up on me. I promise I'll be worth it."

She gave him a light shove to get him moving.

"You'd damn well better be."

CHAPTER 25

Nick hesitated before knocking on Scottie's back door. From the porch, he turned to stare at Cade's Range Rover parked a few feet away, which only served to drive his temper to stroke level.

Without warning, the door swung open. Cade looked as surprised to see Nick as Nick was to see him. The smell of food and coffee wafted through the screen.

"What are you doing here?" Nick demanded. "I want to talk to Scottie."

"She's sleeping. Call her later."

Cade wore such a smug expression that Nick expected to see canary feathers sticking out of his mouth—which would only mean one thing.

Jealousy flushed through Nick like bad water from Mexico. He yanked open the screen door, but Cade blocked his entrance into the kitchen.

"Stay the hell away from her."

"She can decide that."

That bring-it-on look in Cade's eyes used to incite a fight between them every time. Nick sized Cade up and thought better of his gut reaction. There had been a subtle realignment of the balance of power over the years, one most people would never notice, but Nick recognized it and so did Cade, from the look in his eye. This brawl wouldn't be a matter of pummeling a punk teenager. Much as he hated to admit it, the hard, military-trained fighting edge Nick had cultivated as a young man had been dulled by the easy life. From the looks of him, Cade had put on fifteen or twenty pounds of solid muscle since he was a teenager, whereas the most Nick did lately was hit the gym a few days a month to keep his waistband loose.

Cade's pale eyes held the same brazen challenge that had earned him a grudging respect from Nick back then, though he wouldn't have admitted it. The kid never backed down from a fight, no matter how hard or how often Nick pounded him. But now there was another glint in those eyes. A fearlessness no doubt embedded in prison. And Nick wasn't stupid enough to go up against that.

Besides, what he wanted most was the land. He was pissed off that Scottie had obviously chosen Cade over him, but he could deal with that as long as he pulled off this land deal. There were plenty of other women in the world, but none of them would give the time of day to a bankrupt real estate agent.

"You're the one I wanted to talk to anyway," Nick said when he saw Cade was not going to relent.

"Hard to believe. You're usually hiding behind my sister's skirt."

Nick wrestled with the fury inside, knowing that a knee-jerk reaction to the insult would end the conversation. "I heard you bought her off with a trust fund and a house."

"You're wasting my time, Nick. Do you have a point?"

"I want to sit down with you, discuss the benefits my development would bring to Cumberland Cove. I think you'd see why Silas was willing to sell to me."

"In the first place," Cade said, "I've got no reason to believe my uncle intended to sell an acre to you. And in the second place, after the way you used Trish to get what you wanted, I wouldn't sell you an acre of the worst bottom land I own." Cade stepped onto the porch and

191

locked the door before he pulled it closed. "I'm leaving and you are, too. Scottie's tired and needs to sleep."

The unfairness of it all galled Nick. Cade acted like he owned the town and ruled Scottie's house. He'd be gone in a matter of time, leaving Scottie heartbroken, and Nick would be ruined.

All out of stubborn vindictiveness. Cade had no use for the land, and Nick wondered if he cared anything for Scottie, either, or was just using her to get even. He would probably never bother to set foot in Cumberland Cove again.

"Damn it, Cade, Silas promised me that tract. We were going to draw up papers. And I've made a lot of promises to a lot of people." Nick clenched his fists and tried to keep his voice even, businesslike. "You don't live here. The land means nothing to you, and you don't know what's best for this community. Don't let our past stand in the way of doing something good."

"I'm following the instructions laid out in the will."

"Are you saying your uncle lied? Or are you just welshing on his verbal agreement? He probably made that will out a long time ago. Before we negotiated the land sale."

"I don't know what you conjured up in your head, but I guarantee you my uncle didn't have any intention of selling his land to you or anybody else. That mountain has been in our family for generations, and he would never let it be destroyed by the kind of development you're famous for. And neither will I," Cade said evenly. "And just so you know, the land means a lot to me. And so does my sister, which is another reason I'll never sell it to you. You used her to get to me, and the way it looks, neither you or your mother tried to help her when she needed it."

"Look, Cade, your sister's messed up from your situation, not anything my mother did. She tried her best to raise that child, but she's got a lot of Youngblood in her."

"As far as I'm concerned, this conversation is over."

"I'll pay you whatever you want," Nick said. "Name your price, you son of a bitch. I've got to deliver that land, even if I take a loss."

192

"Find your land somewhere else," Cade said, unlocking the door to the Range Rover. "And leave my sister out of it."

Nick grabbed Cade by the front of his shirt and slammed him against the SUV.

"You are not going to ruin my life out of vengeance!"

The sharp corner of the mirror caught Cade's shoulder, eliciting a curse. In one hard, upward sweep, Cade broke Nick's grip. Nick threw a punch. Cade caught his fist and twisted hard to the outside.

Nick's arm bent at a sharp angle behind his back. With his free hand, Cade shoved the side of Nick's face down onto the hood.

"You're breaking my arm!" Nick moaned.

"Damn straight I will."

Cade jerked Nick's arm enough to make him whimper but not enough to do damage.

"Leave me and my sister alone," Cade growled into Nick's ear. "Do you understand?"

For the first time in his life, Nick was afraid of his stepbrother. He nodded and Cade released him. Nick leapt away, nursing his injured arm and face, the fight gone out of him, at least for the moment. Nick retreated to relative safety of the driver's side of his Jag before the anger overrode fear. He jerked the door open and looked over the roof at Cade.

"This is not over. I need that land. I don't care what I have to do, I will get it!"

DAY 6

CHAPTER 26

I
N HIS uncle's quiet house, Cade worked long past midnight. His project in the Gulf was moving forward now, and he wanted to keep the momentum going. He leaned back in his chair and stretched, deciding whether to make a fresh pot of coffee or go to bed. He opted for bed, turned out the lights, and headed upstairs. When he was unloading his pockets to go to bed, he realized he'd left his cell phone charging in the Range Rover. Hoping Scottie had called, he headed back downstairs to get his cell.

Moving through the kitchen by the light of the laptop, he went outside onto the darkened back porch and down the steps toward the Range Rover parked on the gravel driveway behind Silas's pickup, his soft-soled shoes silent on the dewy grass. As he approached, he clicked the remote to unlock the doors.

A curse and the sound of scrambling startled Cade. A dark, broad figure in a black hoodie shot upright in surprise on the other side of the Range Rover.

"Hey! What are you doing?" Cade yelled.

The man sprinted for the woods, and Cade took off after him, but the man had a good head start and disappeared into the night. Shortly, Cade heard a car engine roar to life beyond the woods, where a dirt farm road led to the back pastures. He sprinted around the house toward the main road. Maybe he would recognize the car.

He reached the pavement just as a large, dark vehicle spun out from the dirt road a few hundred yards away, headed fast in the opposite direction, then made a hard right onto the side road leading into the mountains. No sense in trying to follow. By the time he got to his vehicle, he'd never catch up.

Cade leaned over, hands on his knees to catch his breath, as rage and apprehension pumped hard through him. After a few minutes, he returned to the Range Rover to examine the car by the yellow glow of the security light. He was relieved to find all four tires intact. Rounding the car to the passenger side where the man had been, Cade raked the bright beam of the tiny LED flashlight on his key ring along the car.

"Son of a bitch!"

Slashed tires were a pain—this was malevolent destruction. The paint on the side of the borrowed Range Rover had been scratched to a fare-thee-well. Cade ran a hand lightly over the once-slick surface, and an unbidden memory came back: The side of Nick's IROC had felt the same way after Cade had spitefully keyed it as a teenager. Fixing this car was going to cost some money.

Frowning, he stepped back and put the full breadth of the light on the side of the car. Mixed in with the random henpeck scrawling were actual words. Slowly, Cade deciphered the message.

PAYBACK IS HELL.

"Nick, you asshole. You won't get away with this!" Cade grabbed the cell phone from the front seat. Scottie would still be on duty.

***

Ten minutes later, she joined him.

She shook her head at the extent of the damage. "Are you ready to file a report yet?"

"Hell, yes. You can get out your pad."

Scottie pulled her notepad from her pocket and flipped to the page where she had noted the slashed tires that he had not wanted to report.

"This just happened?"

"I ran him off and called you."

She made a note. "So that would have been around 2:30 a.m."

"Close enough."

"Tell me about it."

Cade gave a recap of the night.

Scottie considered him damned lucky he had not been hurt. Cade was never one to back down from a confrontation.

"He apparently left his car on the pasture road, but I couldn't get around front in time to see it before it turned up the mountain."

"Did you recognize the person? Are you sure it was a man?"

"It was a man."

"Can you give me a description?"

"Nick."

"What do you mean? Did you witness Nick doing this?"

"No, but it's a sure bet it's him. He came by your house as I was leaving, and we tied up again. He wants the land, and he was not happy to see me at your house. He basically said he would do whatever he had to do to get what he wanted."

"I didn't want things to end up like this between you and him."

"It's always been this way, and you know that. Just remember this when you have to decide between the two of us. I love you. He loves land."

A simple enough statement, but the truth of it was so powerful that Scottie had to look away from him. She had known what Nick truly loved from the beginning of their relationship, but she had overlooked it. Did she doubt Cade's passion for her? Not for a minute. The doubt in her mind was whether she could survive the dangerous, white-hot love that Cade had always offered. Unless he was a man changed deep in his heart, she might face losing him again. And that she was not ready to chance. Yet.

She took as many details from him as possible then flipped the notepad closed and stuck it in her pocket. The area bordering the gravel parking area was thick with grass and showed no trace of footprints. She squatted near the defiled automobile, running the beam of her flashlight along every inch of the car and the ground before pulling out a small camera to snap pictures. She took particular care to get a clear photo of the words. It was not lost on her that Cade had done the same thing to Nick's expensive car once upon a time, and this could well be payback, but she was reluctant to go there.

Scottie followed Cade along the route of the short chase, alert for a footprint or other trace of evidence. She marked anything suspicious with yellow tape, made more notes. She dusted the SUV for prints, suspecting she would come away with Cade's alone. When she was done, she joined him on the porch, where he had watched in silence as she took the prints.

"I'll be in touch."

"That's it?" Cade asked.

"For now. I'll talk to your neighbor in the morning, and I'll come back in the daytime to have a better look around for evidence. I don't know if Ray will leave the case with me or give it to Rickey."

"Do I have a vote?"

"No. I am sorry about this, Cade. I know the whole week has been tough for you."

"Most of it, anyway," he said with a smile that softened the hardness around his mouth for a moment. "I'm not going to be intimidated. Especially not by Nick."

"I hate to think Nick did this, even though there is a sort of precedent."

"And motivation."

Scottie conceded that, too. Nick had been pretty conspicuous in his attempts to get Cade's land, but until she could talk to him, she would not make him the bad guy.

As if reading her thoughts, Cade said, "When you discuss this with Nick, tell him killing me is not the solution. Even if I die, he can't get my land. My new will is air-tight, and Trish doesn't get an acre."

"It's not going to come to that, I assure you. I need to get back on patrol. I'll take care of this when I get to the station."

"Will you arrest me if I kiss you on duty?" Cade said, lifting her chin.

She glanced around in the predawn darkness.

"Who's to know?" she said, rising on tiptoe to meet his lips. Bad idea, of course, because now she wanted to stay for more. She disentangled herself from his embrace. "I really have to go."

CHAPTER 27

SCOTTIE yawned as she cleared out her mail slot and walked down the hall toward Ray's office. Fatigue settled into her bones, and she was ready to get home to a hot shower and a long sleep. The last couple of days had been stressful and left her frustrated and angry. But she knew Ray would want to talk to her about the vandalism to Cade's SUV, so she might as well get it over with.

"Good morning, Scottie," Ray said as she entered. "Close the door and have a seat."

His tan uniform shirt was starched so crisply that Scottie expected it to crackle when he moved, his brown pants creased to a fault. The scent of his aftershave mingled with that of the furniture spray used by the janitorial service. In spite of his fresh clothes, Ray's eyes were puffy, and the creases around his mouth seemed more pronounced than usual. He straightened the papers on the edge of his desk and cleared his throat.

"So Cade had some trouble this week."

She nodded, knowing he would have read her report already.

"Are you sure he didn't damage the car himself just to stir up trouble?"

"No, I don't think so. There are a lot of people who want him gone."

"Since he's implicated my father and me, I'm turning it over to the county sheriff's office to investigate. They've already been notified. Don't want any insinuation that we didn't do a thorough investigation."

In a way, Scottie was relieved. She would have done an impartial investigation, but it would be better handled by another agency.

In spite of Rickey's warning, she couldn't get Cade's conviction off her mind. Now was as good a time as any. She hesitated before taking a deep breath and broaching the subject.

"What's the possibility of reexamining some of the evidence in Angela's case? Her shirt, for example. Might be enough DNA on there."

Ray let out a short, ugly snort. "You've got to be kidding me. Where did you come up with such a brilliant idea? From Cade? Well, it's not going to happen."

Inwardly, Scottie bristled, although she struggled not to show it. "No, he hasn't mentioned it to me. But it would put to rest any doubt about Cade's guilt."

"There is no doubt about Cade's guilt."

"He denies killing her. Silas was convinced he was set up. I think we need to know for sure."

Ray leaned forward on his desk, his intense gaze appraising her. "Do you know how much it would cost the department to confirm an old conviction just to ease your mind? We're not rolling in dough here, Scottie, like the Atlanta PD. I can't cover that expense, and I'm sure not going to the town council with it. Besides, how do you know what evidence we have?"

"There's a lot of information out there if you know where to look."

"And of course, you know."

"I did that sort of work in Atlanta."

Ray pulled a pen from the pencil holder on his desk and played it between his fingers like a majorette's baton.

"And what all did you find, 'Detective' Townsend?"

She ignored the taunt. "Angela's blouse had blood on it. New testing methods might turn up more evidence. I understand only blood typing was done on it before the trial, and it was inconclusive."

"It wasn't necessary with the other evidence. DNA testing wasn't on the radar for us back then. The prosecution had an open-and-shut case against him, more than enough evidence to convict."

"But no body. What if he's telling the truth?"

"Scottie, lay off. He did it." Ray pulled out a file drawer beside his chair and thumbed through the folders. He glanced up at her and said, "That's it."

Scottie hated fighting a losing battle. "What if—"

Ray slapped the file folder onto his desk and flipped it open. His amber eyes took the look of a feral animal. "Let me be clear, Scottie. If you want to continue to work for me, back off this idiocy, and stay away from Cade Youngblood. Now, get out of my office unless you want me to write you up."

Scottie rose, the tips of her ears burning with anger at Ray's threat. With her hand on the doorknob, she turned back, knowing she could be opening herself to a charge of insubordination. "What if there's a killer still out there?"

She left Ray cursing as she closed the door behind her. Quickly, she gathered her belongings and exited the building before he decided to fire her on the spot.

Before going home, Scottie drove to Nick's office on the glass-and-steel side of town. Because Cade was so convinced that Nick was responsible for the damage to his vehicle, she wanted to talk to Nick off the record. As she parked in the visitor's area outside his building, she blinked at the blinding sunlight glinting off the dark-tinted windows.

She had watched Nick become extremely wealthy developing this pristine land. The Golden Boy of Cumberland Cove, he had little trouble persuading people to sell to him. Only afterward were some townspeople disgruntled at the modern Emerald City in their midst, destroying the pastoral ambiance of the mountain village. She understood Cade's reluctance to see more of the mountain fall to development, but she wondered, in light of his threat to cancel some of the business leases in town, how much was concern for the mountain and how much was revenge against Nick.

Even though it was early morning, she banked on Nick being in the office, especially with his current land problems. The outer office was empty, his secretary not yet in, but sure enough, Scottie found Nick on the phone when she knocked lightly and opened his door.

He held up a finger for her to wait and ended the call quickly. Coming around his desk, he started to catch her in his arms, but she took a step back, and he dropped his hands to his side and gave her a glowering look.

"I guess you're not here to patch things up."

"No. You're going to have to get past that. We're not getting back together."

"Yeah, I should have gotten the message when I caught Cade there yesterday. It was pretty obvious what you'd been doing, but guess what? I don't give up that easy. He'll be gone in a few days, and you can come to your senses, but we'll let it slide for the moment. What do you want?"

Scottie let his premonition settle in the air between them. He might be right about Cade taking off again. She didn't know what she would do then, but for now, she had no plans of getting back together with Nick.

"I want to ask you a couple of questions."

He perched on the edge of the glass-topped desk. "Shoot."

"Where were you this morning from midnight until around two a.m.?"

"Well, obviously not with you. Why?"

"Cade's car was vandalized during that time. He thinks you might have done it."

"He's accusing me?" Nick asked angrily.

"The thing is, the side of the vehicle was keyed. A lot of damage. It's similar to what he did to your car that time."

"So wait, you and Cade think that after a decade and a half, I'm going to pull some juvenile prank like that? Come on, Scottie. I gave you more credit for common sense, if not him."

"I don't want to think so, but he said you threatened him yesterday. Somebody made a mess of that car. And slashed his tires at the caverns the other morning."

Nick laughed. "That gives me so much pleasure, I can't tell you. To know somebody else is harassing him, and I can just sit back and watch. He's such a crybaby."

"It worries me that it's escalating. You know, you really have shown a motive to try to scare him into selling you his land. You should think about that."

"Maybe, but he's got a lot of other people in this town worried about the future of their businesses and even the future of the town. So, I might have to stand in line to get to little brother." Nick gave her a disdainful look. "I'm not too concerned. Looks like he's got you to protect him. I can't believe you turned on me this fast just because the bastard's back in town."

"I'm not turning against you. I'm actually trying to assure myself you had nothing to do with it. You've hammered pretty hard on him about the land."

"I've tried to deal with him through Trish, but obviously that didn't work. I've pretty much resolved myself to bankruptcy. If I ever tried to kill him, it would probably be over you, not the land." Nick tapped his pen on the desk. "Although if somebody else wants to do it, I wouldn't object. And like I said, there are plenty of folks around here of a mind to."

Scottie knew she'd never get a straight answer from him, but she gave it a shot. "Want to give me a list of names?"

Nick smirked at her. "No way. Maybe one of them will get lucky."

Nick's phone rang, and he turned his back on Scottie as he answered it.

CHAPTER 28

W HERE are you going?" Gina asked, locating Bull in the garage of their home after hearing the electric garage door open.

She had been in a snit for days now, and Gina in a snit was bad news. She made sure of that. She tried to aggravate Bull in any tiny, insignificant way she could think of. Enough to rile him but not enough for him to fly into a rage and torture her. To her ire, however, he seemed particularly preoccupied lately and barely paid attention to her.

That wasn't all bad. He didn't want sex, and she could do what she wanted behind his back.

Bull pulled himself up into his Tahoe. "I'm going to get the oil changed in my truck. I'm heading for the farm this afternoon."

Gina hurried to the open door before he could close it. "How long are going to be gone this time?"

"I don't know. There's a lot to do up there in the spring. I plan on staying several days."

That sounded promising.

"Zeb," she said, giving him her most alluring gaze. "Since you're gone to the farm so much, I need something to do around here to occupy my time. I've been thinking about ways to redecorate the house."

"Help yourself. You can move that furniture around any way you want to."

He tried to close the door, but Gina squeezed in close to his knee to prevent it. She drew a long, pink fingernail up his thigh. "I was thinking more like changing the furniture, and then I'd have to change the rugs and the paint and everything."

"You just did all that not much more than a year ago, and it looks fine."

Gina pouted in the sexy way that always got her what she wanted from men.

"It's so out of style, and I want you to have a beautiful home."

"What kind of money you talking about?"

She breathed an inward sigh of relief. As always, he was putty in her hands. "Oh, if you'd just put around twenty thousand in my account, then I'd give back what I didn't spend."

Bull laughed out loud. "Are you serious? Like I could expect a penny back from that."

"I promise I won't spend it all."

He chucked her under the chin and shook his head. "Gina, you used to provide me a little entertainment for my buck, but lately you've given me nothing but grief. You just hang around and clean the house you've got. Like a good wife."

"Zeb—"

"Not a penny, Gina. Now back up, I've got things to do."

"I'm not your maid!" she snapped.

"You're not anything to me anymore. Move. We'll talk about this when I get back from the farm."

Gina stamped her foot. "And what if I'm not here when you get back? What if I want a divorce?" She immediately wished she had kept her mouth shut and gone through with her plan without showing her hand.

Bull pushed her out of his way and slammed the door. He leaned out the open window, his cold eyes boring into hers. "My pet, you will never get a divorce from me, and if you try to run away, I will hunt you down like I would a coyote and have you stuffed. Then you'll truly be my trophy wife."

He backed out of the garage and roared off toward town, leaving Gina stunned. He'd been mean to her and forced some rough sex on her now and then, but he'd never threatened her before. And from the look in his eyes, he just might be serious.

She didn't want to be his wife any longer, but she'd never considered the possibility he didn't want her. Swallowing hard, she thought of the plan she'd been working on for days, ever since he'd accused her wrongly of messing around with Cade. She had no intention of redoing the house, she just planned to replace some of her most precious objects with cheaper ones and secrete her things in a rented storeroom in a nearby town until she could make arrangements. She planned to go somewhere beautiful and exotic. The exact opposite of backwoods Tennessee. A place where she could spend the rest of her life and never be found.

But if Bull wouldn't give her some money, she had no hope of escape. Stupidly, she'd blown through every penny he'd ever given her, not thinking about a future when she might be out on her own. Frankly, she'd expected him to die before now, especially with the heart problems.

She went into the house and began making a list of things she could take with her. Not much unless she was willing to risk staying longer to rent a moving van, because her 'Vette would never pull a trailer. Now that she had made up her mind, she had to act fast. Take no chances.

Money! She needed lots of it. She could do without her things, but with no money, she couldn't even get out of town. Bull controlled all of the checking accounts, and the one credit card she had opened on her own he had canceled when he found out and warned her not to get another one.

Taking her list to the kitchen table, Gina sat down dejectedly, her chin resting on her fist. She doodled aimlessly on her pad, trying to conjure up somebody who would lend her the money and not snitch her out to Bull. Having alienated herself from everybody over the years, she had absolutely nobody in Cumberland Cove to turn to now that she needed help.

As she heard the Tahoe rumble into the garage, she squeezed back her tears, quickly hid her list in a drawer, and dabbed her moist eyes dry with a paper towel. It wouldn't do to let Bull see her weakness or her list.

***

That morning, Cade slept late for the first time in years. The winter-shuttered upstairs windows kept out the intrusion of dawn and muffled the sounds of intermittent traffic on the country road outside. He woke to tranquil silence around nine o'clock. For a long time, he stared at the ceiling, still half-asleep, luxuriating in the soft warmth of the heavy quilt against the chill of an unheated room and mentally bracing himself for whatever the day ahead might bring.

A hot shower revitalized him. With a couple of pieces of toast and scrambled eggs on a plate and a cup of strong coffee, he sat down to take up work where he had left off the night before. Before he got into his own work, however, he pulled up Trish's bank account to see if she had accessed it since she disappeared. She had not, but he made a mental note to check daily. If she used it, Scottie might have the authority to track the location.

Engrossed in the details of his project, he lost track of time until he hit a snag and needed more data to move forward. It was after one p.m., and he had promised Guy he'd stop by the store and go over the books with him.

Now was as good a time as any. He found the data files he needed and started a download, which would take a couple of hours, and set the computer to power off after the download. He could work when he got back then maybe catch Scottie for a quick dinner at Nelda's before she went to work.

As he parked in the back lot of the hardware store, the pleasant memory of his afternoon with Scottie was tempered by the ominous message scrawled on his vehicle. His suspicions were torn between Nick and Bull. Either of them was crazy enough to try to scare him out of town, and both of them probably thought they had good reason.

Three men he recognized from the wake sat hunched over a checkerboard on a table near the pot-bellied stove. One of them was Bobcat Jones, the mountain man who thought the caves were haunted and the very man Cade hoped to find here. The other two were Big-un Johnson and Old Man Peters.

Cade greeted the men cordially. All three responded in kind.

"Hey, Cade, we was just talking about you," Bobcat said.

"That doesn't sound promising," Cade said.

"Wondering if you're going to close the hardware store."

"No plans at the moment."

The men nodded approval, and Big'un said, "That's good to hear. It's kind of a fixture around here. But shore seems empty without Silas."

"You all just make sure it keeps making a profit, and I'll keep it open as long as I can."

"Not much profit in checkers," Guy said, grinning.

"Oh, I don't know. Silas kept the place going for years on checkers," Old Man Peters said without looking up from his game.

Cade watched the slow game for a few minutes until Bobcat lost to Old Man Peters.

"Bobcat, can I talk to you for a minute?"

The two men walked into Silas's office in the back of the store with the curious eyes of the others following their every step.

"Whatcha need, Cade?" Bobcat asked.

"How far into the caverns have you been?"

"I told you I don't go in there anymore."

211

"But you used to." From the nervous look in Bobcat's eyes, Cade knew he was right. "What made you stop?"

"I said they're hainted, didn't I?"

"How far back have you been? As far as the waterfall?"

"No. And I ain't going, neither, if that's what's on your mind. I used to have a still in that little cave on the hill, but I don't have that no more. I just hunt around there sometimes."

"Have you ever seen anybody else in the area when you were hunting?"

"Nah, can't say I have, but I don't hunt that land much anymore. Police department cracked down a few years ago, and I pretty much steered clear since." Bobcat cocked his head sideways. "Why? You seen somebody up there?"

"I didn't see them, but I know they were there." What Cade really wanted to know and didn't know who to ask without opening a can of worms was who put the cross at the waterfall and how long ago.

"I'll keep my ears open. If I hear anything, I'll let you know."

"I'd appreciate it."

Out in the store, Cade heard Guy tell the old men he was closing up for the night followed by the sound of chairs scraping across the floor.

"I better git outta here before Mr. Guy locks me in," Bobcat said with a grin. "And hey, thanks for okaying my credit with him."

"No problem. See you later. By the way, Bobcat, you haven't seen my sister around anywhere, have you?"

"She's run away again? I ain't seen hide nor hair of her, sorry." Bobcat jogged out the door, yelling to Guy, "I'm comin', Mr. Guy, don't lock that door yet."

Cade waited in the office until Guy secured the outer doors and joined him. By then, Cade had removed the store ledgers from the safe and had them opened on the desk. For the next hour, they went over the books and discussed the store's potential. In the end, they both agreed to keep the store open for the foreseeable future. Guy wanted to keep working, and Cade wasn't ready to turn loose this connection with his uncle.

Cade replaced the ledgers, preparing to leave. He needed to finish his work in case Scottie had time to get together.

Guy cleared his throat. "Can I talk to you about something before you go, Cade?"

"Sure, what?"

"Rumor has it you might not renew some leases around town."

"Gossip travels fast."

"I have to tell you, I think that's a bad idea."

"What goes around comes around." Cade drew his jacket on. What he did with his property was his business.

"Be careful with vengeance, son. I know you think you got a bad deal from these folks, and maybe you did. Silas always said so, and he was a no-nonsense man. If he'd thought you were guilty, he would have been just as up-front with that."

Guy glanced at a wall hung with plaques and awards. A key to the city hung beside photos of Silas with the mayor, the governor, and other celebrities.

"This was his town, and he loved it, same as he loved you. For you to go destroying it now just because you have the power would break his heart." Guy looked hard at Cade until Cade was forced to meet his eyes. "Silas loved you enough to give you the power to punish your enemies. But I believe he trusted you not to. I think he meant for you to become the man he knew you could be. All I'm asking is that you give your uncle some consideration before you do damage you can't undo."

Cade knew Guy was right, but the bitterness against this town had been pent up in him for a long time, and it might take an exorcism to get rid of it. Still, he knew the guilt would be a hell of a lot worse if he let his uncle down. Again, he was going to have to regroup and rethink his priorities.

"I'll keep that in mind," he said. "Has Trish been in here the past day or so?"

Guy shook his head. "No. I saw her last at the funeral. Why? Should I give her money if she asks?"

"No, don't give her money. She's got plenty now. She got in an argument with Johanna and took off in her car. Nobody's heard from her since, and I'm a little worried."

With a guffaw, Guy said, "Don't give it another thought. The girl runs off about twice a year or more. She always comes back in a few days."

Guy's words didn't ease his mind completely. In spite of what everybody told him, the niggling worry about his sister was growing stronger the longer she was gone.

CHAPTER 29

T HE CUP of coffee in Ray Drake's hand had long ago cooled off as he sat motionless in a rocker on the front porch, staring into the gathering gloom. In this old section of Cumberland Cove, the lots were spacious, and houses had character and charm with their large, high-ceilinged rooms and loving craftsmanship. The close-knit neighbors looked out for one another, most having lived in the same house for decades, raised their families here, watched their children move away and begin their own lives. Ray had chosen to relocate to his childhood home after Bull married and moved his whore wife to a new subdivision that more suited Gina's crass taste. Ray enjoyed living alone, and from this location, he could be at work in less than five minutes.

The familiar sounds of the evening surrounded him. A slight breeze rustled through the trees, a hound dog bayed in the distance, and a frog orchestra gave a midnight serenade from the shallow pond behind his house. Ray listened for a while, trying to identify the different species by their voices. The rumbling bass chorus of bullfrogs stood out most, punctuated by off-key banjo plucking from green frogs and high-pitched tree frog trills.

Ray stared at his department-issue car that sat in the driveway to his left with the seal of the Chief of Police, Cumberland Cove,

Tennessee emblazoned on the door, the banner of his success in life. A big fish in a tiny pool. Despite the stillness of his body, Ray's mind reeled with feverish thoughts that flitted from one bad memory to another. All triggered by the random piece of metal that Cade found on the roadside, possible evidence that his own experienced detective hadn't found in spite of assurances that he and his team had combed the area twice.

The oversight bothered Ray on many levels. First, overlooking crime scene evidence made his department look incompetent, even if the part turned out to be irrelevant. Second, as much as he wanted to reject anything that Cade Youngblood brought forth, either tangible or theoretical, he couldn't afford to ignore the discovery. Third, if the lab found fragments of Silas Martin's DNA or clothing, Cade had more fuel for his long-standing accusation that Rickey and Bull had botched Angela's murder investigation. On top of that, tonight he couldn't get Angela off his mind.

Ah, he missed her. He rocked back in the chair, staring at the star-studded night sky. How long could a man hurt like this? He managed well enough throughout the year until spring came with its promise of new life. Only not for Angela anymore. And, really, not for him, either. Tomorrow was the anniversary of her death. The date seemed to come around faster every year.

A part of him had perished when Angela's bloody clothing was found in Cade's truck, when he had followed the blood trail to the waterfall deep in the caverns and been forced to accept the fact that the asshole had murdered her. That she was never coming back—that their future had been destroyed by a drunken, worthless, punk teenager who had no respect for anybody or anything and who still would not admit his crime.

Cade's audacity to stay this long in Cumberland Cove amazed and infuriated Ray to no end. How many times over the years had he contemplated the most satisfying method to kill the bastard if he ever saw him again? Yet, when imagination turned to reality, he couldn't. He had sworn to uphold the letter of the law when he took office, and he wouldn't back down on that promise to the citizens of Cumberland Cove. But his blood pressure rose, and his fingers twitched whenever Cade's name was mentioned.

At least Cade had shown the good sense to stay out of Ray's line of fire, although he had ventured close to the crosshairs when Trish vanished. If Trish had not already established her penchant for running away from home, Ray might have nailed him. But there had been no sign of any foul play concerning Trish, even though the girl had not been in contact with anybody since. Ray still had a niggling theory that Cade had something to do with her disappearance, but he couldn't act on it without some kind of lead.

He'd heard that talking helped ease the pain of losing a loved one, but he couldn't open up to anybody about the love between him and Angela because nobody had known. Not his best friend, Nick. Not even his father. Possibly the love affair between the teenage mountain beauty and the son of the police chief had been the one secret ever kept in this nosy little town. He didn't even have a photo of Angela, only the vision he carried in his mind and the memory of her taking his hand and moving it to her small belly to touch the tiny solid bump growing inside her.

They had made plans that very night to run away before she started showing and drew attention. Ray figured he could eventually persuade his father to forgive them, but he knew better than to tell anybody beforehand. Then, a few days later, their secret became irrelevant. No need to make clandestine schemes, no need to slink into the mountains to love one another.

The night she disappeared, Ray was tied up on a complaint on the other side of town that turned out to be a bust, since the suspicious person reported was gone. By the time Ray finally made it to their trysting place, Angela wasn't there. He assumed she'd gone home, and it wasn't until the next day that he learned she was missing.

Suddenly, there was no longer a reason to admit to their relationship. No point in trying to justify marrying her because he wanted to be a good father to their child, to be a loving husband, to make a life outside the microcosm of Cumberland Cove and out from under Bull Drake's shadow. His beloved Angela had vanished into thin air, leaving behind only the memories to haunt him for the rest of his life.

The gaping void that opened in Ray that day had never been completely filled since. Probably never would as long as Angela's murderer walked the earth.

Bull's Tahoe turned into the driveway. Ray leaned forward as his father got out, slammed the door, and mounted the steps to the porch. The sallow light threw harsh shadows across the old man's weathered face and turned his thinning white hair a sickly yellow, giving him a haggard look.

"I didn't expect you tonight," Ray said.

"Thought I'd drop by for a few minutes. I'm on my way up to the farm."

"This late?"

"Lot to do up there. I want an early start in the morning," Bull said. "Got to pick up groceries first, though, so I can't stay but a minute."

"It's a good thing you've got that old place to occupy your time."

He thought about those occasions in the autumn when deer-hunting season started and he spent a night or two at the old house on the property to hunt with Bull. But he no longer had the time or patience to stay long in such an isolated location. Still, the place had served as a lifeline after Bull had been relieved of his duties as police chief. He had spent months up there at first then tapered off over the years. Now he mostly used the place to piddle with his hobbies without being disturbed.

Ray reached over and slid a rocker closer to his own chair. "Stay awhile. How's Gina doing with Cade in town?"

"Like a bitch in heat," Bull muttered as he sank heavily into a nearby chair.

"He should be gone soon."

"I hope so. Don't know how much longer I can deal with her," Bull said with a weariness Ray didn't like to hear in his father's voice.

"I caught her sneaking in the other night. I know she'd been with him, even though she denied it. I put a tracking device on that hotrod of hers a long time ago so I could keep up with her, but she really ain't worth the trouble anymore."

"Why did you marry her, anyway?" Ray said after a while. He had never had the gall to ask that before, but tonight, in the mood he was in, the words just came out.

His father reflected for a few minutes then simply said, "I had my reasons."

"Must have been good ones."

Bull grunted. "Good enough. Time was I could halfway keep up with her, but now it takes Viagra, and the doc told me to lay off that. I ignored him at first, but then a couple of times, I got some bad chest pains afterward, so I gotta do what he says."

From the time Bull married Gina, Ray fully expected to get a call that the old man had died in bed servicing the nympho, but he didn't like to hear it had almost happened. "You never told me you had chest pains."

"They went away," Bull said, sitting forward in the chair, his elbows on his knees. "Gina's young. I know she likes to run around and have a little fun."

"A little fun? Dad, that woman—" Ray clamped his mouth shut. No need to alienate his father over a decision long made and probably regretted a hundred times. "Never mind."

Bull slapped Ray's knee. "Ain't your problem, is it, son? I made my bed, and I gotta lay in it, no matter how dirty it is."

Bull's bitterness made Ray feel guilty. His dad had been through a lot since Ray's mother abandoned them, back when Ray was a child. Ray had grown up without her, and the maid his father hired had been like a mother to him, so he had compartmentalized the loss like he did most unpleasant things. Bull never spoke her name, but Ray knew her infidelity had changed his father, made him cynical and bitter. Ray understood even more after he lost Angela, though Angela had never been untrue to him. Life had hardened both of them, made them more alike than the genes they shared.

To change the subject, Ray said, "Cade's threatening to refuse to renew the lease on our building. We'll be in a bind if he does that."

"You better be looking for another place for the department, son. Even if he gives in now, he might not next time."

"I've got Nick looking into it. He's having to deal with his own problems now that he can't buy Silas's land for his development. Silas did the wrong thing leaving everything in Cade's hands. He laid the groundwork to destroy this town. Then today I got a court order to release the physical evidence from Angela's murder. He's going to stir all that up again, having that evidence tested."

"That damned Cade needs killing," Bull said, rising to go.

Ray looked around at his father. "Well, don't you be the one to do it."

Bull grunted as he headed for his SUV.

"You just keep doing your job, son. It'll all work out in time. Always has."

CHAPTER 30

Back at his uncle's house, Cade put away the few groceries he'd bought on the way home. He had talked to Scottie, and she needed to go in to work early, so he would settle for another sandwich tonight.

He powered up the laptop to check his download and waited for the familiar password screen. Nothing. He could hear the hum of the hard drive, but the screen remained black. No mouse click, no keyboard stroke wakened the computer. He couldn't even look for a problem because he couldn't get past the black screen.

Was it hardware failure or a virus? He had a serious security system on all the company files, but his uncle's wireless access was unsecured. He dialed the home phone number for his computer geek who kept the network humming.

"Jake, this is Cade," he said when the man answered. "Have you got the network down for some reason?" Cade knew before Jake answered that the situation was worse than that. It was after hours, and even if the network was being updated, the password screen and a message should have come up.

When Jake told him the network was operating fine, Cade said, "I'm sorry to bother you at home, but can you get into my computer from Timbuktu and see what's going on with it?" Cade described the problem and what he'd been downloading.

After a long silence on the other end, Jake said. "This is bad. I can't get control, but apparently somebody else has."

Just then, the screen flickered. "Hold on, something's happening," Cade said.

Another flicker, then a bright horizontal line appeared in the center of the screen growing until it became a line of red text.

...we have redemption through his blood, even the forgiveness of sins.—Col 1:14

"What the hell?" Cade muttered.

"What's the matter?" Jake asked. "Are you up again?"

"Apparently I've been hacked. Somebody's sending me scripture. How can that happen with our security?"

The clicking of Jake's keyboard came through the earpiece. "I still can't get in," Jake said.

He explained to Cade that a savvy computer hacker could buy a root kit and load malware on Cade's laptop. "He could basically drive by the house if the wireless connection is not secure and pick up the IP address. Then when the computer is connected to the Internet, he would hack into the computer remotely. Once in, he has access to do whatever he wants."

Jake pointed out that it would be very difficult to detect that type of malware and might take him some time to find.

The red scripture disintegrated into pinpoints, which turned into drops of blood that swirled into another line of writing.

And almost all things are by the law purged with blood; and without shedding of blood is no remission—Heb 9:22

"Christ," Cade whispered.

"Another one?" Jake asked.

"Yep."

"What do they say?"

"You don't want to know. Keep trying to get in, but don't destroy anything. Try to find out where it's coming from, if you can. Make sure this is isolated," Cade ordered. "Do whatever you have to do to protect the network and the data files."

"Will do. I'll call back in a few and let you know how it's going."

"I appreciate this, Jake."

The screen went black for a few seconds. Cade eased down into the chair, staring at the computer. A bright white circle appeared in the center of the screen, expanding until Cade could make out the contours of a woman's face, her eyes closed. The rest of the screen was still dark, but her face was illuminated as if somebody had a light on it. Long black eyelashes brushed chalk-white cheeks. Short black hair fringed her forehead. Just as he recognized the face, the screen blacked out again.

Trish! But Cade couldn't tell if she was sleeping or dead.

For the wages of sin is death—Romans 6:23

"Come back!" Cade muttered, repeatedly clicking the mouse where the face had been. "Come back, damn it."

And cast the worthless servant into the outer darkness. In that place there will be weeping and gnashing of teeth.—Matthew 25:30

Then Trish's sobbing voice came through the speakers, thin and frightened. "Help me! Please, somebody help me!"

Without taking his eyes from the screen, Cade groped for his cell phone nearby on the table. He glanced at it long enough to speed dial Scottie's number.

When she answered, he said, "Can you come to Silas's house right now? Or send somebody."

"What's wrong? More vandalism?"

"No, worse. Somebody's hacked my computer. Whoever it is has got Trish."

"How do you know that?" she asked.

"They're sending me some pretty cryptic messages. I can't figure out where she is."

"I'm on my way."

You serpents, you brood of vipers, how are you to escape being sentenced to hell?— Matthew 23:33

"Where are you, Trish?" Cade whispered, straining to see or hear anything that might give him a clue. "I'll help you. Where are you?"

Now the scriptures came one after another, tumbling onto the screen.

These two were thrown alive into the lake of fire that burns with sulfur.—Rev 19:20

Eye for eye—Exodus 21:24

And all the while in the background, he could hear Trish's pitiful sobs and pleas for help. Who the hell had her, and what were they doing to her? His inability to help her ate at Cade like the beast that had gnawed on him for years that he had not been able to save Angela.

He listened intently to the odd static in the background. It sounded familiar, yet he couldn't place it intermingled with Trish's weeping.

A car pulled up outside, followed by the scuffle of feet on the wooden porch and a knock at the door. Relieved that Scottie was here, he called out, "Come in."

The *click click* of heels across the wooden floor prompted him to look up. Gina gave him a simpering smile from the archway.

"Hey, Cade."

A new frisson of anxiety ran through him. If either Bull or Scottie caught them together, he was mincemeat. He went around the table to meet her as she staggered into the kitchen. He didn't want her to see his possessed computer.

"What are you thinking, coming here like this?"

She looked up at him with shrouded gray eyes. Her hot breath smelled strongly of mint and whiskey. "There's shumting I need."

"You need to go home," Cade said. "I'm in the middle of a work project."

She frowned and looped one arm around him to press against his chest. "I don't want to go home."

Gina had never minded close encounters. Cade pried her arm loose. She slid her other arm around his waist.

"Gina, stop it!"

Getting her off him was like dealing with an octopus. If he managed to free himself of one hand, another wrapped around him.

"Kiss me, Sugar. If you're worried about ole Bull, he's gone off to his farm." Gina steadied herself against him. "We're shafe."

The smell of whiskey on her breath enveloped him like a shroud. She was trying to seduce him now as if he were the hell-bent teenager he'd once been, with nothing on his mind but trouble and sex. A kid spiraling down into delinquency. Hopeless, helpless, angry, and self-destructive. A lost boy powerless to save himself.

No way in hell! He had fought the devil and worse to crawl out of that abyss—to change—and he did not intend to go back.

He caught Gina by the shoulders and forced her away from him.

"Just get out of here, will you?" All Bull Drake's trophy wife had to do was whisper rape, and he would be on the chain gang the rest of his life. And if Scottie caught them together again...well, the chain gang might look good.

Gina's pique was obvious when she sat down dejectedly at the kitchen table, apparently much more sober than she'd been pretending. "I've got something to tell you, if you'd listen. I need your help, and I'm willing to make a trade for it. You ought to listen to me."

He glanced at the computer with concern, afraid that she would hear Trish's voice. But to his surprise, his normal sign-on screen was back. That concerned him worse than the scriptures. What if he'd lost the opportunity to find his sister because of Gina?

A look of comprehension crossed Gina's face when she looked at the computer. She narrowed her eyes at him.

"You're not working. You just want me gone because you're waiting for Scottie."

When he didn't answer, she ran her tongue across her teeth and made a sucking sound.

"I see. Well, I suppose I'll just tell you what I need and see if you want to help me. I don't have anybody else to go to. I'm leaving Bull, only he doesn't know it yet."

Cade's stomach lurched. A sure death trap.

"He's not going to sit still and let you leave him."

"I know that. He already told me he'd hunt me down like an animal and stuff me. And he just might because of all I know. That's why I need your help. You've got money. I don't have a penny unless he gives it to me. He controls everything. That damned 'Vette belongs to him, so he could report it stolen, so I'm going to ditch it as soon as I can and catch a flight somewhere far away."

There was a look of desperation in Gina's eyes that Cade recognized well. He'd seen it reflected in his own eyes years ago when he saw no escape from the quagmire that had swallowed him up to slowly digest him alive. But he'd been given grace for some reason: His uncle had been there for him. Gina had nobody. Now might be his time to pay forward.

"How much?" he asked, pulling out his wallet. It was worth paying her to get rid of her.

"Enough for a plane ticket out of the country somewhere and to keep me from starving until I can find work."

"Do you have a passport?"

She nodded. "Bull let me go to Europe with his cousin right after we got married. I've kept it renewed."

Cade pulled out his wallet and withdrew a thick sheaf of bills. "Three thousand. That's all I've got."

Her eyes grew wide. "Are you kidding me?" She swiped at her damp cheeks and smeared lipstick. "Do you always carry that much money?"

The computer screen went black.

He had to get her out of there before Trish started crying again.

He pressed the folded money into Gina's hand and herded her to the door. She reached up to kiss him, and he gave her a quick buss on the lips.

"Get away while you can, Gina. I hope you make it."

She gave him a quizzical look. "You okay?"

"I'm fine. I have work to do."

As soon as she was out the door, Cade rushed to the computer. As if somebody were watching and knew Gina was gone, the scriptures appeared again.

...tooth for tooth—Exodus 21:24

... life for life—Exodus 21:24

Then nothing...black...silent. The brilliant white dot appeared center screen. Gripped by the spreading light, sucking in one hard breath after another, Cade watched as the screen flared white-hot and his sister's face appeared. As the blinding light struck her face, she opened her eyes. Like the worst horror flick imaginable, her face contorted in terror. She shrank back, tears streaming down her face. Blue eyes showing the whites in panic, her blood-curdling screams echoed from the speakers. The screen went dark with her shrieks filling the room.

...sister for sister— Ezra 7:7-7

Ezra!

"Jesus Christ, I'll kill you!" Cade yelled at the computer. He recalled Ezra's words at Silas's wake: *But I read my Bible until I understood what I had to do...* Was this Ezra's mission, to sacrifice Trish in order to punish Cade? A wild loop cycled before his eyes like the flashing of a strobe light intermingled with Trish's face and the scriptures.

Trish's terrified face... *thrown alive*...the static in the background... *into the lake of fire.*

The static noise grew louder. The rush of water. The rustic cross with an A on it flashed on the screen.

And Cade knew where Trish was.

He grabbed his coat from the back of a kitchen chair. As he started from the room, he heard Trish's screams again. He jerked around to see the large words splattered in blood red across the screen.

0000 hours...

Over the falls...

Just like Angela...

Sister for sister...

An ear-splitting explosion followed, and the screen went black.

The kitchen clock showed 10:30 p.m. He wasn't sure he could even get to the waterfall by midnight. He jerked open the kitchen drawers one by one looking for a weapon of some sort. If his uncle had a gun anywhere in the house, Cade hadn't seen it, but he would give a pretty penny for one right now. Running out of time, he gave up and sprinted for his car.

One thing Cade did know—if Ezra Wright had hurt Trish, he was a dead man, if it meant throttling him with bare hands!

CHAPTER 31

THE distinctive rear end of a red Corvette came into view as Scottie pulled up to the house.

Déjà vu in the worst way.

Scottie shifted into reverse. She didn't intend to relive any Cade-Gina sexcapades. If he didn't have any better sense—his problem.

To her surprise, Gina appeared on the lighted front porch, waving her hands wildly.

"Wait!" Gina yelled, tripping down the steps as fast as her high-heeled mules would allow.

Scottie shot backward to turn around. Gina trotted toward her car as fast as she could.

"Scottie, please!"

Scottie ground her teeth, but she braked to keep from running Gina over, although the idea was entertaining. She powered down her window.

"Do you have a freaking death wish, Gina?" she said, using her anger to disguise the hurt and bitterness she was feeling at the moment.

"It's not what you think," Gina said, bracing on the window frame, trying to catch her breath. Probably the most exercise she'd ever had in an upright position. So maybe Cade had a heart attack screwing her.

"Frankly, Gina, I don't care. And you can relay that message to Cade. Back off, I'm leaving. I'm so angry right now I can't think straight."

"It's not what you think," she repeated through clenched teeth. "Something real bad's wrong."

Through her jealous pique, Scottie recalled Cade's phone call. But then again, she remembered the message on the typewriter, too.

Scottie glared back at her. "Talk fast, Gina."

"I came to get money from Cade so I could leave Bull. Nothing happened between us, I swear. He gave me money. See?" Gina pulled a wad of money from her pocket.

In the glow of her dashboard lights, Scottie could see apprehension in Gina's eyes. Her heady perfume drifted into the car.

"Go on."

"Cade was on his computer and acted weird. Said he was working, but there wasn't any work, just the blank screen. He kept trying to get me to go, but I really needed the money. Finally, he gave it to me and put me out on the porch. But I had to find my keys in my purse. All of a sudden, I hear, like, Trish screaming her head off, and Cade yelled, 'I'll kill you.' Then this explosion, and I didn't know whether to run or what, but after a minute or two, I went back inside because I was afraid he was killing Trish." Gina stopped, her eyes wide and scared. "But there wasn't anybody in there. Then I heard him take off in his car."

"When?"

"Just a few minutes ago. I'm surprised you didn't see him."

Scottie wondered why, too. He must have turned up the mountain.

"Do you have any idea where he was headed?"

Gina shook her head. "No, but I hope he doesn't have Trish with him. I can't find her in the house, though, and it sounded like she was dying."

Scottie's phone vibrated, and she checked the caller ID. She held up a hand for Gina to be quiet.

"Hey, Cade, what's up?" She frowned as she listened to his agitated voice trying to explain what he'd seen on his computer.

"Cade, don't go in those caverns alone. You're walking into a trap."

"Just send somebody as soon as you can."

"I don't know how to get to the waterfall. You've got to wait."

"Rickey or Ray will know the way. God knows they went there enough investigating. Tell them they might have to cut off the lock. I'm going in the back way."

"You wait until we get there! I'm calling for backup, and I'm on my way."

"I can't afford to wait."

Cade disconnected, leaving her listening to a dead line.

"He's in trouble, isn't he?" Gina said. Her hands shook as she gripped the window frame. The concern in her voice took Scottie aback. It had never occurred to her before that Gina might actually be in love with Cade.

"Yeah, he is," Scottie said. "Thanks for stopping me. I've got to get some help now."

Gina wouldn't turn the car loose.

"I heard him talking. He said Ray knew the way to the falls." Gina hesitated, as if struggling with some internal demon. "Scottie, I swore I'd never breathe this, but you've got to know. Don't go to Ray."

"Why not?"

"He killed Angela. I'm sure of it. And Bull's been covering up for him ever since. I know this, Scottie, 'cause I was the one who told Bull that Ray got Angela pregnant. I know now that's why Bull married me and why he sent me off during Cade's trial. So I couldn't testify against him and prove Cade's innocence."

Stunned, Scottie stared at her, open-mouthed. "Why the hell didn't you say something before now? When you could have helped Cade?"

"I'm helping him now, the only way I know. Don't go to Ray."

"We're going to talk about this later, mark my words."

"No, I'm not going to be here." A hard rain had started that plastered Gina's flaming hair to her face. She swiped impatiently at it. "Bull will kill me when he finds out. You just help Cade."

231

Gina fled to her car. The 'Vette roared to life, the back-up lights streaking the wet hood of Scottie's squad car neon red. The sleek car whipped around in the clearing, spewing gravel in all directions, and tore by, narrowly missing the cruiser's back fender.

Scottie was right on her tail. Gina turned away from Cumberland Cove; Scottie went the other way, immediately turning up the mountain road, headed for the caverns.

***

Cade slammed on the brakes in front of the caverns. The door of the lean-to stood ajar, an open invitation to enter. Good, the responders could get in that way, but he had to find the short route in.

He gunned the engine again and steered the Range Rover up the seldom-used dirt road that led to the family cemetery—and to the little-known entrance to the caves higher on the mountain and closer to the waterfall. Halfway up, he caught a glint out of the corner of his eye.

He threw the car into reverse and backed down almost as fast as he'd gone up. His headlight glanced off of a vehicle half-hidden in the brush. Grabbing his Mag-lite, Cade set the emergency brake but kept the SUV running as he jumped out to have a look.

He remembered this clunker, had ridden in it before, when he and Ezra Wright were friends. He approached the old, jacked-up Ford Bronco cautiously from the side to shine his light inside. Empty. The tattered seats were too messed up to tell if any of the stains were new.

He raked his flashlight beam the length of the vehicle. The dented driver-side fender caught his eye first then the headlight—and the missing metal trim.

His mouth went dry as his throat constricted. *Uncle Silas.*

This psychopath who held his sister captive had run down his uncle in cold blood!

Minutes later, Cade ducked into the hidden entrance to the caverns carrying a bright battery-operated lantern with his Mag-Lite as a backup. The small cave was littered with the refuse that indicated a long-abandoned still and that its owner had once occupied the area.

He had less than a half-hour to meet Ezra's deadline, and he'd never made it to the waterfall that fast before from the front entrance. From here, he might have a chance. First, he had to figure out the maze that led from this cave to the main caverns. Twisting through needle's-eye passages and hustling down rock-strewn drop-offs, he finally saw a dim light at the end of a tunnel. At least Ezra was making it easy to get there. Which meant the man was seriously looking forward to the kill.

Alert and watchful, Cade hastened through the familiar caves as fast as the terrain and lighting would allow. When he heard the dull roar of the waterfall from a distance, he stopped to gather his wits before continuing on, slowly, cautiously. As he got closer, the rhythm of the plummeting water pounded into him, a thudding that reverberated through his very bones, dislodging a seed of foreboding that he wouldn't find Trish alive, if he found her at all.

The sound almost deafened him as he rounded a final bend and stepped into the vast, open space, encased in darkness except for a candle burning in front of the altar to Angela. Dampness trickled down the sheer walls like the cold sweat running down Cade's body.

Out of the darkness above, a heavy curtain of water cascaded into a deep pool. The overflow cut a narrow, swift-flowing channel across the floor of the room until it reached the edge of the abyss and plunged into oblivion. Cold spray from the thundering water beaded on his face and hair, ran in rivulets down his jacket.

Cade scanned the area, his hope diminishing. Where was Trish? Thrown to her death over the cliff? The obvious answer seemed to be yes, but in his gut, Cade still felt a connection to his sister—his living sister. He flashed the light around, peering into the crevices, looking for any hint that she had been there. Looking for Ezra.

Setting his lantern in the crevice of two abutting stalagmites to protect it, he pulled the heavy Mag-lite flashlight from his belt.

A high-pitched scream bounced off the rock walls until it seemed to come from every direction at once. Cade used the shadows of the rock formations for cover as he followed the rushing stream toward the lower waterfall. Topping a slight rise, he had a clear view of the terrain below.

Near the brink of the abyss where the churning water ultimately disappeared, Ezra held Trish in a death grip, his sinewy arm wrapped around her neck. Kicking and flailing, Trish fought with all her might, her hands locked onto his arm, fingernails gouging into his skin.

"It's about time!" Ezra yelled. "I was afraid you might miss the main event."

***

As she raced down the back roads, Scottie picked up her radio to call dispatch for backup then thought again. Worried about Gina's accusation, she hesitated to go through the department. There was no time for delay, and if Cade was Ray's scapegoat, Ray might just as soon be rid of him. Instead, she phoned Rickey Chambers at home.

She explained what was going down and told him to meet her at the caverns.

"Ezra was a loose cannon when he was on the force. You know that's why Ray let him go, don't you? He was working with our computers, and Ray found out he was hacking into confidential files where he had no clearance."

"I didn't know that," she said.

"Ray kept it pretty quiet. I was the one who figured out something was wrong with the files, that's how I know. Ezra bragged a lot about his expertise and training in the military, so it's no surprise he could hack Cade's computer. Do you want me to notify Ray?"

"No."

She was met with a brief silence, then Rickey said quietly, "Why not?"

"I don't have time to explain it now, just trust me on this. We'll need backup, though."

"I'll get somebody from the county. I'm on my way right now."

She was asking for trouble by going around Ray. It might mean her job and her career, but if Gina had told her the truth, she couldn't afford to take a chance.

Scottie regretted not taking Trish's disappearance seriously, although if Ezra had imprisoned her in the caverns, finding her would have been a stroke of luck.

How long had Ezra been planning this? It seemed too well thought out to be a sudden, random action. She had never once heard him mention Angela, so his attack had broadsided her.

Tears threatened to blur her vision as she remembered Cade as the child she'd loved so well. She recalled how her young heart would thump like a tom-tom and she couldn't wipe the silly smile off her face every time he came in sight. She was not prepared to lose him just when they had made the first step to recover the love they had lost. As far as she was concerned, she still possessed the soul that he had entrusted to her the day his mother died. She didn't intend to give it up tonight.

The squad car fishtailed as she whipped onto the gravel road to the caverns. The chain gate was down, and she sped through, parking in the clearing before the main entrance. Odd, she thought, that neither Cade nor Ezra's vehicle was there. After a rapid assessment of her immediate surroundings, she approached the open doorway of the lean-to. All the lights were blazing, and the cavern was quiet, its serenity masking whatever was happening in its bowels. Impatient, she turned to watch down the road through the pouring rain. She was tempted to go in alone, but she would be wasting time not knowing the way.

Where are you, Rickey?

CHAPTER 32

ET her go!" Cade shouted, sidestepping down the incline. Loose rocks and gravel, skittering down the slope ahead of him, made the footing treacherous. "It's me you want, not her."

Ezra lifted a lip in contempt. "You destroyed my whole family. Now you're going to lose what's left of yours. A sister for a sister, like I said. She's going first."

"Cade!" Trish wailed, struggling anew.

Cade was afraid she would make Ezra lose his balance. "You'll burn in hell for killing an innocent girl."

"You killed my innocent sister. I'm just following God's word." Ezra retreated a step.

"You know the Bible better than I do," Cade said, easing down the slope. "But I thought God passed judgment, not man."

Ezra stiffened. "I'll be the one to punish you as you deserve. I just want to know why you killed Angela."

Cade's eyes never left Ezra's face as he inched down the slope toward them. "And I want to know why you murdered my uncle. How are you going to explain that on judgment day?"

"He had to die. He bragged about you one time too many. Besides, I knew you'd come back if he died, so I could avenge my sister," Ezra said.

Trish's eyes grew wide, and she tried to look up at Ezra. He pulled a wicked knife from a sheath on his belt and put it to her face.

"Be still," he ordered then turned his attention back to Cade. "Now you tell me why you wanted to kill Angela, else I'm going cut your sister's face to ribbons before I throw her over."

Tears welled in Trish's eyes as she pleaded with her captor. Did Cade confess to something he didn't do to mollify a madman—to save his sister's life?

Ezra and Trish were dangerously close to the deadly precipice and creeping ever closer. Afraid to rush Ezra's hand, Cade could only keep talking, trying to get an edge.

"Listen to me, Ezra. Angela was like family to me, too. You know that. I took her up to the end of the road past the cemetery every day after work. She never would let me walk her the rest of the way home, even though I always offered. She had been given a hard time at school that day because everybody thought she was pregnant."

"You're lying," Ezra roared. "Angela would never do that!"

Cade held up his hand in appeasement. "I'm just telling you what happened. I don't know if she was or not. She and I did argue that afternoon at the store because I wanted to know who she was seeing. I swear, Ezra, if I'd found out who he was, I planned to beat the hell out of him."

Cade had quietly closed the distance between them, and Ezra seemed to just now notice that.

"Stay where you are. One more step and I cut her."

Cade stopped. "Okay, okay. Don't hurt her."

"So go on with this lie of yours. It's giving me even more incentive to kill you."

"We were both in an ill mood by the time we got to the end of the road. I did ask her if she wanted me to walk with her. She told me to mind my own business, that she didn't care if she ever saw me again, and I basically said the same."

Their parting words still stung Cade every time he remembered them.

"Sadly, I was too interested in getting to my moonshine jug back at the cabin, and I let her go off mad. We never saw one another again, and that's something I live with every day."

"I wish I believed you. Your sister's kinda pretty. Pity."

The sharp blade flicked against Trish's cheek, and blood spurted. The shedding of his sister's blood triggered a swift, primal instinct: Protect what he loved.

Trish's hysterical struggle gave Cade an opening. He rushed Ezra. Ezra jerked Trish out of Cade's reach and punched him hard in the chest and shoulder. Only when he felt the weakness did Cade realize he had been stabbed. By then, he would have sold his soul to the devil rather than surrender. Logic and reason gave way to a tunnel-vision focus with one goal: Destroy Ezra Wright.

Choking, Trish struggled with all her might. Cade grabbed Ezra's head with both hands and head-butted his face hard. With a howl, Ezra dropped the knife, groping his bloody, broken nose. Cade wrenched Trish free. He flung her up the incline as far as he could then drove a knee into Ezra's groin, doubling him over.

Cade was losing blood, his strength ebbing fast. He attempted to scramble away, but Ezra caught his leg and dragged him downward.

"You are going to pay!" Ezra growled, yanking him to his feet.

Ezra seemed to have superhuman might. His crazed eyes bored into Cade's then shifted to Trish, who was trying to claw her way up the incline. In that moment, Cade knew he had to keep this man away from his sister at all costs.

They teetered on the brink of the black abyss. Muscle against muscle, wit against wit, man against man: One fought to avenge the family he'd lost, the other to protect the only family he had left.

Cade threw all his weight against Ezra. Their balance shifted.

"We're going to hell together, Ezra!"

***

Scottie topped the rise in the dim cave just as the two grappling men disappeared over the edge. She stopped dead, unable to comprehend what she had witnessed.

The cascade of water shivered with feeble fibers of light and fell like luminous satin from above. An eerie, greenish glow shimmered off the wet cliffs. The power of the waterfall was palpable this close, reverberating through Scottie's body, making rational thought difficult. She had only seen the two men. Where was Trish?

Then she heard the wails. Sweeping her light around, she located Trish lying near the brink. Scottie scrambled down the incline, her boots skittering on the loose gravel.

"Scottie! Get back," Rickey shouted from behind her. "Get away."

Instead, Scottie sat down and scooted on her butt until she reached Trish.

Trish grabbed on to Scottie and clung to her in terror. "He went over!" she cried. "Cade went over the waterfall!"

Scottie hugged Trish close as she took in the blood, diluted from the spray of the falls, running in rivulets along the rock crevices. The stream of her light ran off the edge of the cliff and disappeared into a black void.

Rickey scrambled down to them.

"Don't go any closer, Scottie. You'll go over, too." Rickey had to yell to be heard this close to the falls. "Backup is coming. There's nothing we can do. Just wait."

Her cold hands shook as she clenched her arms around Trish, trying to warm and reassure the quaking girl. She ground her teeth to keep from crying. Cade was gone; in the beat of a heart, he was lost to her. She felt an ominous presentiment that if she abandoned him now, he would be gone forever.

Despair overtook her as she stared dry-eyed into the dark nothingness before her. Some unfathomable intuition tugged at her. She couldn't just let him go like this.

She surrendered Trish to Rickey in spite of his protests. Rolling onto her belly, she inched to the brink, shining her feeble flashlight into the black hole that gave nothing back.

"Cade!" she yelled at the top of her voice. "Cade! Where are you?"

At first, she thought the noise of the falls was playing tricks on her ears. She swept the light back and forth along the sheer embankment, her eyes blurred from the fine mist rising from the depths.

"Cade?" she shouted again.

No, it wasn't her imagination. She heard his voice, weak and distant, but it was him. Through the fog, she saw a bluish gleam. Aiming her light for that, she saw him, about fifteen feet down, huddled on a ledge no more than ten feet at its widest. He had his cell phone on and was waving it at her. A yelp of joy escaped her lips.

"Hang on, Cade. Help is coming. Hold on!"

CHAPTER 33

SHE WAS going straight to hell, she had no doubt of that whatsoever. Gina took the rain-slick mountain curves at breakneck speed, trying to outrun the fear and self-loathing she felt. She was following the back roads over the mountains to Knoxville to stay out of sight of Cumberland Cove's finest. She wished now she had not told Scottie anything.

For years, she'd regretted not speaking up, but the absolution she hoped for was missing now that she had. And now Scottie held the useless truth of what had happened, because nobody would believe her, and she would lose her job for threatening Ray. Truth was, probably nobody in that rat-hole town would believe Gina, either. She should have just kept her mouth shut and made a run for it.

Except for the lack of money. She patted her pocket, reassured by the wad of cash tucked there. She'd always been able to count on Cade, and tonight had been no different. Why the hell couldn't he count on her?

She could have been a good wife to the right man, she was sure of it. But she would be long gone by the time Bull came home, because she wasn't going to be a wife to him, good or otherwise, anymore.

Tears clouded her eyes anew at the thought of the home she would never see again. The only pure and beautiful thing ever in her life. She envisioned the pristine rooms she had created in an attempt to redefine herself, to escape the squalor of her childhood and become a better person.

Her efforts had failed. At least as an unhappy teenager, she had retained a shred of self-respect and, in her heart, knew there was some good in her. Now, she saw nothing inside but ugliness. She had prostituted herself to Bull Drake in the worst way possible.

Was she evil? Gina could not stop the hard sobs that suddenly wracked her body.

Yes. Evil. And a coward. Evil to have let Cade rot in prison for something she knew he didn't do, yet too much a coward to come forth. And now, running away from everything, leaving Cade out in the cold again, because nobody had ever believed the truth when he told it.

Steady rain was fast turning into a downpour, and she switched the windshield wipers to high. Maybe for once, she should do something right. Scottie might be able to prove Cade's innocence if Gina testified against Ray and Bull. Maybe that would salve her seared conscience. At the next opportunity, she would turn around and go back to face the music.

A sudden jolt sent the 'Vette flying forward. The glare of bright headlights blinded her as she glanced in the rearview mirror. Somebody had rammed her! She fought to control the powerful car as a sharp bend in the road flew toward her. The headlights were taller than her sports car, and she recognized the massive bumper on the front as it closed in for another hit.

Bull! He truly was going to kill her.

As the 'Vette lurched forward from another smashing blow, Gina slammed on the brakes, snatched the wheel to the left to avoid the edge. Overcorrected. The 'Vette twisted and bucked as it hurtled down the steep road, gathering speed as Gina fought frantically to steer.

A voice came through her OnStar system, calling her name, asking if she needed assistance. The system had registered an impact.

"Yes, help me!" Gina shrieked. "He's pushing me over. Help me, please!"

The road-hugging 'Vette took the curve, but Bull's top-heavy Tahoe could not. In her rearview mirror, Gina saw the lights of the SUV go airborne over the side of the mountain like a rocket into black space. She slammed on the brakes, shifted into park, and jumped out. She could still hear tree limbs splintering as the heavy vehicle continued its downward plunge.

In shock, she stared at the wide swath torn through the underbrush. *Serves you right, you old bastard.*

She thought of Silas Martin's death and how Bull had talked about the penalties being so much harsher because whoever hit him had left the scene. She at least had to call for help. Her OnStar contact said she was sending somebody, but Gina wasn't sure that was enough.

Shivering in the cold rain, afraid to stay, afraid to run, Gina ran back to her car and locked herself inside. She swallowed hard then dialed a number she never thought she would dial for help. When nobody answered, Gina left a message in a shaky voice then started the engine of the 'Vette, turned the heater on, and hoped the air heated up soon. Her teeth chattered, and she hugged herself and rocked back and forth in the seat, trying to warm up.

"Please call me back," she whispered, staring at her phone as if she could make it ring.

Maybe she could. The phone buzzed in her hand. Quickly, she answered.

"Oh, God, thank you for calling me back, Scottie. Are you on patrol?"

"No, not at the moment, but I am busy," Scottie answered. "What's the problem?"

"I need help."

"I thought you were going to Knoxville." Scottie sounded aggravated.

"I was. Bull tried to run me off the road," Gina said, trying to control her shaking hands and steady her voice. "I don't know how he found me."

"Are you hurt?" Scottie broke in.

"No, but Bull ran off the road, down the mountainside. I can't get down there to him. I don't know what to do."

"Where are you?"

Gina told her what road she was on.

"Have you called for help?"

"When Bull rammed my car, it activated the OnStar. They said they were sending somebody. I was afraid to call the police department. I don't know what Ray will do. I know he won't believe me."

Scottie hesitated for a moment, and Gina doubted that Scottie gave a hoot about her or her problems. She really couldn't blame Scottie. Gina had done her dirty more than once.

"I'm on my way. Stay in your car until the responders get there. I'm going to go pick up Ray. He'll have to be notified anyway. This way I'll be there with you."

Gina began to sob. "Thank you, Scottie. Thank you."

***

Scottie slipped the phone back into its holster on her belt as she watched one ambulance pull out of the clearing in front of the caverns. Trish was inside, hypothermic, hysterical, but not seriously hurt. At least Ezra had not abused her, only kept her captive until he could lure Cade into the caverns. Still, three terrifying days alone in the cold darkness had traumatized her, and Scottie wondered how the experience would affect Trish's already unstable psyche.

She turned to see another stretcher coming from the cave lean-to. Crossing the clearing, she fell in step with the EMTs as they hauled Cade toward the other waiting ambulance. She dared not think about his fate if he had not hit the ledge. As for the injuries sustained when he fell, there was no way to know the full extent until he reached the emergency room.

"How's he doing?" she asked one of the medics.

Cade opened his eyes and lifted his head slightly. "Why don't you ask me that?" His voice was weak, but he was smiling.

"Okay, so how are you doing?" she asked him.

"Considering where I was a couple of hours ago, this is the best I've ever felt in my life."

"I believe that," she said, returning his smile. "I have to leave you in the care of these guys. I'll catch up with you at the hospital."

"Hurry. I don't intend to stay long," he said.

"Don't leave without me."

As they loaded him into the vehicle, she gathered her resolve. If what Gina told her last night about Ray was the truth, she might be arresting her own chief before the night was out.

DAY 7

CHAPTER 34

R AY WAS roused from a sound sleep by loud knocking on his front
door. He pulled on his pants and shirt and padded through the
house barefoot, knowing that nothing good came from a visit
this time of night. Scottie waited outside, her expression grim.

"What is it?" he asked as he held the screen door open for her to
come in.

She declined. "I'm wet. I'll wait out here. Your father's been in an
accident in the mountains. I didn't want you to hear it from dispatch."

"I'll get dressed."

Minutes later, pulling on his rain slicker as he crossed the yard,
Ray climbed into Scottie's cruiser. She flicked on full lights and siren
and pulled out of his driveway, running code. The windshield wipers
threw a frenetic spray in all directions, and the slick roads made him
think twice about their speed, but Scottie was an excellent driver, had
aced every one of the driver training courses.

On the way, Scottie filled him in with all she knew, including
Gina's assertion that Bull tried to run her off the road. "Gina said she
had no idea how Bull figured out where she was."

Bull's words rang through Ray's head. Words he dared not repeat
aloud.

I put a damn tracking device on that hotrod...she ain't worth the trouble anymore....

Had his father really tried to kill Gina? But why? Surely not just because Cade had come back to town. God knows, Gina had screwed everybody else in the county. She'd even come on to Ray a few times when they were young.

"Something else you need to know," Scottie said.

"I'm listening."

"Ezra Wright kidnapped Trish. We recovered her tonight from the caverns."

"Alive?"

"Yes. Fortunately, Cade got to them before Ezra could kill her, although that was his intention. That and murdering Cade in retribution for killing Angela."

"What about Cade?" Ray wasn't sure what he wanted to hear.

"I think he's going to be okay."

"I'll want the details in your report."

"One other thing. I'm pretty sure Ezra ran down Silas to force Cade to come home."

Ray stared at the slick, white lines of the country road whipping underneath the speeding cruiser. "I am sorry about that. Silas was a good man, even though he never would accept Cade's guilt."

Something in Scottie's silence put Ray's nerves on edge, but he was too worried about his father to dwell on it.

Once in the mountains, Scottie was forced to slow down even more. This seldom-traveled back road had once been the main route to Knoxville before the interstate and a more recent four-lane bypass made it obsolete.

Red strobe lights on the road ahead made the misty air pulsate with urgency. Ray leapt from the car as soon as Scottie braked to a stop. Emergency workers and firemen moved down the mountain toward the wreckage with practiced efficiency. Gina stood on the roadside, in one of the department's yellow slickers, her hair plastered to her face, watching the efforts. Her Corvette sat halfway off the road a few yards farther on.

Two Cumberland Cove officers and two county sheriff's deputies were on the scene, along with the EMTs. There was no point in trying to get down to the wreck and better to keep out of the way to give the responders room to work. Ray's mind reeled with an overload of questions. Nothing made sense.

"What happened, Gina?" he said, as he joined her.

Gina wouldn't answer him. In a minute, Scottie came to them after talking with one of their officers.

"They've reached the Tahoe," she said. "He's alive, but they're going to have to cut him out."

Ray's concern for his father manifested itself in anger toward Gina. He fully blamed her for his father's downfall over the years, and he held her responsible for this accident, right or wrong.

"I'm asking you again, Gina. What happened? Where were you two headed in two cars?"

Finally, she said, "I was headed for Knoxville. He appeared behind me, though I don't know how he knew where I was unless he's been following my every step. He thought I was sneaking around seeing Cade, but I wasn't." She leveled a brazen stare on Ray. "He tried to push me over. I'm lucky the 'Vette stayed in the curve."

Ray wanted to shake her senseless. Gina stared at the 'Vette. "You can look at the back end and see where he rammed me."

"Why the hell would he want to do that?"

"I was leaving him, and I guess he figured it out."

Gina caught Scottie's eye for a long moment then turned to Ray with a defiant look. "I don't know how this is going to turn out with Zeb, but in case he's dying, I think you should know. I've kept it in all these years, even though I knew it was wrong. I finally figured out why Bull married me to begin with. So I wouldn't testify against him for covering up what you did."

"Covering up what?"

"I was running away from him because I knew he was going to kill me. He was afraid when Cade came back to town, because he knew it might all come out if Cade forced the issue."

"What are you talking about?" Ray said, an edge of dread creeping into his mind. Had he triggered this by mentioning to his father that Cade had filed a lawsuit to reopen his case?

"I was the one who told Zeb about you and Angela back then because you wouldn't have anything to do with me. Then she disappeared, and Zeb made me help cover up her murder." Gina spoke in a fast, breathy whisper. Ray had to lean close to hear her. "Cade went to prison for it, but I know you killed Angela. And I'm going to testify against you. I'm not afraid anymore."

"What are you talking about? I didn't kill Angela." Ray wanted to throttle her, to keep her from saying anything else. Ultimately, he sensed that his whole world was about to implode and there was nothing he could do to stop it.

"I told Zeb you met Angela on the logging road every day and that she was pregnant."

In shock, Ray fought down bitter bile as he stared at Gina. She had told his father? Bull had never once mentioned to Ray that he knew about Angela. Then she was gone without a trace. The evidence, all circumstantial, had pointed at Cade. But now Ray wondered if there really had been a cover-up.

Rickey, a rookie detective, eager to please his boss. Evidence of foul play, easy to pin on Cade, even without a body. Had his father purposely manipulated the case to redirect attention away from the real killer? And had Ray himself wanted somebody to blame so badly in his grief-stricken angst that he'd been blind to the truth? Had he been a party to sending an innocent kid to prison?

And the possibility that terrified him beyond all others—had his own father killed the woman he loved and their unborn child?

"I didn't kill Angela," Ray repeated quietly.

Gina looked him in the eye, and they both knew the truth.

Scottie placed a hand on his arm. "What do you want to do about this, Chief?"

Ray shook his head slightly. "I don't know yet."

The three of them watched in silence as the rescue effort continued. When at last they brought Bull up, Ray waited at the back of the ambulance. The old man lay motionless, thin purple veins lacing the pasty skin of his face and hands.

"Can I talk to my father?"

"Sorry, Chief Drake, gotta scoop and scoot on this one."

The medic rushed around to the passenger side, and the ambulance made a careful U-turn and headed down the winding road as the grayness of dawn slowly spread across the mountain.

"Come on, Chief," Scottie said. "I'll take you to the hospital. You, too, Gina."

At the hospital, Scottie convinced Gina to be seen by a doctor in case she had whiplash injuries from her car being rear-ended. She went to check on Cade, who was having X-rays and a CT scan then joined Ray in the waiting room.

They sat in silence. The world had tilted for a lot of people tonight, and she wondered what the new balance of power would be tomorrow when the facts were known. At the moment, Ray looked dejected and confused. Every few minutes, he glanced at the clock or walked to the nurse's station to ask about his father.

When he was finally called back, he turned to Scottie. "Will you come with me, Officer Townsend? I'd like to have a witness when I speak to my father."

Scottie followed him to Bull's bedside in a cubicle cluttered with monitors, IV equipment, and portable lifesaving equipment. The old man opened bloodshot eyes when Ray called his name.

"Son," he said weakly. "I'm glad you're here."

Ray took his hand, squeezing it lightly. He seemed not to know what to say to his father. Scottie could see the warring emotions flitting across Ray's face as he stared at his father's battered face.

Finally Ray choked out, "What did you do, Dad?"

"I was trying to stop Gina from..."

"No, Dad, I mean what did you do when Gina told you about Angela and me? All those years ago."

Bull had a defeated look in his eyes. "She shouldn't have told you anything about that."

Ray extracted his hand from Bull's clinging fingers. "Well, she did, and I need to know the truth. Things have to be set straight after all this time. Before it's too late."

Bull closed his eyes. His hands trembled as he picked at the thin sheet over his body.

"I loved her, Dad. Why would you...take her away from me?"

Without opening his eyes, Bull began to speak in a low voice. Ray motioned Scottie closer so she could hear.

"When Gina told me about you and Angela, I had to fix things. I caught her on the way home one evening. Gina told me you met her up there every night. I sent you across town on a wild goose chase so I could talk to her. I told her to leave you alone. I offered to pay for everything—an abortion, a nice place for her to live somewhere else. I tried to reason with her! She fought me. She fell backwards, hit her head. I didn't mean to hurt her. I never meant to. Forgive me, son."

Ray leaned down and modulated his voice in the thin-walled room. "I loved her! We were going to marry, have a family. My life has been pure hell without her."

"I know, I know. Even if you never forgive me, I did what had to be done. You couldn't marry her, and I couldn't tell you why."

Ray took him by the shoulder and gave him a wrench. "But you are going to tell me!"

The old man threw up his hands in defense. The heart monitor beeped urgently. Bull winced in pain but did not utter a sound of protest. Every muscle in Ray's body quivered.

Bull shrank under Ray's fury, his words barely audible. "She was your sister, Ray. Her mother raised her after we had an affair. Nobody knew Angela wasn't her husband's child or that I gave her money so my daughter could have a little better life. When Gina told me about you and her, I knew I couldn't let it happen. Don't you see that? I loved her because she was my daughter. I never meant to kill her."

Scottie thought Ray might come apart, he was shuddering so hard. She tore Ray's hands loose from Bull before he throttled the old man. Ray jerked away from her, his eyes wild and haunted. He stared at Bull, who had fallen back on the bed, his face mottled blue. The heart monitor flatlined. Ray backed away and pushed through the horde of ER personnel alerted by the screeching monitor.

Scottie knew the old man was past reviving. She'd seen that look too many times in her career, but this time she felt no emotion, only numb disbelief at what Bull Drake had done to his own blood kin and to an innocent teenager.

CHAPTER 35

C ADE?"

The soft voice near his ear brought Cade out of a slightly drugged reverie. Trish leaned over him, his hand in hers. He blinked back to reality, remembering that he had been settled in a regular room some time earlier. Trish wore a set of blue scrubs, and her hair was freshly washed, though not styled, and still becoming to her pretty face.

"Hey, Sis. You okay?"

"Yes, thanks to you."

She straightened, still clinging to his hand. She stared at the floor, as if summoning her courage. Finally, she said, "Cade, I'm so sorry for the way I treated you." Her voice broke, and she struggled to continue. "I was messed up, and I didn't know."

"It's okay. I understand why you didn't trust me. I don't blame you."

"Mom—Johanna admitted everything you told me. I couldn't believe it. I'm just so, so sorry about all of it." She buried her face in her hands. "I've always loved you so much. Thank you for coming to save me."

Cade grunted, aware of every bruise and scrape on his body. He said with a grin, "Too bad we couldn't have found something tamer for our first brother-sister outing."

To his surprise, Trish gave a snuffling chuckle. "At least now I know you would still jump in after me. Cade, I want to get my life back together. You were right about the drugs, but I don't think I can get off of them on my own."

"Do you want to go to rehab? There are some good facilities around."

"I don't think I can afford one of the nice places."

Cade squeezed her hand. "We'll make it happen. Have you talked to Johanna?"

"Just to tell her I was okay. She wanted to come to the hospital, but I told her not to. There's just too much hubbub in the ER right now with Bull dying and everything."

Cade sat bolt upright in spite of the ripping pain. "What?"

Trish's eyes went wide, and she covered her mouth. "Oh no, you didn't know. You've been having tests run. I'm sorry. I should have waited and let Scottie tell you."

"Well, it's out now, so you tell me."

"I don't know if I should."

"You'd better. You owe me big-time for last night."

"Okay, but you've got to promise not to get upset. I'll be in huge trouble if you pop stitches or something."

Trish closed the door to his room and came back to the bedside. Cade eased down on the pillow to alleviate the wooziness that had plagued him since he hit the ledge.

She took a deep breath. "I got most of this hearsay, but I think it's probably true. Gina was trying to leave Bull, and he found out and hit her car from behind."

So Gina's fears had been well founded. "Was she hurt?"

Trish shook her head. "She managed to stay on the road, but Bull's Tahoe went down the mountain. He was half dead when they got him here." Trish pulled up a chair and sat down, her face on level with Cade's as she whispered. "But, Cade, Gina had told Scottie that Ray killed Angela and Bull covered it up all these years."

Cade blinked hard, thinking he was hallucinating. "Say that again," he said.

Trish told Cade the gossip she had heard from her nurse friends in ER. They had overheard Gina telling Scottie that she had squealed on Ray and Angela in exchange for Bull getting her off a prostitution rap in Chattanooga. Then when Angela disappeared, Bull married Gina and sent her on a long vacation to Europe with his cousin. By the time she got back, Cade had been tried and convicted.

"Gina said she was afraid of Bull and Ray, so she never breathed a word about what she knew. She told Scottie she didn't think her testimony could have helped you then. And Scottie basically agreed with her, because Bull had done a good job of skewing the investigation."

Cade lay back on the pillow, staring at the ceiling, trying to grasp what Trish was telling him. He could prove his innocence now.

"They said Ray was about to kill his daddy in ER after he heard everything. Scottie stopped him. Bull was dying anyway. But Cade, here's the crazy thing...Bull admitted he was Angela's father from an affair. That he couldn't let Ray marry her because they were brother and sister. Is that not just unreal?"

"Go find a doctor. I'm ready to get out of here," Cade said.

"I'm not so sure," Trish said, straightening and shaking her head. "How will you manage?"

"I'm not that bad off. You're a nurse. You can stay at Uncle Silas's house and take care of me as well as the staff here. You'll need a few days to find a good rehab facility, and I'd rather you were with me than anyplace else."

"You mean it?"

"If you want to."

"Oh, I do. I want to."

He caught Trish's arm as she rose. "Thanks for telling me."

"Thanks for saving me," she said, planting a kiss on his cheek.

★★★

By the time Scottie could leave the station late that afternoon, she was exhausted, but she wanted to see Cade. He had left a message on her phone while she was in a meeting, saying he was home at Silas's house. She wasn't sure how he'd managed that, but they needed to talk, so she headed that way before going home.

He was sitting on the front porch waiting for her.

"Excuse me if I don't get up," he said as she climbed the steps to the porch. "My nurse made me promise not to try to walk unless she's with me. She seems to think I might have a head injury."

Scottie laughed at the understatement. "You hired a nurse? I wondered how you escaped so handily."

She pulled a rocker close to his. "I can't tell you how glad I am to see you looking this well."

"Hey, I always look good."

"Hi, Scottie," Trish said, pushing the screen door open with her hip as she brought out a tray of iced tea and glasses.

Scottie smiled. "I approve of your nurse."

Trish set the tray on the table beside Cade's chair. "I know you two have a lot to talk about, so I'm going inside to get your bed ready, Cade. You need to rest soon."

As soon as Trish was out of sight, Cade turned his full attention to Scottie.

"Is it true, what Trish told me about Bull Drake?" he asked.

She nodded, clasping her hands in her lap. "Yes, it's been quite a day."

Cade summarized Trish's information from the hospital gossip mill. Scottie was amazed at the detail Trish had gleaned from her friends.

"Basically, that's the gist of it. Between what Gina told me and Bull's confession, we're piecing the puzzle together. I'm sure you'll hear from Rickey soon. He is devastated that he didn't follow his intuition and get backup from the sheriff's office. Bull Drake was an intimidating man, and Rickey had a family to support. Who knows what decision any one of us would have made."

"Don't make excuses for any of them, Scottie. Rickey didn't do his job, and I'm the one who paid the price."

"I know. Still, life's not ideal. There's no accounting for the human factor. The truth is spreading. The whole town is in shock."

"What's next? I want my name cleared."

"You won't have any trouble. That's one of my top priorities."

"Good, I'm glad you're in charge of my case."

Scottie smiled slightly, surprised that she was taking the rapid changes in stride. But maybe she had prepared herself for this day for years. She wasn't sure how Cade would react.

"Ray resigned this afternoon, and the city council appointed me interim Chief of Police."

Cade stared at her in silence for a long time. Dusk had fallen, but a security light at the end of the driveway illuminated the porch with a soft glow.

"What are you thinking?" she asked, unable to read his expression.

A slow smile spread across his face, lighting those pale blue eyes Scottie loved so much. He reached out to lift her chin with his fingers.

As his lips touched hers, he murmured, "I think it's about damn time—for both of us."

ABOUT THE AUTHOR

Elaine Grant is a multi-published, award winning author who lives in the Shenandoah Valley of Virginia.

She is a member of International Thriller Writers, Sisters in Crime, Novelists, Inc., and Romance Writers of America.

Two of her books were finalists for the prestigious RITA Award.

Contact Elaine at elaine@elainegrant.com
www.elainegrant.com
www.facebook.com/elainegrantauthor

Other Novels by Elaine Grant

ROSES FOR CHLOE

MAKE BELIEVE MOM

AN IDEAL FATHER

NO HERO LIKE HIM

COMING

THE VALLEY

Book 2
Tennessee Mountain Home Series

Cumberland Cove had survived the worst—or so they thought. Murdered teenager Angela Wright's case was closed when her real murderer confessed. Then months later, Scottie Townsend, acting Chief of Police discovers that Angela's story is being repeated every year. But who's taking the missing girls and where are they?

Cade Youngblood, the innocent man railroaded to prison for Angela's death, now holds power over the entire city. Will he take revenge? Or will he find reason to put the town to rights to make Cumberland Cove his home once more and salvage the love he and Scottie once shared?

The cop and the felon are on opposite sides of everything now, yet their passion still smolders just beneath the surface. Will the murders and mayhem pull them back together or push them apart?

www.ingramcontent.com/pod-product-compliance
Lightning Source LLC
Chambersburg PA
CBHW021956170626
46808CB00001B/183